# Dodging Bullets
## A Detective Liv DeMarco Thriller

## G.K. Parks

Copyright © 2025 G.K. Parks

A Modus Operandi imprint

ISBN:
ISBN-13: 978-1-942710-48-6

*For my mom and dad*

# ONE

A blade of grass scratched his cheek. The itch had been nagging at him for the last few minutes, every time the wind blew, but he remained still. Even when test-firing, he liked to simulate actual conditions. His target wouldn't be out in a field in the middle of nowhere, so grass wouldn't be a problem. But something else would. There were always distractions, especially in the concrete jungle where the man he intended to kill would be hiding.

Releasing the tension from his shoulders, he exhaled slowly, aware of the rhythm of his own heartbeat. Even something as simple as that could ruin a shot. He'd done his research, studied, and practiced so he knew every tiny intricacy that made the best sharpshooters stand out. He also knew the act itself was a ritual, highly individualized and deeply personal.

He waited to feel the thump in his chest before he squeezed the trigger. The bullet hit too high. The degree off, the angle wrong.

Getting used to a new weapon took time and patience. The sights were never aligned right, not for that first shot. After adjusting, he waited a few counts for the stress to decrease. Emotions made his heart beat faster and his muscles tense. Both would ruin his aim. This had to be spot-on. He wanted it to be perfect.

After a few calming breaths, he fired again. Despite the suppressor, the sniper rifle was far from silent. However, it shouldn't matter here. He had chosen this place for the quiet tranquility.

Peering through the scope, he searched to see where the bullet hit. It was much closer to the target this time. In fact, his instructors would have said it was a perfect shot, but not to him. It wasn't precisely centered. It was a smidge to the right. He wanted perfect. He didn't want his bullet to go through his target's eye. He wanted the shot to be dead center.

He made one final adjustment, confident as he reloaded with what he hoped would be his final test round. The wind shifted before he could fire. Military snipers usually had a spotter, someone to keep track of these things and advise on adjustments, but he always worked best alone.

Glancing down, he ran the numbers in his head, something he'd always been adept at doing, made a final tweak, and fired. The bullet soared through the air. Two seconds later, he watched it impact with his target. That was the perfect shot. Now all he had to do was repeat it under different conditions.

He unscrewed the suppressor and slid it into the case first before removing the rifle from the stand. Before he could put it away, the crack of a twig caught his attention. Turning, he spotted a man with a hunting rifle, camouflage pants, and an orange safety vest. Why the hunter bothered with the camo pants made no sense, but the things most people did made little sense to him.

The hunter peered down at the open case, the long silver barrel of the suppressor shining in the late afternoon sun. "Are you hoping not to scare away the animals?"

"Something like that." He had come here for a reason. He didn't want anyone to see him. He was supposed to be a ghost. This was supposed to be the perfect hit—a kill that would make him a legend. Now this man with the orange vest stood to ruin it all. He could almost see it now, the newscast with some nosy reporter thrusting the microphone into the hunter's face while he told the story of the man he saw that afternoon pheasant hunting with a silenced sniper rifle. "Are you here for duck or pheasant?"

The hunter looked even more leery. "It's deer season."

"They tend to spook easily, especially when it comes to cars and headlights. I didn't want to scare them away." He slid another round into the rifle. "That's why I made this trek to the middle of nowhere. No one was supposed to be here."

"That's the same reason I like this spot." The hunter reached into the flap of his vest and pulled out his cell phone. "No signals either." He eyed the sniper rifle again. "I like coming here for target practice. I take it you're doing the same."

"Uh-huh." He slid the sniper rifle over one shoulder while he folded the stand and put it away. After picking up his spent casings, he turned to the hunter. "You really shouldn't have come here today."

The hunter nodded, his hand on his own rifle. "I could say the same to you." At this range, the shorter barrel gave the hunter an advantage, or it should have. But the man with the sniper rifle wasn't a hobbyist. He had every intention of becoming a legend. "How about I go about my business like this never happened?"

"I think that'd be best for everyone involved." He gestured with his free hand. "By all means, enjoy the rest of your day."

"Yeah," the hunter said, "you too."

The hunter made it halfway across the clearing before the back of his skull blew through the front of his face.

\* \* \*

"Liv and Brad cannot be together," Emma said. "I won't allow it. In fact, I forbid it."

"Why not?" I asked.

Emma glared at me. "You know exactly why not. The last time the two of you partnered up on game night, you decimated the rest of us. I am not going to stand by and let that happen again."

Brad chuckled, amused by her dramatics. "Are you

afraid, Em? You don't think you and your fiancé stand a fighting chance against us?"

Before Emma could lunge across the coffee table and strangle Brad, Mac intervened. "How about we make this a battle of the sexes? Girls versus boys."

"No." Emma's tone remained sharp. My best friend was as competitive as they came. "That wouldn't be fair to Dino. He only met Jake tonight, and he barely knows Brad."

"Okay, how about I play with you and Dino?" I asked.

"No," Brad said. "You and Emma playing together would be just as devastating."

I held up my hands. "It's not my fault I'm the best player here."

They both glared at me.

"Fine. I won't play."

"We could play Monopoly instead." Mac pointed to the stack of board games on my shelf. "That doesn't involve teams."

"No," Brad and Emma said at the same time.

Mac held up her palms. "It was just a suggestion."

Jake Voletek finished his beer. "Liv and Mac are on my team. Problem solved."

Neither Brad nor Emma looked particularly pleased, but it made the most sense. Had I realized game night was going to be this complicated, I would have figured out something else for us to do. On the bright side, no blood had been shed and everyone seemed to be enjoying the snacks I'd made.

After several different party games, we ended in a tie. Brad had been giving me suspicious looks throughout the night. I wasn't sure if he hoped to throw me off my game or if he had a bone to pick with me for letting him get stuck with Emma and Dino. It wasn't like my best friend and partner hated each other. The threats and bickering were how they showed their affection. It was their love language, or so I hoped.

"Good game." Mac closed the lid on the Taboo box and added it to the growing pile beside the coffee table. "So how's the wedding planning coming along?"

Emma curled up beside Dino, resting her hand on his stomach. "We're still touring venues. In between, Maria's been nagging us about cake tastings and putting the menu together."

"That's because she wants you to have it at the house or at her sister's restaurant," I said. "You know my mom. She wants to be involved."

"The other day she came out with a giant book of linen and lace samples," Dino said. "It's sweet she's so into this." He pressed his lips to the top of Emma's head. "It's nice she loves you so much. My mom wants to be involved too."

"Oh, I know." The look on Emma's face said it all. In fact, Dino's parents' involvement nearly led to their break-up. "Maybe we should run off and elope."

"You can't elope," Mac said. "The two of you are absolutely adorable. You deserve a fairytale wedding. Ooh, have you thought about doing a custom cake topper? Instead of the generic bride and groom, you could put yourselves on the cake."

"Don't you think we're a bit big?" Dino asked.

I wasn't sure if he was joking or if he thought Mac was being literal.

"I was talking about a 3D print. I could scan in your photos, turn them into 3D renders, and print a custom cake topper." Mac turned to Emma. "Please. Please. Please. Let me do it. If you don't like it, you don't have to use it, but I want to do something. It's not every day I get asked to be a bridesmaid."

"You could really do that?" Emma asked.

"Yes." Mac's rainbow-colored pigtails bounced as she nodded her head enthusiastically.

"This is my cue to leave," Jake whispered before getting up. He grabbed a few of the empty trays and headed for the kitchen. I followed, grabbing the empty bottles that had collected on the end tables. "Tonight was a lot of fun. Thanks for inviting me."

"Anytime. It's not as awesome as spending the night in the arcade, but the company's better."

"Agreed." He gave me a hug, grabbed his service piece from the counter, and slipped it back into his holster before putting on his jacket. "Do you need help cleaning up?"

"I got it."

"Okay, princess." He winked, flinching when I slapped his arm. "You know I couldn't resist."

"Try."

He headed for the door. "Emma, it was nice to see you again. Dino, it was great to meet you. Congrats on the pending nuptials."

"Thanks, man." Dino waved.

"Are you taking off?" Mac asked, making a pouty face.

"Yeah, I have court tomorrow. ADA Winters likes it when I show up rested."

"I'll walk you out." Brad got off the floor and returned the abandoned cushions to my couch.

"You're leaving too?" Mac asked.

Brad nodded. "I'll see you tomorrow at work. Don't stay out too late." He looked at me. "Are you bringing coffee, or is it my turn?"

"I'll do it," I said.

"Okay. Night, Liv." Brad turned and waved to Dino. "Good night, Dino. This was fun. Next time, we'll dominate."

"You bet."

Emma made a harrumph noise. "You already stole my best friend. You are not stealing my fiancé too, Bradley."

Brad smiled. "We'll see."

After he and Jake left, the conversation turned to nothing but wedding prep. As maid of honor, I forced myself to focus on the details. But aside from Mac 3D printing figurines of Dino and Emma, nothing else was decided.

"Doesn't Emma need to have a dress picked out before you can do the printing?" I asked.

Emma's icy look sent chills through me. "When are we going dress shopping?" she asked.

"When do you want to go?"

"This weekend. I'll get the girls together, and we'll make a day of it. How's Saturday?"

"That should be fine." Being a homicide detective made a social life difficult. Putting game night together and inviting two other homicide detectives, the PD's resident computer expert, an ER nurse, and a radiologist had practically taken an act of congress, but we pulled it off somehow. However, I wasn't sure I'd get that lucky twice.

Fifteen minutes later, the conversation fizzled. My guests were ready to say their good-byes. Emma had worked a double and was seconds away from crashing, which would explain why she'd been a little cranky this evening. Mac, on the other hand, had gotten a mysterious text that had made her giggle.

"What do you have planned after this?" I asked as she made her way to the door.

"D&D." Mac grinned. "Do you want to come? You'd have a blast. We dress up and everything."

"I've never played."

"That's okay. You'll catch on quickly."

"Another time," I said.

She gave me that look that said she knew better. "Okay, but think about it. And let me know if you change your mind."

Once Mac left, Emma gave me a hug. "I had fun tonight."

"I'm glad."

She gave me a strange look as she pulled away. "What was up with Brad?"

"What do you mean?"

"I don't know, but there was something different about him. I don't think he liked you playing with Jake." She gave me a sideways look. "We'll talk about this on Saturday."

"No, Em, we won't."

She waved it off, waited for Dino to give me a hug, and hooked her arm through his. "At least this place is nice. Try to keep it that way."

"Yes, Mom."

Closing the door, I surveyed the damage. Maybe it'd be easier to move than clean up. Grabbing the remaining platters from the table, I brought them to the counter, pulled out the storage containers, and scooped the leftovers inside. At least I'd have snacks and lunch for the rest of the week.

I had started washing the dishes when someone knocked on my door. "Did you forget something?" I asked, expecting to find Emma on the other side.

"I thought you might need help cleaning up." Brad grinned. "It's the least I can do, neighbor."

I laughed. "That beeline out of here wasn't to avoid the

clean-up?"

"No. I didn't want anyone to get the wrong idea." He moved closer, snagging a plate off the counter and placing it on top of the stack beside the sink.

"What would that be? That you're a considerate human being?" I elbowed him as I settled in front of the sink to wash while he dried and put the dishes away. "Everyone at the precinct already thinks you're a nice guy."

"I am a nice guy."

I knew why he left. It was the same reason he asked about coffee in the morning. Now that we lived in the same building, we were worried rumors would spread. I never wanted to get that kind of reputation. The one I had was bad enough. Brad knew it. He'd known it since the day we met. But in the two plus years that we'd been working together, we'd grown closer to the point where I wasn't sure keeping my distance was as important as it once seemed.

"What are you thinking?" He brushed against me, curious as to my thoughts.

I shook it off. "Did you throw the game so Emma wouldn't win?"

"Me?" Brad feigned innocence, clutching the dish towel to his chest. "Why, I'd never."

"You would."

"Maybe, but I didn't."

"Are you sure?"

"For the record, Jake, Mac, and I would have mopped the floor with you."

"Mop this." I splashed sink water at him.

He wiped his face. "Oh, so you really want to mop the floor?" A mischievous glint came over him. The next thing I knew, he had the sprayer aimed at me. "Take it back."

"Take what back?"

His caramel brown eyes danced, and then he squeezed. I shrieked and dashed away. He spun, shooting water at me while I grabbed another towel and positioned myself near the remaining ranch dip. Picking up the spoon, I held it up.

"You are so cleaning my apartment after this," I said.

He smiled. "That's why I came back. Weren't you paying attention?"

"You came back for this?"

"I came back for you." He held the sprayer in both hands and gave it a squeeze. I tossed the spoon at him, but he sidestepped and it landed in the sink.

I ducked, wiping my face and hair with the towel. "Remember when I asked if you were going to flood my apartment? I never thought you'd do it from inside my kitchen."

"Okay, okay. I'll stop." He made a show of moving the sprayer toward the sink. "But you were going to wash down the counter anyway. This is the fun way of doing it."

"You're insane."

He waited for me to get closer and gave the sprayer another squeeze.

"Brad." I smacked him with the towel. He grabbed the end and gave it a tug, pulling me close.

I collided with his chest, my hair on the left side of my face soppy and dripping. He laughed, that velvety smooth sound which only grew deeper when I splashed more water on him. He grabbed my hands and backed me against the counter, away from the sink.

"Truce?" he asked, letting go of my hands and taking hold of my hips.

"Truce."

He lifted me onto the counter and grabbed a dry towel to wipe my face and hair before wiping his own. He stood in front of me, inching closer by the second, while we laughed. I didn't think it was a conscious decision. More like gravity or magnetism.

"Hey," he said softly, his hand brushing my wet hair back before caressing my cheek, "I've been thinking about that conversation we had."

My voice caught. "Yeah?"

"Mm-hmmm."

"I thought we were playing it by ear, that we hadn't made any decisions."

"We haven't. Yet. But I've been thinking about it all night."

That explained the looks he'd been giving me. "Okay."

"Okay?" His brows knit together. "Help me out, Liv.

What does that mean?"

I slid my hands up his chest and grasped his face. "I say we let it play out." And then I kissed him.

# TWO

Brad held me in his strong arms and kissed my neck, avoiding the side with the scar. He had enough of his own. Some from shrapnel, others more recent from burns. Who knew we'd have his and her scars?

I turned to face him, another round of giggles escaping my lips. We'd been doing a lot of that tonight. Honestly, I wasn't sure I'd ever heard Brad giggle before, and when I pointed it out, he said that was a chortle, not a giggle. But it was a giggle. He was giddy and completely at ease. We'd always been comfortable with one another, but this was different.

He pulled the sheet, forcing me closer, his mouth open like he wanted to playfully bite me, only to plant a big, wet kiss on the side of my face. I wiped his slobber away and rubbed it against his shoulder.

"Eww."

Laughing, he gave me a quick peck on the lips before brushing his nose against mine and settling on the pillow we were sharing. I could see it in his eyes. But he didn't say it. Instead, he rolled me onto my back and buried his face in my neck before kissing along my collarbone. Who would have thought this was how game night would end?

My fingers ran through his short hair, my back arching. "Brad."

That's when the switch flipped. He stopped, locking onto my eyes. Even though he held that playful, sexy smile, his eyes were clouded with thoughts and fears. My partner was freaking out, which made reality slam into me like a semi. What were we doing?

"We should slow down," he said, rolling off me and onto his back. "This isn't even a proper date. We shouldn't...not like this. Not tonight."

"Brad, hey," I moved onto my side, tracing the stubble on his cheek, "talk to me. What are you thinking?"

"I don't know. I just...I don't know."

"I'm right here. I'm not going anywhere."

He gave me a sad smile. "Not yet."

"Not ever."

"Don't make promises you can't keep, DeMarco."

"When have I ever done that?"

"C'mon, Liv, you know how this will go. I never should have instigated. I shouldn't have come on to you. We work together. There are rules."

"Is this because Emma said we couldn't be together? Did you do this to prove her wrong?"

He rubbed his eyes, laughing. "Jeez. I never even thought of that." He peeked at me from beneath his fingers. "If I say yes, do we pretend none of this happened and chalk it up to a drunken indiscretion?"

"We're both stone-cold sober."

"We can pretend we're not."

All jokes aside, I asked, "Do you want to?"

"No."

"So what's the problem?"

"Besides our work dynamic?"

"We can keep this quiet. It's no one's business." Regulations stipulated otherwise, but rules were made to be broken, especially if it meant losing my partner. "Nothing has to change at work."

"Even if we can pull that off—"

"We can."

"Even if, you're my best friend, Liv. You're my everything. I always mess things up. Nothing ever lasts. I don't want to lose you. Lose us. I don't know how to do this."

I cracked a smile. "You're wrong, Fennel. You're exceptionally gifted at this." I nodded at the rumpled bedding surrounding us. We were only half undressed. We hadn't crossed any lines we couldn't come back from, yet. "I've seen and heard enough that I don't have any doubts."

"Liv, you know that's not what I meant."

"You and I have always been great. None of that changes. We have our coffee ritual, our lunch breaks, our late night working dinners, the fancy chocolates you buy before I leave on tough assignments or to combat particularly difficult days. I don't expect more or less. We stay us."

"Nothing changes?"

"Nothing changes," I said. "Well, except at some point I expect you to put out."

He laughed. "What do you think Emma will say about that?"

"I'm not telling her. Not yet."

Brad's brow furrowed. "Are you ashamed?"

"No, but if Emma knows, my mom will find out, and then my dad."

"How long do you think we can keep this a secret?"

"We both worked undercover. It shouldn't be that hard."

"We'll see." He snuggled against me. "Tell me this isn't a mistake."

"It's not." But I didn't know. However, I couldn't picture any future reality where we weren't together in one sense or another. Hopefully, I wasn't wrong.

He flicked a strand of my hair over my shoulder. "You don't look convinced." He sighed. "It's okay. I'm not either. Let's take things slow. Like molasses. As soon as it starts to take a turn, we pull the ripcord. Agreed?"

"Brad, we don't need a ripcord." But I nodded anyway. From here on out, we were playing by a different set of rules.

\*     \*     \*

The next day at work was business as usual. I brought the coffee, as promised. The only thing different about my partner was the glint in his eye. We hadn't had sex, so that didn't explain the glint. Maybe I was projecting. Or maybe for the first time since I'd been attacked in that liquor store, Brad was back to his old self.

"Hey, Fennel," Detective Lisco called from the other end of the bullpen, "you and DeMarco are next up. It looks like you caught a weird one."

"Weird how?" Brad asked.

Lisco shrugged. "I hope you packed your hiking boots. You're going on a field trip."

"Hiking boots?" I peered at her, but she had gone back to organizing the case files.

Before Brad could inquire as to what was going on, his phone rang. He gave me a look and picked it up. "Homicide." He waited, listening. "Uh-huh. When?" He scribbled something on the legal pad. "What does that have to do with us?" His eyes went skyward. "Yeah, all right. We're on our way." He put the phone down.

"Do I want to know?"

"A hunter was killed. A hiker found his body, called the park ranger, who called the police. It's not our crime scene, but the locals wanted someone from homicide to check it out."

"That's out of our jurisdiction."

"Yeah." Brad grabbed his keys from the drawer and reached for his jacket. "No one cares. They want us to shadow the investigation."

"Is Lt. Winston okay with this?"

"I assume so."

On the way, I pulled up what I could find on the victim. Ryan Dugrey, forty-seven, married twice, divorced once, two stepsons, no children of his own. He worked as an actuary but enjoyed hunting, fishing, and all that outdoorsy stuff. He was a member of several hunting clubs. He had a license to deer hunt, which explained why he'd been at the wildlife reserve in camouflage and a hunting vest.

When we arrived, Brad parked as close to the trail as he could, but we still had to hoof it a mile and a half through the wooded terrain. Brad didn't come off as an outdoorsman, but he knew everything he needed to survive in the wilderness. For him, this was no different than a walk in the park.

"Did I ever tell you about the time Emma made me go camping?" I asked as we followed the markers left by the park rangers.

"You went camping?"

"We slept on the roof of our college apartment building in sleeping bags on top of an air mattress. We'd just fallen asleep when it started to rain."

"You're making this up."

"Nope."

He shook his head. "You know, that doesn't count as camping."

"We slept outside and made smores. It counted."

"Emma let you have smores?"

"Yeah, homemade marshmallows and grain-free graham crackers."

"It's still not camping. You didn't have a tent."

"We did too. It was a pop-up tent. Is that what they're called?"

"Yeah, but—"

The scene before us made Brad stop mid-sentence. Several park rangers and members of the sheriff's department were scattered around the field. Compared to the dense woods we'd traveled through, the slight smattering of trees and overgrown vegetation made it look like a clearing.

Crime scene tape marked a large rectangular area. I couldn't see the body from here, but I could see blood spatter, bright red against the otherwise green and brown environment. A park ranger intercepted us before we could get too close.

"Detectives Fennel and DeMarco." Brad held out his credentials. "Someone requested our presence."

The sheriff turned, having heard the announcement. "Let them through, Kent. I called them." The sheriff moved toward us, his hand extended. "Sam Evans."

Brad introduced us again, and we shook hands with the sheriff. "What are we looking at? A hunting accident?"

"You tell me." The sheriff led us to the body.

I hadn't seen anything like it before. At first, I thought someone had collapsed the back of the victim's skull with a sharp blow from a pointed instrument, like a pickaxe. But then I realized what I was seeing was bone fragments and brain matter covering the grass from the other side. Whatever had killed this guy had put a hole right through his head.

My partner pulled on a pair of gloves and knelt beside the body. "When's the ME arriving?"

"They're on the way." The sheriff glanced behind us, as if expecting them to appear on command.

Brad straightened. He'd gone pale, but he didn't look like he was about to get sick, which made one of us. Something had spooked him. "Did anyone see or hear what happened?"

"No."

My partner scanned the area. "Did you find any shell casings or the bullet?"

"I'm assuming the bullet's in that mess." The sheriff pointed at what was left of the victim's skull. "I'm thinking that must have been made with hollow points or an explosive round."

Shaking his head, Brad stepped away from the body and headed toward the other side of the clearing. "We'll need metal detectors. The trajectory should be a straight line. The in and out would have slowed the bullet. It couldn't have traveled too much farther. Forensics should see about reconstructing the scene. They may be able to pinpoint the exact location of the bullet if we can't find it." He approached a tree and studied the markings. Hanging from the branch was a yellow ribbon. "We need that bagged and tagged."

The sheriff chuckled, eyeing me. "Is this guy for real?"

"Fennel, what's going on?" I asked.

Brad eyed the ribbon before moving to the left. He was almost out of earshot when he stopped in front of a different tree. "Sheriff, you should have this entire area contained. The killer used this whole place for target practice. Two bullets are lodged in that tree." He indicated the location.

"How do you know the killer did that?" the sheriff asked. "Lots of people hunt around here. Those bullets could belong to anyone."

"If I'm not mistaken, they're 7.62 NATO rounds." Brad returned to the body. "No one hunts with rounds like that except a killer. We're looking for a sniper."

# THREE

Brad hadn't said much since we returned from the crime scene. He'd been right about the bullets. He'd also been right about the sniper using the area for target practice.

"This shouldn't be our case," Brad said. "It's out of our jurisdiction. We shouldn't have to make the notification."

"The sheriff offered to handle it for us," I reminded him.

Brad's icy look indicated he didn't find my comment helpful. He scrunched up his nose, like he was about to say something, shook it off, slammed his palm against the steering wheel, and cursed. "Fuck."

"Hey, talk to me. What is it?"

"I don't think Ryan Dugrey was the target. I think he saw something he shouldn't have and died because of it. That spot in the woods, it was off the beaten path. In fact, it wasn't on any path. It was quiet. No cell signals. No trail markers. No nearby camp grounds. The sniper didn't want to be seen. He went there for solitude."

"According to the park ranger, a few of the more adamant hunters like to find secluded spots like that. That appears to be why Dugrey was there. He had his hunting rifle and gear with him. It wasn't like they were in the middle of nowhere."

Brad and I often took turns playing devil's advocate. My points were sound, but he dismissed them anyway. "You saw that place, Liv. The sniper had several different targets set up at different distances. Guaranteed, there's more lead that we haven't found, spread farther out in other directions. He could have been testing out different weapons and types of rounds. The killer wasn't there for sport. He's planning a hit."

"Since when do you jump to conclusions right out of the gate?"

"I'm not. I'm telling you someone else is going to die if we don't ID the sniper and stop him."

My partner's words sent chills through me. Brad wasn't one to sound alarms prematurely. Every time he did, there was always a good reason. "Okay, let's assume you're right. Dugrey stumbled into something and was killed before he could share the details. The wildlife reserve is huge. Someone must have heard those shots. A sniper rifle sounds different from a hunting rifle. Any number of people could have gotten suspicious and went to check it out. Dugrey may not have been the only one who saw something. The sheriff's department and the park rangers will question everyone in the vicinity. They'll figure this out. In the meantime, Lt. Winston wants us to find out who killed Ryan Dugrey and why."

"I already told you."

"I know." I held up my hand. "And while I have no problem taking you at your word, the LT isn't as easy to please."

"Tell me about it," Brad mumbled.

"We need to be sure before we sound this alarm. If not, the investigation will go in too many directions. Let's make the notification, speak to the current wife, see if there are any red flags, and take it from there. Who knows? Dugrey was an actuary. Maybe he predicted his own death."

Brad rolled his eyes. "That's not funny."

"It's a little funny."

He glanced at me. "Do you honestly believe the sniper set up in that spot to wait for Dugrey?"

"I don't know, but we owe it to the dead to find out."

"I hope you're right, Liv. I hope Dugrey was the target. It would mean the killer's done."

"Do you think Dugrey's murder could be a hired hit?"

"We've never had a sniper as a suspect before, at least not

that I recall. It's not common that someone with that skill set murders someone, at least not stateside. I've seen a few guys lose it and go on rampages, but those were war zones. Not that that's any excuse. I've also seen the guys who had been trained to kill discover they had a taste for it. Those were the ones who became contractors or worse."

"You think our suspect falls into that second set?"

"I do."

"Why?"

"I can't quite put my finger on it, but there was something about the scene and set-up that feels eerily familiar." Brad parked in front of Ryan Dugrey's brownstone. Either from nerves or an abundance of caution, Brad carefully examined our surroundings before opening the car door. "I'll make the notification."

"Are you sure?" We both hated this part. Usually, we'd argue over who got stuck delivering the bad news.

"Uh-huh." He went up the porch steps, his head on a swivel. After ringing the doorbell, he peered up at the windows before glancing behind us and checking the windows in the nearby buildings.

I kept my attention on the front door. We had no reason to believe this was an ambush situation, but one could never be too careful. We had walked into more than our fair share of traps.

The door opened twenty seconds later. A bone thin woman stood on the other side, a dish towel in her hands, a sweater neatly tied and hanging over her shoulders.

"How may I help you?" she asked.

"Mrs. Dugrey?" Brad flashed his badge. "May we come inside?"

"Yes, of course." She unlocked the screen door and stepped back. "What is this about?"

"I'm Detective Fennel. This is my partner Detective DeMarco. We work homicide." Brad searched her face, but there was nothing but puzzlement reflected on her angular features. "May we sit down?"

"Yeah...okay." Sensing something was wrong, she went to the sofa, an expensive cream-colored piece that looked like it was for show and not to be used, and perched on the edge.

Brad took a seat on the wingback chair across from her. "Mrs. Dugrey, I regret to inform you that your husband Ryan was killed earlier today."

Her eyes went wide. She opened her mouth to ask a question, but no words formed. Instead, she pulled her jaw back up, her front teeth latching onto her bottom lip while she stared at him in a mix of horror and confusion. "I don't understand. Today's Ryan's day off. He..."

"Ma'am," I tried, but she was processing the words, forming ideas and theories that would help her make sense of the news.

"He likes to hunt. He has a permit. Was this a hunting accident? Did someone mistake him for a deer?" Her voice rose an octave, resonating somewhere between a laugh and a sob.

"The park ranger found him a mile from the normal paths and trails. He'd been shot," I said.

"Oh god." Her hand flew to her mouth. She sucked in several breaths, which sounded like wheezing gasps, before waving her hand in front of her face a few times and forcing her composure to return. "Did anyone try to help him?"

"It was too late for that." Brad inched forward. "I am so very sorry for your loss."

She reached out, and he grasped her trembling hands. "Ryan grew up hunting. He knew to be careful. I'm sure he had his vest. Did he have his vest?"

"Yes, ma'am." Brad held her hands, grounding her. "We're not certain this was an accident. Do you know if anyone wished your husband harm?"

She blinked rapidly, thoughts racing through her mind. "I," she shook her head a few times, "don't know."

"Did anyone threaten him?" I asked.

She looked up, surprised to see me standing beside Brad's chair. "Um...not that I'm aware, but Ryan predicted when people would die. That was his job. It was for insurance. He didn't do it to be mean or as a carnival act. But people hated it when he'd run the numbers and give them the news. He always made sure they knew he was more of a statistician than a fortune teller, but several people were upset when they found out how their premiums were calculated."

I pulled out my notepad and pen. "Where did he work?"

"Smith and Smith."

"How were his relationships with his coworkers?"

"Fine. Everything was fine. Ryan was easy going. His job wasn't particularly stressful. He made good money. We," she sniffed, choking, "we were good. Things were good."

"How long have you been married?"

"Six years." She wiped her eyes with the dish towel that had been in her lap. "Did you speak to Vivian yet? She was his first wife. They were together for a decade. She must be devastated."

"Not yet," Brad said. "How was their relationship?"

"It was good. They're friends. We had Viv and her wife over a few weeks ago."

"Oh."

A smile tugged at Mary's lips, her chin trembling which contorted the smile into more of a grimace. "The divorce had nothing to do with Ryan. It had everything to do with Vivian realizing she made a mistake. They still loved each other, but it wasn't a romantic love."

"And you were okay with that?" I asked.

"Of course. Viv wasn't a threat. She was Ryan's best friend." She swallowed, pressing her hand to her mouth and squeezing her eyes closed. "She introduced us. Vivian and I worked together at the antique store after their divorce. She thought we'd be perfect for one another. And we were." Mary's gaze went to the wedding photo hanging on the wall. "I don't understand how he could be gone. We had breakfast together this morning before he headed out. He didn't leave early, which meant today was more of a nature hike than a hunting expedition." A sob escaped, and she shoved her fist over her mouth to make sure it didn't happen again. Once she was calm enough, she took her hand away. "Are you positive this wasn't an accident?"

"It's unlikely." Brad peered around the room. "Would you mind if we looked around? It'd help the investigation if we could have access—"

"Whatever you need," she said. "I have to know what happened to my husband."

Brad pointed to a room off to the side with a large mahogany desk in the center. "Is that Ryan's office?"

She nodded. "Help yourself."

"Thank you, ma'am."

I hung back, offering my condolences. "Are those your sons?" I indicated a framed family photo.

"Yes. That's Billy and Joey. They weren't Ryan's, but he loved them just the same. Of course, they're away at college. They were already teenagers by the time Ryan came into their lives. He never got to do all the fun things with them. Y'know, catch in the front yard, pee-wee soccer, things like that, but he did get to teach them how to drive. He went through so much to adopt them." She wiped at her eyes. "They'll be devastated when they hear the news."

"What about their biological father?"

"He died when they were babies. They barely remember him."

"How did he die?" I asked.

"An accident." She stared at the floor. "I thought that would be the hardest thing I ever had to endure. Now it's happening again."

"I'm sorry."

"Did Ryan suffer?"

"No. He probably didn't even feel it."

"Thank god for that." She sniffed again before standing up. "Excuse me while I clean myself up. Feel free to look around. Let me know if there's anything else you need."

"We will." I hesitated. "Is there anyone we should call for you?"

"No. I'm fine."

She didn't seem fine. She seemed like she was struggling to hold it together, but this wasn't the first time she'd been through this, which automatically placed her on our suspect list. We'd have to dig through everything.

I joined Brad in the office. My partner appeared overwhelmed, which was something I wasn't used to witnessing. He rubbed a hand down his face and indicated the chest of oversized drawers where the Dugreys kept their records.

"They have everything we could possibly want and more.

All of it is categorized and labeled."
"What's the problem?" I asked.
"It'll take forever. We don't have that kind of time."
"Then let's get some reinforcements down here."

# FOUR

"Are you sure this wasn't a hunting accident?" Lt. Winston asked. The moment we returned to the precinct, Winston had called us into his office. "The sheriff's department figured it was an accident. They wanted us to consult, not tell them how to do their jobs."

"In that case, they shouldn't have called," Brad mumbled.

"What's that, Fennel?" Winston stared at my partner. "Are you saying this is an accident?"

"No, sir. But if they believed that's what it was, they never would have contacted us. They would have taken care of it themselves. They asked for us because they wanted to pass this off. Homicide investigations require a lot of resources. Time, money, and manpower."

"The PD is better equipped to handle a homicide," I said. The look of betrayal in Brad's eyes put a pit in my stomach. "But you're right. This shouldn't be our problem."

Winston rocked in his chair. "That's why I was hoping you would have determined this was an accident. I could try to kick it back, but there's no point. The dead man lived here. He worked here. If we chuck this back to the sheriff's office, they'll pester us for our assistance with their case. So we keep it." Winston flipped through the crime scene photos. "One shot. Back of the head. Ballistics came back. Dugrey was killed with a 7.62 NATO round, but not all the rounds they pulled out of the sniper's targets were the same caliber. He could have had multiple weapons or that area is used for target practice by several different hunters."

Brad reached for the report and flipped through the pages. "The killer's using an MRAD. I'd guess an Mk22."

"MRAD?" I asked.

"Multi-role adaptive design. The gun parts are interchangeable, giving the shooter the ability to fire different rounds. The barrels and cartridges can be swapped out. With a weapon like that, he could go for more stopping power or for greater accuracy or distance." Brad rubbed a hand over his mouth before stuffing his hands into his back pockets. "That's what I couldn't place. The varied target distances. He wasn't changing weapons or perches. He was testing out his different options with the one gun."

Winston's eyebrows lifted. "You sound certain. How can you be sure?"

"I've seen this before."

"Where?"

"Afghanistan. The snipers would set up in the desert the same way this guy set up in the woods. One perch, different target areas."

Winston turned back to his computer screen, but from his expression, he wasn't buying Brad's theory. "Ryan Dugrey didn't have money problems, but he frequented that wildlife reserve. According to his wife and the members of his hunting clubs, it was no secret that park was his favorite spot. Plenty of people knew it. Any one of them could have lured him to that location, waited until his back was turned, and popped him." Winston looked at me. "You said Dugrey's second wife's first husband died in an accident. I had someone pull those records. He was the victim of a hit and run. The person responsible was never caught. Since she granted us access to their financials, we've discovered a two million dollar life insurance policy for Ryan Dugrey. Mary is the sole beneficiary. Dig deeper into that. Find out just how happy the couple was."

"Yes, sir." Since this wasn't a hunting accident, we had to assume Ryan Dugrey was the intended target until the evidence proved otherwise.

"Fennel," Winston turned to my partner, "since you're knowledgeable when it comes to weapons, I want you to look into the hunting clubs Dugrey belonged to. Find out who possesses a weapon like the one you described. My money's on one of these sportsmen. Surely, someone had the means. I bet they even knew when Dugrey planned his next hunting trip. That would give them opportunity. All you need to come up with is motive."

"Assuming he was the target." Brad stood up straighter. "I think Dugrey stumbled into the wrong clearing and lost his life because of it."

"You have no basis for thinking that." Winston pulled out a photo of the body and pointed to the hole in the center of Dugrey's skull. "That wasn't an accident. That's a perfect shot."

"I didn't say it was an accident."

Winston tilted his head to the side, as if his brain glitched leading to a physical manifestation. "If that were the case, Dugrey should have run for cover. According to the crime scene, the park rangers didn't believe his tracks indicated he was running away. No branches were broken. His footsteps had been even and in a straight line. He wasn't evading enemy fire. In fact, besides the shots that went into the targets, the only bullet found was the one that went into Dugrey, which was recovered twenty meters away. If this had been an impetuous act, one in which Dugrey walked into danger, where's the evidence to prove it? The shot looked like it had been meticulously planned, most likely by someone Dugrey trusted."

"I'm telling you—"

"You're speculating." Winston put the photo back into the file and closed it. "Explore the most likely scenarios first. I gave you orders. Follow them. Once you exhaust those possibilities, move on, unless something changes. Keep me apprised of your progress." Winston glanced at the door. "Get to it."

"Yes, sir." Brad hated this, and he mumbled to himself as we made our way out of the LT's office. "This is bullshit," he said when we were halfway to our desks.

"I warned you."

He pointed at me. "Not helpful."

"This is really bothering you. Do you mind telling me

why?"

"Most of the time, we get there too late. This time is different. We can stop this guy before he takes down his target. I know it. But not if we go by the book."

I glanced back at Winston's office. "Are you sure about this?"

"Ninety-nine percent."

"All right. Do what you have to. I'll cover for you."

"Liv." Brad looked like he wanted to protest, but saving someone was more important than keeping my ass out of hot water. Even if I hated being a legacy, the daughter of a decorated retired police captain, the rumors were mostly true. I was Teflon. Winston had his sights set on moving farther up the ranks. He already made one giant misstep when it came to the members of his unit. He may have given us orders, but as long as we got the guy and didn't break any rules of procedure, taking a creative detour to avoid following his orders wouldn't come back to bite me in the ass. "I'll start with the hunting clubs, like Winston wants. From there, I'll move on to gun ranges and dealers. Long guns aren't that common." He reached for his phone. "I'll see if Mac can look into black market sales on the dark web while I check the more legitimate routes. If I can find the gun, I can find the shooter."

"At least that'll make it easier to appease Winston." I typed in Mary Dugrey and ran her background. "In the meantime, I'll go after the usual suspects, starting with the wife. We'll trade notes later tonight."

Brad smiled, as if remembering our previous night which had been forgotten due to current events. "Deal."

Even if Brad was correct, that Dugrey wasn't the target, retracing his steps could shed some light on the killer's identity. Since the wildlife reserve was part of the park system, most of their security measures had to do with keeping an eye on who entered and exited. Aside from the security cameras which covered the parking areas and public restrooms, surveillance was at a minimum.

The park rangers had already been tasked with providing plate numbers for everyone who came and went. The sheriff's department would be scouring the rest of the feeds for anyone carrying a sniper rifle or acting particularly suspicious. But that wasn't my concern.

Instead, I dove head first into Mary Dugrey's background check. She didn't have a criminal record. No history of violence or mental instability. Aside from her first husband's accident, nothing else triggered a red flag. Two husbands over the course of twenty-two years didn't exactly scream black widow.

However, Mary Dugrey had the most to gain from Ryan's death. Not only did she stand to gain full ownership of their house and everything in their bank accounts, but she also had his insurance to fall back on. Was that enough of a reason to kill him?

Her husband made good money. He had a salary, pension, and benefits. She, on the other hand, worked on commission at the antique shop which his ex-wife owned.

When I spoke to Mary, she didn't seem jealous. She was happy with her life. I couldn't help but wonder if Vivian Hall, Ryan's ex, felt the same way.

I ran her background, finding nothing significant. The details of their divorce showed it had been amicable. Ryan paid alimony for the first two years they were separated. Their assets had been split. Vivian kept ownership of the antique shop they co-owned, and Ryan kept the house. The rest looked like it had been cut down the middle. Frankly, Ryan may have gotten the worse end of that deal since he was the primary breadwinner.

On a whim, I looked into Mary's dating history. As far as I could tell, she had only dated men. Besides her first husband and his accident, one previous boyfriend had met a tragic end. Cancer. But that had been a few years after they had stopped dating. I couldn't see how that could possibly connect to her or this.

I performed the same review of Vivian's dating history. Everyone in Vivian's past remained alive and well. Unlike Mary, Vivian maintained friendships with her exes. I almost wondered if she and Mary had ever been romantically involved. Based on their social media accounts, they were especially close, but it didn't seem romantic. However, their lives were completely intertwined, personally and professionally. With Ryan out of the picture, I wondered if they'd become closer or drift apart.

Instead of wasting more time on these pointless contemplations, I copied the address to the antique store and went to pay Vivian a visit. The bell above the door chimed, signaling my arrival.

The shop was neatly arranged, each item tastefully displayed. A few people browsed on the other side while a couple spoke to a woman I recognized as Charlotte, Vivian's wife.

I headed toward the rear of the shop, figuring I'd find a desk or cash register hidden somewhere in the back. The price tags on most of the items made me reconsider my chosen profession. It also made me glad that I wasn't carrying a purse for fear I'd bump into something and spend the next five years paying off the damages.

A woman appeared beside me. "May I help you?"

"Vivian Hall?" I recognized her from her photo.

"Yes. Did you call earlier about the writing desk?"

"No, ma'am." I showed her my badge, a little afraid of pushing my jacket out of the way and knocking over a Ming vase. Not that I spotted any Ming vases, but public servants couldn't be too careful. "I'm Detective Liv DeMarco. Do you think we could find somewhere quiet to have a conversation?"

"What is this about?"

"Your ex-husband." I looked around, but the shop didn't appear overly busy. "I don't want to take up too much of your time."

"We can talk in my office." She pointed to a hallway before looking around. "Charlotte, I'll be in the back if you need me."

"No problem."

"Is that your wife?" I asked as I followed her into a tiny, cramped room.

"Uh-huh." She took a seat behind the oversized desk, which looked like it belonged in a mansion instead of the too-small room. I took a seat on the sofa in front of the desk. Unlike the desk, the gray couch had seen better days. The threadbare upholstery had lost most of its luster. From the squeaky give of the cushion, I wondered if the frame would collapse beneath my weight. "You said you wanted to speak about Ryan. I'd like to know why."

"When's the last time you saw him?"

"Three days ago. He came over for dinner."

"You sound like you were close."

"We spoke all the time. Every day."

"Did you speak to him today?"

"We texted." Vivian reached into the front pocket of the half-apron she wore and pulled out her phone. "He sent me photos, like he always does."

"Photos?"

She held up the screen. "Nature photos. We both love the outdoors. He's into hunting and fishing. I like to paint landscapes and flowers. That's how we first met. I had found a beautiful spot at the wildlife reserve near the creek where the most gorgeous wildflowers were growing. Every day, I'd take my canvas and paints and stay until I lost the light. We stumbled into one another, and that led to coffee, which led to dinner, which led to the next decade and a half of my life." She smiled at the photo and put her phone down on the desk. "He still sends me beautiful images for inspiration."

"How does Mary feel about that?"

"She doesn't mind. She likes to tease he sends me pictures of flowers but he brings her actual flowers." Vivian bit her lip. "Why are you asking about Ryan? Did something happen? Is he okay?"

"No, he isn't."

Vivian stared at me. "What happened? Where is he?"

This was the part I dreaded. Telling her flat out would make the rest of the interview more difficult, but I couldn't conceal it any longer. "I'm sorry to tell you, Ryan was killed earlier today."

"Killed? How? Where?"

"At the park." I nodded at her phone. "May I?"

She nodded, swallowing as her entire body trembled. "Do you know...does Mary know? Did you tell her? How is she? May I call her?"

"We notified her a little while ago. You can speak to her as soon as we're finished."

Vivian nodded, her head bobbing up and down while she bit her lip and wrung her hands.

I read the text chain, noting the other photos he sent. Nothing sounded inappropriate. They weren't having an affair. And they weren't fighting. The conversation read like the texts I exchanged with Brad, Jake, or Emma.

"Was Ryan having problems with anyone?"

"Not that I know of."

"Did he talk about work?"

"Work was good."

"What about his hobbies?"

"You mean the hunting and fishing?"

"And whatever else he liked to do."

Vivian sniffed. Tears streaked her cheeks, which she wiped with the back of her hand. "Ryan liked what he liked. Hunting, fishing, camping. He was meant for the great outdoors. He always teased as soon as he retired, he'd move to Montana and become a mountain man. I told him he'd be bored with spotty internet and cell phone service. He wanted both. He needed the bustle of the city and his time in nature. I can't believe...how did he die?"

"He was shot."

"Do you think it was a hunting accident?"

"We're looking into every possibility. Did he have someone he'd go hunting with? A friend? A group of friends?"

"He belonged to several hunting clubs. They'd have competitions and events. He liked participating in those things, but he preferred his time outdoors to be solitary. It was part of that balance he needed." She shook her head, predicting my next question. "As far as I know, he wasn't with anyone today. He went to the wildlife reserve alone."

"Who knew where he'd be?"

"Me, Mary, Charlotte, anyone who knew what he liked to do with his days off."

"So everyone he worked with?"

"Pretty much."

Charlotte appeared in the doorway. "Viv, what's wrong?" She maneuvered through the clutter and wrapped Vivian in her arms. "Sweetheart, what is it?"

Vivian gave me a final look. "Are we done?"

"For now." I put my card on her desk. "If you think of anything or anyone who may have wanted to hurt him, let me know. I'll be in touch."

I made it as far as the door before Viv said, "Ryan's dead." And then she burst into tears.

I glanced back into the office, finding Charlotte rocking her gently while she smoothed her hair and hugged her. Based on that scene alone, I didn't think Charlotte had anything to do with Ryan's murder either, but jealousy was another common motive for murder. However, that didn't fit what I was seeing. My gut said Brad was right, which meant we were running out of time.

# FIVE

Today wasn't supposed to go like that. The area should have been empty. Why wasn't it? Why did that guy have to show up? If the hunter had only waited three more minutes, he would have lived.

The sniper stared at the black gun case. After taking the shot, he didn't stick around. He couldn't relish in his kill or celebrate the pinpoint accuracy. He had to get out of there. But damn, if that hadn't been perfect. On the bright side, he no longer had any doubts that the sights were properly aligned and he was ready. Losing the gun would be smart, but it was the perfect weapon. He hoped it'd become part of his signature. Too bad the shot hadn't been silenced, like the test fires before it.

But since the wildlife reserve was so large, he hoped no one had heard the shot. Had he been thinking clearly, he would have screwed the suppressor back on, but he hadn't wanted to spook his prey. That was the number one rule. The target should never see it coming.

Originally, he hadn't had an exact timetable established for his first hit, but once the hunter's body was found, he'd have to set the other dominos in motion. After all, legends weren't made by accident. Every step had to be carefully planned. A murdered hunter wasn't supposed to be his first move. But since the shot turned out so superbly, he didn't want to waste the notoriety that would be associated with it.

He'd have to keep his ear to the ground. Once the body

was found, the police would investigate. He was confident he could stay a step ahead. That had always been his plan. Maybe today hadn't been a waste. Maybe it was a glimpse into what was yet to come. A Frank Sinatra song played through his head.

The smile tugged at his lips. Unlike those insane killers who taunted the police or did foolish things that ultimately led to their capture, he didn't want to get caught. He wanted to be a whisper, a shadow, the boogeyman. That's how he'd become the most sought-after assassin in the world.

*       *       *

The Dugreys' financials and internet history didn't indicate anyone in their house had an interest in sniper rifles, hiring hitmen, or committing murder. Not that any of those things would be blatantly obvious, but there were usually breadcrumbs or something that didn't feel quite right. But nothing set off my spidey sense. The discrepancies in Mary's background, namely the previous dead husband, proved to be inconclusive.

Unlike Ryan, Mary's first husband didn't have an exorbitant life insurance policy. In fact, he didn't have any life insurance at all. They were young with two small children. They weren't expecting tragedy to strike. Given their financials at the time, they didn't have any extra to spare.

Mary had been a waitress who took online courses in art history and business. Somehow, that translated to getting a job at an antique store. After her first husband's death, she moved back in with her parents who provided childcare and financial support until she was able to get back on her feet. If she had something to do with her first husband's death, her involvement wasn't motivated by money. And now that she had enough to live comfortably, I didn't think the two million dollars in life insurance would have been reason enough for her to want her current husband dead.

On a whim, I looked into her children. The twins were sophomores at the same local college. They lived on campus. They received scholarships which covered a third of their expenses. The rest was paid for by the college fund Ryan had set up and their work study. Neither had ever been in trouble. No known issues with drugs or alcohol. I checked, but they didn't have gun permits or any firearms registered in their names.

No police reports had ever been filed and no 9-1-1 calls had been placed. Nothing indicated Ryan Dugrey was abusive or violent. If he was, the police had never been alerted. I had seen Mary. She didn't have any visible bruises and wasn't covered up to hide marks on her arms. Most likely, she hadn't had her husband killed as a way to protect herself.

"The wife's not involved."

Brad looked up from his desk. "Told you."

"How's the search for the gun going?"

"Not great."

"Did you get anything from the hunting clubs?"

"They're game hunters. Every member owns a hunting rifle. As far as the administrators know, none of the members own sniper rifles, even though several have large gun collections."

"Gun collections of hunting rifles?" I asked.

"And handguns, assault rifles, the usual. You got your side arms, classic artillery, and your AKs and AR-15s. Nothing out of the ordinary. Nothing like what the killer used."

"Did you ask specifically about the Mk22?"

"They didn't know of any member who possessed one. I've reached out to some contacts. I'm still waiting to hear back. The gun shops I've called are sending over what they have on everyone who purchased a sniper rifle, specifically any gun that can fire the rounds used to kill Ryan Dugrey."

"That should help."

"Except we both know a weapon like that wasn't acquired through legal means."

"It never hurts to check."

"Sure." But the way Brad said it told me he didn't believe it.

I looked at the time. It wasn't five yet. The work day would be wrapping up soon, but if I hurried, I should be able to make it to the insurance company where Dugrey worked before close of business.

"I'll see what Ryan Dugrey's coworkers have to say. Call if you find something," I said.

"You do the same."

My trip to the insurance firm was a bust. Everyone at the office knew of Dugrey's outdoor hobbies. When asked, every member of the firm could tell me where Dugrey would be on his day off—the wildlife reserve.

Dugrey was well liked. No one showed any outward animosity toward him. When told he was dead, most exhibited shock and sadness. None of his coworkers stood to benefit from his demise. His death wouldn't lead to any promotions or bigger offices. Still, I added the names to the list, asked the usual questions, and got a list of his current clients and policies he'd been working on. Maybe someone didn't like the new premium quote and offed him or was denied coverage and went berserk. Stranger things had happened. I'd be remiss not to consider the possibilities, but I knew it was a waste.

After passing those details off to some uniformed officers to run down, I decided to check out the three hunting clubs. Brad had phoned them, but matters like this required a personal touch. My partner had been trying to save time. That was his prerogative, but Winston wouldn't be pleased to find out about this. By showing up, I hoped to get something relevant and appease our CO. Two birds, one stone.

I'd never been to any hunting clubs before. The image I had in my head was a cross between a lodge and a shooting range. But the first place I visited wasn't either. It looked more like a cigar club with nice furniture, a lot of polished wood and leather. Animal heads and antlers hung from the walls over fireplaces, and nice bookshelves were lined with leatherbound classics and display cases featuring antique weaponry.

Only a handful of people were inside. Two women and four men. The man at the door hadn't stopped me when I entered since I flashed my badge, but now that I had time to get a look at the place, he cleared his throat.

"Are you seeking membership?" he asked.

"No. I was hoping you could tell me something about Ryan Dugrey."

The man smiled politely. "He is a member."

"I know. That's why I'm here."

"May I ask what this is about?"

"Mr. Dugrey was killed earlier today. It was his day off."

"Was it a hunting accident?"

Everyone had asked the same question, which made me curious. "Why would you think that?"

"Ryan was deer hunting." He lifted his phone off the desk, unlocked the screen, and showed me a photo. "He sent this to me earlier today. He always sends photos when he starts his day."

"Were you two close?"

The man shrugged. "Ryan texts everyone the same thing. All the members do it. We have a shared social media account. Everyone has access. We all post our photos." He wrote down the handle and slid it toward me.

"You post photos of fresh kills?"

"It isn't distasteful. Mostly, it's sunsets or sunrises, empty fields, the quiet woods, our gear for the day, the sandwich we ate while hiding in the weeds, or the squirrel or bird we spotted."

"Did Ryan post any photos today?"

The man tapped his screen a few times before shaking his head. "If you recovered his phone, you should have access to this information."

I nodded, not willing to tell a potential suspect that the phone had been damaged and we hadn't been able to access the information saved on it yet. We had phone records, but that was only half the picture. The rest would take more paperwork and time, which Brad was convinced we didn't have.

"How well did everyone know Ryan?" I asked.

The man indicated a photo hanging on the side wall. It showed a dozen and a half people in camouflage, holding their rifles while posing in front of the fireplace. Ryan was left of center, smiling brightly. "We're a tight-knit group."

"Did anyone have any issues with Ryan?"

The man shook his head.

"Was he exceptionally close to anyone?"

The man shook his head again. "We socialized together. We'd have barbecues and dinners. We did some charity fundraiser stuff. Ryan always participated. But mostly, this was a place for people to hang out. He'd stop by maybe once a week, when we didn't have any events going on, have a drink, and share details on his latest find or perch he really liked."

"Did he mention anything about a clearing he found at the wildlife reserve?" I did my best to describe the area where we'd found the body.

The man flipped through the photos on the hunting club's social media page. "Are you talking about this spot?"

I looked at the photo. The targets weren't set up in the trees, but it looked like the same place. "Yeah."

"About a month ago, Ryan found that place. It wasn't close to any water or food sources. The rangers put out salt licks and the like for the animals, but they always do that in more wooded areas. This was out in the open. Besides some birds and geese, he had never spotted anything worth shooting there."

That phrase made me raise an eyebrow. "Someone else felt differently."

The man looked uncomfortable. "You're right. I didn't mean to...I will help however I can."

"Can you get me access to this social media account?" I pointed to his phone. "I'll also need names and contact information for all your members." I nodded toward the group assembled near the fireplace, sipping cocktails out of crystal glasses and chatting easily. It must be five o'clock. "I'd also like to talk to them."

He gestured to the doorway. "By all means."

"Thanks." I hadn't expected that kind of treatment. Instead, I'd expected the stereotypical anti-police response.

Relieved I didn't get it, I went into the other room and repeated the process with the group assembled. Every single person had received photos and texts from Ryan.

Ryan had shared that spot with everyone in his hunting club, but according to the six people I questioned, none of them had bothered to make the hike to visit that location.

"It didn't seem worth it," the woman on the left said. "It was quite the trek. No waterfalls and nothing but squirrels, geese, and rabbits. I have nothing against them, but if I was going out for the day, I'd want to bag a stag."

"You and me both," the woman on the right said. She almost laughed before she remembered what happened. "Do you think someone intentionally killed Ryan?"

"We're still investigating."

The man beside her looked uneasy. "You think one of us is involved."

"I was hoping you had something insightful to share."

The man snorted. "This is a fishing expedition."

"Let me guess. Lawyer?"

The smug look evaporated. "Corporate, mostly. But my firm has a division that specializes in criminal defense cases."

"Did you kill Ryan Dugrey?"

"Don't be absurd."

"Then let's not worry about your firm's specialties." I asked a few more questions, but no one knew of anyone who had gone to check out the location Ryan had found. "If it was such a terrible place for hunting, why would he go there?" I finally asked.

"Ryan liked the journey more than the endgame. He wanted to commune with nature. Hunting didn't exactly fit his personality. He would have been better off taking nature hikes. That's what he enjoyed. But every so often, he'd get it in his head that he had to prove something. That's when he'd bag a wild turkey or some fowl. He shot a deer two years ago. It took him almost another year to finish off the venison and jerky," the lawyer said.

"That's why he got a permit this year," the woman on the right said. "He was feeling that itch to get another one."

"But none of you ever went hunting with him?"

They shook their heads. "Ryan preferred it that way."

"What about the rest of you? Do you go out together?"

"It's an outing for sure," the woman on the left said. "We make a day of it. We may not come home with anything, but it's fun."

"That's because your big mouth scares the critters away," the man with the beard said.

I gave him a look. "You seem to take this seriously."

"I understood Ryan's point. He liked the quiet. He was respectful of nature."

"Even when killing Bambi's mom?" I asked.

"Especially when he was hunting. We do it for sport. It's not like we can't go to the grocery store and pick up steaks, but Ryan made use of what he killed. He didn't do it to be showy." He glanced at the lawyer.

"It's a sport. We're sportsmen," the lawyer said.

The bearded man shrugged. "To each his own."

After checking alibis, I handed out copies of my card, collected the member list and contact sheet from the man at the front desk, and headed to the next hunting club where Ryan Dugrey was a member.

# SIX

"You can take the last one." I indicated the cauliflower wing leftover from last night's game night. After the day we had, I couldn't believe that was only yesterday. It felt like decades ago.

Brad stabbed it with his fork and popped it into his mouth. He didn't even look up from the screen. I would have made a joke, but now wasn't the time. This case was getting to him.

The three hunting clubs hadn't been able to provide any insights into Ryan Dugrey. The only useful piece of information I had gleaned from them was that Ryan had shared that quiet clearing with everyone—his wife, his friends, his coworkers, his hunting buddies.

"If someone wanted Ryan Dugrey dead, it wouldn't have been hard to figure out where he'd be and when he'd be there." I reached for a carrot stick, dipped it into the ranch Brad had made, and took a bite. He was right. The ranch was better than hummus.

Sighing, he rubbed his eyes and leaned back in the chair. It was the first time he'd relaxed since we arrived at my apartment. Even his eating was tense. "He was shot from behind. No one was lying in wait to pop him. If they were, he would have been shot from the front."

"Couldn't it be argued that Dugrey knew his attacker and trusted him enough to turn his back to him?"

"I see you've been hanging around ADA Winters again."

"Brad."

He scrubbed a hand over his face before grabbing a carrot stick, smothering it in hummus, and biting down on it. "That's not what happened."

"Were you there?"

He glared at me, got up, and grabbed a jar of almond butter from the pantry. After finding a bag of raisins, he returned to the living room, covered a celery stick in the nut butter and grabbed a handful of raisins and stuck them on top before taking a bite.

"The hummus is about the same color." He indicated the dip bowl before grabbing another celery stick and repeating the process, this time with hummus instead of almond butter. "Pretend the hummus isn't on the table. All you see is a platter of these." He indicated the two celery sticks. "I tell you they're both ants on a log. You see the ingredients, so you assume that's what it is. It looks like it, right?"

"Brad, I don't need you to make infantile comparisons."

"But that's how it looks. This," he picked up the unbitten celery, "looks like it could be that. But upon closer inspection, it turns out it's something else entirely."

"I said I didn't need the comparison."

"I know, but something tells me the LT will. I thought it'd be best to practice on you first." He ate the celery with almond butter before picking up the second stalk. After taking a tentative bite, he shrugged and ate the rest.

"How was that?"

"It would have been fine without the raisins." He wiped his hands and went back to staring at the computer screen. "You're right, though."

His theatrics left me confused. "About what?"

"Dugrey went past his attacker. We found the phone destroyed, but his wallet remained. The killer wasn't after his money. But he smashed the phone, which means Dugrey may have had something on it that would have helped us identify the shooter."

"Maybe he snapped a photo."

I scrolled to the top of the hunting club's social media page, but the newest photos didn't cover the clearing. They had been taken much closer to the entrance. "Cell service is spotty. We had a hard time getting a signal to call out."

"The park ranger had to radio it in and let someone else call the sheriff." Brad balled up his napkin and tossed it from hand to hand. "Dugrey must have realized something wasn't right. He was a hunter. He would have sensed danger. He must have come up on the guy, realized he was in trouble, and tried to walk away."

"A random act of violence."

Brad got up to clear the table. "You know how hard those are to crack."

I checked my messages, but the sheriff's department and park service hadn't found any witnesses. We had the surveillance footage from every camera in and around the place, but that wouldn't be helpful unless the guy had a record or we knew who to look for. "Did you get anything from your black market contacts?"

"Not yet."

I checked my phone again, but no messages had appeared in the last half a second. "Mac hasn't gotten back to us yet either." I grabbed my own plate and left it in the sink. "What did she say she was working on yesterday?"

"I don't remember."

Neither did I. "Do you think she's still bogged down with that?"

Brad shrugged. "She knows this is a top priority. I told her there's a clock on this."

"How much time do you think we have?"

"I have no idea, but I hope it's enough."

*     *     *

He kept one eye on the TV hanging above the bar. The sound had been muted, leaving only the captions. Today was supposed to be nothing more than target practice, something to break-in the new gun and bolster his confidence. Instead, it turned into a mess in both the literal and figurative sense.

"Do you want another?" The bartender indicated the beer bottle beside his plate.

"One more," he said.

The bartender grabbed the longneck, popped the top, and put it down. A bead of condensation rolled down the side. "Anything else?"

"A few more napkins," the man said. "I don't like to make a mess." It was true. He liked things to work out neatly. Nothing today had been neat, not even the burger he ordered, which had dripped sauce all over his plate and fingers. Why did today have to be one of those days?

To make matters worse, the eleven o'clock news came on. Normally, he didn't concern himself with the talking heads, but he wondered if the body had been found and word had spread. Even though he believed that area was quiet and secluded, the hunter never made it home that night. Surely, by now, someone was missing him. That would result in a search. Once the body was discovered, they'd have to rule it a homicide. A perfect shot like that couldn't happen by accident.

He pointed to the TV. "Do you mind turning it up?"

The bartender glanced around, but the place was practically empty. Grabbing the remote from the shelf beneath, he cranked up the volume. "Is that loud enough?"

"Yeah, thanks." The man finished his fries and wiped his fingers.

*"A body was found in the wildlife reserve earlier today. An investigation has been opened into what police believe to be a homicide. If you have any information, please call."* The number and website flashed at the bottom of the screen.

He remained on the stool through the first commercial break and finished his beer before the weekly weather forecast had completed. Once he knew conditions would be pleasant the next day, he paid his bill, left a tip, and headed out. Tonight, he'd make a few final tweaks to his weapon. In the morning, he'd scout the various vantage points he'd scoped out and select a location. After that, all he'd have to do is wait for his target.

He didn't want to waste too much time. Even though it was unlikely the police would ever figure out he was to blame for today's murder, he wanted to stay a step ahead. The sooner he finished the job and got out of the city, the better. He wanted to be a legend. That meant he couldn't be caught or killed.

# SEVEN

Brad jumped, nearly giving me a heart attack in the process. I'd fallen asleep on the couch while watching surveillance footage from the park entrance. The dim gray filtering in from behind the curtains told me it wasn't quite dawn.

He gasped a few times, his eyes wild as he searched for some unseen danger.

"Brad," I said from across the room, "are you okay?"

He blinked a few times, his left hand shaking. "Yeah. Fine."

He wasn't, but there was no reason to point it out. He ran a hand over his face and squinted at the digital clock over my stove. "I should go upstairs. We have work in three hours. I need to get some sleep."

"Do you want to stay here?"

"No. You need to sleep too. I'll give you a ride in the morning."

"Are you sure you're okay?" I knew that look. Brad had another one of his nightmares. This case, like a lot of our cases, brought up bad memories for him. Snipers. Wars. None of it was good. "I'm here if you need me."

He gave me a lopsided smile. "I know, but I'm okay." He went to the door, turning to find me behind him. "Thanks, though."

"Yep." I leaned against the doorjamb, watching him go down the hall and disappear into the stairwell. Once he was out of sight, I closed my door and bolted it shut. Then I stared up at the ceiling, waiting to hear him enter his apartment. That was the good and bad of living beneath him. I always knew when he was home. Once he was settled into his place, I closed my laptop, piled our notes into a neat stack, and crawled into bed.

When my alarm went off, I resisted the urge to throw the annoying device across the room. Instead, I forced myself out of bed and into the shower. The not quite hot enough water jolted me awake. By the time I was dried and dressed, I was more than ready to hit the ground running.

With two travel cups filled with high test, I grabbed my things and headed for the door. Brad must have heard me open my door because he met me in the stairwell before I could go up to his apartment.

"Is that for me?"

I handed him the cup. "I grabbed your notes too." I indicated the messenger bag hanging from my shoulder.

"And my laptop?"

"I got everything."

He flipped open the lid and took a sip. "You're too good to me."

"I know."

He smiled, but it didn't quite reach his eyes, which were dark and red. More than likely, he hadn't slept. I wasn't sure what he spent the last three hours doing, but he smelled strongly of aftershave, which was usually a sign he'd been drinking. However, I didn't think he'd want to dull his senses by doing something that stupid when he was so convinced the clock was ticking.

"Did you have any revelations last night?" I asked.

"Not really. Our best bet is tracing the weapon, but I've been thinking the shooter has skills. That kill shot was dead center."

"Pun intended?"

He scowled. "Too early in the morning, Liv."

"Sorry."

"Anyway," he unlocked his car and we got inside, "we know the shooter was using that area for target practice, but he's already a good shot. Nothing was too far off. He was precise. I'd say the discrepancies were due to conditions or unmade adjustments rather than lack of skill."

"I agree." I let the words sink in. "Our killer must have another place where he practices."

"There are only one or two ranges that could accommodate someone with his skills."

"You don't think he has his own private target area set up someplace else?"

"If he did, why would he have gone to the wildlife reserve to practice?" Brad turned to look at me. "If you say because he wanted to kill Dugrey, I will let you out here and you can walk to work."

"You wouldn't do that to me."

"Do you wanna bet?"

"I could call Jake. He'd pick me up."

Brad shook his head. "We haven't even been out on an actual date yet, and you've already figured out how to twist the knife. Explain that to me, Liv."

"Fine, if calling Jake bothers you so much, I'll call Logan Winters instead."

Brad fished out his phone and held it in my direction. "Go ahead. In fact, you can use mine."

"Now you're the one twisting the knife."

Brad laughed. "What? From what I remember, you did spend a night in the ADA's bed."

"I spent the night alone in his bed."

"Sure, whatever you say." But he knew I wasn't interested in Winters, just like how he knew I wasn't interested in Jake. There was only one person who ever made Brad feel threatened, and that was a complicated and sticky situation which would never be fully resolved.

"Seriously though," I said, getting us back on topic, "the killer found what he thought was a secluded place in a wildlife reserve where he could fire off as many shots as he wanted without arousing too much suspicion. What makes you think he'd take his fancy gun to a range and fire in front of other people when he didn't want to attract any attention?"

"But he would have attracted attention." Brad scratched his cheek, something he did whenever he had a thought. "Yesterday, you pointed out that the gunshot would have sounded different coming from a sniper rifle than a hunting rifle."

"So?"

"So, the wildlife reserve is full of hunters. They'd expect that thundering boom. They would have realized it sounded different."

"Which could be why—" I stopped mid-sentence. "As far as we know, Ryan Dugrey was the only person who went to that clearing. From what everyone told me, that was his place. That's where he always went to commune with nature or whatever. No one else was with him. No one else went to investigate."

"Dugrey didn't hear the gunshots," Brad said. "If he had, he would have stayed away or gotten a park ranger. He was already there, or he stumbled upon the shooter, who didn't want to leave anyone alive who could ID him."

"But he hadn't committed a crime at that point."

Brad gave me a look. "Not yet, but he has something in the works and got caught preparing. That's how I know Dugrey wasn't the intended target and why we have to hurry up and stop this guy before it's too late."

That was a lot of supposition. "I'm not sure. Dugrey may have heard something and went to investigate on his own, came across the sniper, and—"

"And what? Continued past him like nothing happened? If Dugrey was expecting trouble, he would have snuck up behind the guy, found out what was going on, and tried to backtrack. He stumbled into something."

"Which is what you said yesterday at the scene," I pointed out, "which means Dugrey didn't hear the gunshots."

"Our sniper had a suppressor."

"You're sure?"

"It's the only thing that makes sense. Not a single person the sheriff's department and park rangers interviewed remembered anyone or anything out of the ordinary, including suspicious gunshots besides the one that killed Dugrey."

"All right, so what does that mean?"

Brad parked in his usual space. "I don't know."

I laughed, even though it wasn't funny. For a second, I

thought he was about to say something brilliant that would blow this thing wide open and point us directly at the sniper. "Okay, so..."

"So it's something else to run down. However, I hold to the fact this guy was practicing at a range. The only reason he would have deviated and went to the wildlife reserve was because he needed somewhere secluded to test out the suppressor. He couldn't do that in front of prying eyes. It would have led to a lot of questions."

"That perch couldn't have been the sniper's normal spot. Dugrey would have noticed. He went there all the time." The wheels turned in my head. "How do you think the killer found it?"

"He could have stumbled upon it while hunting."

"Do you think he's a hunter?"

"Possibly."

"All right, I'll run down every member of those hunting clubs again. Even if he wasn't part of the club, he may have accessed their social media accounts. Those photos had been posted for a while. He may have thought it was the perfect spot too."

"Okay, check in with Mac."

"Will do." I got out of the car, my mind turning over the facts. "Dugrey shared that location with everyone he knew. Maybe Dugrey knew his killer, even if he was never meant to be the intended target. He could have seen what one of his friends or acquaintances was doing, asked him about it, and when he tried to leave, that person stopped him."

"That would explain a lot," Brad said. "And it would mean yesterday wasn't a waste. Let's hope you're right. While you do that, I'll continue working the gun angle. Even if I can't find the gun purchase, I may get lucky with the suppressor." He shook off the question before I could ask it. "A man can dream, right?"

"Sure."

After checking in at our desks, I unloaded my materials from the bag and left the rest with Brad. I had my own mess to sort through. But it was nothing compared to Mac's workstation which was covered in half a dozen oversized cups and just as many candy bar wrappers.

"Tell me you didn't sleep here," I said.

"I can tell you, but it won't be true." She tilted her head back and peered up at me. "Well, it's sort of true. I didn't sleep exactly. More like stopped blinking for about twenty minutes. I don't think my eyes even closed, which would explain why my contacts are so dried out they are glued to my eyeballs."

"Mac—"

"I know." She waved it off. "But between Brad's case and what I was already working on, I didn't think I had much of a choice." She made a few exaggerated blinks before grabbing an eyedrop bottle from the drawer and squeezing a few into her eyes. "That's better."

"Did you make any progress?"

"Black market sales on the dark web are scary, scary things. I've been talking to this guy, Cobra, for the last four hours. He says he may have something for me, but it's probably more dick pics."

"Wh—"

"You'd have to be there." She pointed to the black chat box in the corner. "Here. There. Whatever." Her ponytail bounced, reminding me of the tail on a rainbow unicorn toy I had as a child. "But I found several people willing to sell Mk22s. I'm trying to figure out if any of them are local or sold to someone local. It's slow going, backtracking their movements and determining their prior contacts. Any idea when the gun was purchased?"

"I have no clue. The guy's lethal with it, so however long that would take."

"Do you think he has prior training? Military? ESU? Something like that?"

"That's our best guess. Who else would have the know-how or skill?"

"Video game enthusiasts?"

"Seriously?"

"I don't know. Simulations are never the real thing, but what's to stop a guy from training himself?"

"No one does that."

"Except those whackadoo bunker militia types."

I nodded at the screen. "Do you have someone in mind?"

"A few someones. I'll let you know as soon as something pans."

"How long? Best guess."

"Give me an hour." A photo appeared in the chat box, a close-up crotch shot. "Maybe two." She turned to look at me. "But that's not the entire reason you came to see me."

"I need to know everyone who saw the photos of that clearing where Ryan Dugrey was killed." I gave her the details on the hunting clubs and their social media accounts. "You may also need to check the rest of Dugrey's online history and phone records. Dugrey shared his special place with everyone."

Mac pointed to the photo on the screen. "Just like this guy."

# EIGHT

The panel van remained parked on level four of the parking garage. The garage was nearly full, but there were enough spaces scattered throughout the first three floors that he'd only seen two cars circle past since he'd arrived.

He had found a place to park on the exterior wall, where the break in the cement allowed him the perfect view of the insurance firm, Smith and Smith. The security cameras in this particular garage were a joke. He had hacked the system, set it to loop, and deleted the footage of his arrival. Even if the authorities determined this is where the shot originated and recovered the footage, the most they'd get would be a shot of a van.

The pet grooming decals he'd placed along the sides matched a local business he'd found. The van itself he'd borrowed from the back lot of a flower shop that was temporarily shut down on account of a water leak. The license plates he'd swapped with a car he found parked in an assisted living community. The authorities would be twisting, running each of the Frankenstein parts of the van, none of which connected to him. It was brilliant. Everything necessary had fallen into place.

From the driver's seat, he stared through his binoculars at the insurance firm. Ken Yeger's office was on the forty-seventh floor. Yeger had denied the wrong claim. That made him responsible. He had to pay, and since he made sure it wouldn't be in dollars and cents, blood would have to suffice.

He peered around the binoculars at the clock on the dash. Yeger had a lunch meeting at 12:15 with one of Smith and Smith's top clients. Like clockwork, Yeger would take the elevator to the lobby five minutes too soon and take that time to step out of the building, walk twenty-five feet away from the front door, and call his mistress.

*Should I let him say goodbye?* The thought made him chuckle. Having someone hear the shot over the phone would be far more dramatic. The rumor would circulate, but he didn't want to cut it that close. As soon as Yeger was away from the building and he had a clear shot, he'd take it.

After checking the side mirrors, he popped out the windshield and slid it down the hood. Reassembling the rifle with his preferred pieces, he loaded the weapon, set it up on the stand, and shifted out of the driver's seat and into the passenger's seat. He would have preferred a better position, like on his belly, which was how he learned to shoot, but he'd make this work.

The panel van kept anyone behind him from seeing what he was doing. No one would ever see his rifle unless they came up beside him, and if anyone was that stupid, he'd shoot them with his side arm. He was nothing if not prepared. But he didn't like messy. Unlike yesterday, today would be neat and clean. An easy in and out.

Everything was set. He aimed at the area beneath the awning. Days earlier, he had marked the spot where Yeger always waited for his car with chalk to indicate the man's height. Headshots were the best. It left no question. The victim would not survive, which was the point.

According to current weather conditions, winds were calm. Humidity was low. Nothing would interfere with the shot. Still, he wanted to be precise. Searching through the scope, he found a spot above the awning where four bricks met in what looked like a perfect cross.

Easing his finger onto the trigger, he waited for the thump in his chest and squeezed. The bullet took a moment to reach its destination, letting out a little puff of cement as it hit its mark. Zooming in, he made sure the shot landed dead center. It was a hair to the left.

He adjusted a smidge, wondering if the sights were off or

if the calm breeze had been enough to disturb the trajectory over the distance. He was far enough from the insurance firm for his shot to be considered exceptional but not extraordinary. After all, he was just getting started. Legendary status had to be earned, like building up characters in video games. He couldn't go from level 1 to level 100 with only one kill.

Precisely eighty-seven seconds later, Ken Yeger exited the front door. He peered around, as if expecting his driver to be waiting. When he didn't see the town car, he pulled out his phone and moved off to the side, stopping beneath the awning.

The sniper smiled, the giddy sensation coursing through him. *Relax.* He ran through a quick meditation while he stared at the man through the scope. With the magnification, he could make out what was on the phone's screen. Yeger was placing a bet using a sportsbook app. Before he could hit submit, the 7.62 NATO round pierced his skull half an inch above his ear. He would have preferred if the shot had gone between his eyes, but since Yeger was standing sideways, leaning against the brick, that would have to count.

As he disassembled the long gun, placing the pieces back in the case and tucking the tripod away, he glanced across the way. Without his binoculars, he couldn't make out the details, but he could see the frantic scurrying, like woodland creatures escaping a fire.

Leaning forward, he snagged the strings he had tied to the loops he'd glued to the inner frame of the windshield and dragged it closer. After securing it back in place, he started the engine and slowly backed out of the parking space. By the time he exited the garage and was halfway down the street, he heard the first of what would be many sirens. And so, the legend begins.

\*     \*     \*

I'd spent most of the day pouring over persons of interest, but I didn't know if any of this would yield results. For all I knew, the killer could have stumbled upon that clearing in the wildlife reserve by chance, the same way Ryan Dugrey had a few months earlier. It wasn't a secret, but it was off the beaten path, literally.

I put down the phone. The park rangers hadn't been able to help. Visitors were encouraged to stick to trails and common areas. The park staff had no way of knowing who veered away or explored beyond the commonly traveled paths.

Security cam footage hadn't yielded any results. Since we had no idea what the killer looked like, it'd be impossible to find him on the footage. We had a list of names of people who had entered prior to the murder and exited after the estimated TOD. Someone on this list had killed Ryan Dugrey.

Background checks turned up all sorts of things, but I didn't spot any murder charges in the mix. Instead, I found myself comparing that list to members of the hunting clubs to which Dugrey belonged. That made the most sense, but I didn't find a match.

Mac was still tracking down every IP address which had accessed the photos Dugrey had posted on social media, but I didn't expect there to be any real surprises. More than likely, the same people who belonged to the clubs went to the pages. With any luck, the few oddballs would lead us to the killer. But I didn't have the information yet. Instead, I found myself going through Dugrey's phone and internet history while I performed my due diligence and looked for the usual suspects, even if Brad and I agreed it was unlikely the killer and Dugrey had a history. More than likely, they didn't even know one another.

"That can't be a coincidence," I muttered.

Brad came up from behind me, having returned from his trip to a gun range that specialized in distance targets. "Did you find something?"

"No."

"I thought I heard you say something about a coincidence."

"The clearing or whatever it is, Dugrey picked out that spot. That's his spot. I scoured the internet looking for other posts or mentions about that location but there's nothing."

"Did you think the killer was going to post a selfie of him standing there?"

"Y'never know."

"True, but we should assume this guy doesn't have shit for brains."

The mention of brains reminded me of yesterday's crime scene. My stomach did an uncomfortable flip. Usually, Brad was the one who got queasy at scenes, not me. "How did your outing go?"

"I'm not sure." Brad put a folder down and placed a USB on top of it. "I convinced the owner to hand over his records. On the wall, he has a few used targets with the distance, date, and shooter listed, like a hall of a fame. Based on what I've seen, a few guys could have made the shot that killed Dugrey."

"Did you get their names?"

Brad snapped his finger and made an 'aww, shucks' gesture. "I knew I forgot something."

"Smart ass."

"Most of the guys are military. A few are still active. I'll make some calls and see what I can find out. I may know some people who can help us out with this."

"Why am I not surprised?"

"Jealous?"

"Nope. This is the entire reason why I keep you around."

"It's not for my good looks and charm?"

"It's one hundred percent because of your good looks and charm. If not, you'd be useless to me."

His brown eyes sparkled. "You think I'm good looking and charming?" He winked. "I'll take it." After giving me a flirty look that made my stomach do another flip, this time the good kind of flip, he picked up the phone and went back to work.

I leafed through the folder before taking the USB and plugging it into my computer. After copying the data, I put it down, skimmed the list, and cross-referenced it to the data I already possessed. Four names matched.

"Brad," I wrote them down and slid them across to him, "these guys were at the wildlife reserve yesterday."

Nodding, he drew stars beside their names on his list

while explaining who he was and the information we needed. Two of the men had been military. One active. One retired. The other two were a mystery. He drew question marks beside the other two names, and I ran background checks while he spoke on the phone.

Before the results of the first search came back, Detective Jake Voletek approached my desk. He looked at my partner, who had curled himself in toward the phone while furiously scribbling on the notepad.

"Hey, Liv," Voletek gave Brad a concerned look before shaking it off and turning his full attention to me, "you might want to see this." He held out a tablet with crime scene photos. They were dated today and timestamped three hours ago. "The ME said this was the second time in two days he had something that looked like this. I'm guessing it's the same guy."

Today's victim looked similar to Dugrey in that he had a hole through his skull. Instead of going back to front, this shot had gone from side to side, essentially ear to ear. The sight was sickening, but I forced myself to flip through the other photos.

"The MO looks the same." I couldn't find the ballistics report. "Any idea about the bullets or gun used?"

"7.62 NATO rounds."

Brad's chair squeaked. He'd heard Voletek. "When?"

"This afternoon, right around lunchtime." Voletek took the tablet from me and handed it to Brad. "No one heard gunfire. Someone said they thought a car in the distance may have backfired, but that was one report. No 9-1-1 calls came in reporting a shooter."

"The bastard has a suppressor." Brad exhaled a shaky breath. "Fuck." He slammed his palm on the desk before rubbing a hand over his face and flinching. "I knew it. I fucking knew it."

"Who's the vic?" I asked.

"Guy named Ken Yeger," Voletek said.

"That sounds familiar." I reached for a stack of printouts and skimmed. "Where was he killed?"

"Outside Smith and Smith."

"He worked there. He was in charge of..." My mind had

blanked on his official title.

"He's an adjuster," Voletek supplied.

"That's where Dugrey worked," Brad said. "Shit. Did I get it wrong? Maybe if I'd—"

"Stop." I stared into my partner's eyes. "This is not on you."

"Of course, it isn't." Voletek took back the tablet. "The scene hasn't been cleared yet. If you want to check it out, you should hurry."

Brad grabbed a set of keys. "Let's go, Liv."

# NINE

By the time we arrived, the body had been carted away. The spatter remained on the wall and sidewalk. The area had been roped off. Most people were too busy to gawk at the crime scene tape or police officers standing around, which I appreciated. But there were always those few nosy looky-loos who wanted to know what happened. Thankfully, officers were handling it.

"They should have notified us sooner," Brad said.

"You saw the photos. What were you going to learn from seeing the body?"

My partner didn't answer. Instead, he eyed the hole where a crime tech had dug out the bullet. "High caliber. It entered on one side, exited on the other, and still had enough oomph to pierce the brick and mortar." He turned, staring into the distance in the opposite direction. "Has anyone run trajectories yet?"

Ellie Simmons, a crime scene tech, closed her kit. "What are you barking about, Brown Eyes?"

I tried not to laugh. Ellie and Brad were friends. She could get away with that. In fact, her question helped shake my partner out of his foul mood.

"I'm sorry." He shook his head a few times. "This may be our second victim."

"Two sniper kills?" She whistled. "I would have thought I'd have heard about that."

"News doesn't always travel fast." I indicated the hole in

the wall. "You're sure we're looking at a sniper?"

"Yep. Patrol thought it could have been a drive-by or something point blank, given how ridiculously precise the kill shot was. But no one heard or saw anything." She indicated several security cameras in the area. "Footage has already been pulled. A canvass is in the works." She stared at the spot where the blood had soaked into the pavement. "There aren't a lot of vantage points. For it to hit the way it did, I'd say it must have come from above," she stood with her back to the wall, gesturing with her hand and pointing, "given how tall the vic was and where it ended up against the brick. I'm waiting for our gear. We'll get laser pointers set up and run it through the computer to get the exact angle and degree."

Since buildings didn't line the other side of the street, the only structure with a straight shot to this spot was a parking garage at the end of the street. I wasn't sure how difficult making a fatal, precision shot from that distance would be. ESU could answer that question, but Brad didn't need verification. He asked Ellie to call him once the gear arrived and crossed the street.

He didn't even look before walking into what could have been oncoming traffic. However, patrol had closed both ends of the street, given the homicide, so my partner didn't get splattered across anyone's windshield. Maybe he knew it was safe to cross, but my gut said he wasn't even aware. He had tunnel vision.

"Hey, Liv," Ellie nudged me, speaking softly, "what's going on with him?"

"Yesterday, he predicted this would happen. He wanted to stop it, but," I glanced at the crime scene markers, "obviously, that didn't happen."

"Poor, Brad. Do me a favor and keep an eye on him."

"That's the plan." I looked both ways before dashing across the empty street. Even though the roads were blocked, I'd seen crazy motorists and homicidal maniacs run roadblocks and demolish sawhorses too many times not to take the extra second to make sure the coast was clear. And Brad thought I was the reckless one.

Brad stopped a few yards in front of me, turned around,

and pulled out his phone. By the time I caught up to him, he was staring at the screen, the magnification turned up all the way. "See that?" He indicated a mark on the screen above the awning. "The bastard took a practice shot."

"Are you sure that's what that is?"

He took a few photos and sent them to everyone involved in the case. Then he passed his phone to me, saving me the trouble of taking mine out to see the photo. "It's dead center, just like his kills. This guy's a pro. That's why he took the test shot. He wanted to make sure conditions were right. No interference. No nothing."

"Shouldn't he have been concerned test firing would have alerted his target or someone nearby?"

"Patrol said no one heard the shot. Either shot."

"He must have had a suppressor, like we suspected."

"That would make distances more challenging. But the garage isn't too far away. It'd be a tough shot but not impossible. Not for someone skilled." Turning, he headed to our next destination.

The garage was filled but not overcrowded. Brad indicated several security cameras as we entered.

"I'll have someone pull the footage." I called it in while I followed him up the stairs.

My partner didn't even waste time on the first level since Ellie said the shot came from above. Brad indicated the rear and side walls. "He would have had to have been positioned against this front wall."

Brad slipped between two SUVs and peered out the narrow opening where one concrete slab stopped at chest height, leaving a three foot opening before the concrete slab from the level above began.

Spinning, Brad checked for security cameras, finding a few. "Make sure we get footage from every camera in this place."

"Yes, sir." Normally, I'd have a more sarcastic retort, but now wasn't the time. I peered out the opening. "A lot of trees are in the way." The few that lined the sidewalk blocked the path from the garage to the insurance firm.

"He wouldn't have wanted an obscured shot. He must have shot from higher up." Brad reversed course, heading up the ramp to the next level.

On the third floor, we repeated the process. From here, the trees no longer created an obstacle. I started on one end. Brad started on the other, and we searched for evidence or any indication the sniper had been set up on this floor. But we didn't find anything. No spent casings. No scratch marks from a tripod. Nothing.

Brad reached for his phone. "We need CSU in here. They can check for gunpowder residue. But I'm not seeing anything obvious." He called for another unit and dialed Ellie. "How are we looking with those trajectories?"

"We're still getting set up," she said.

"Hey," I got my partner's attention, "I'll check upstairs. Meet me there." After he nodded, I made the trek up the ramp, moving to the side as a silver SUV circled downward.

The female driver appeared to be in her mid-thirties. I flashed my badge, hoping she'd stop, which she did. "Is something wrong?" She peered at me from her half rolled-down window.

The murder took place three hours ago. It was unlikely she had seen or heard anything suspicious, but I had to ask. "When did you park in the garage?"

"A little after two. I had a few quick errands to run."

"Where were you going?"

She gave me a suspicious look. Too many of these and she'd tell me to go to hell. "The bank, the pharmacy, and to pick up an order of cupcakes for my kid's birthday. Why does it matter?" Her eyebrows knit together. "Is this about the police cars blocking the other street? What happened down there?"

"Did you happen to see any suspicious vehicles in the garage when you arrived?"

"No."

"Do you usually park here, ma'am?"

"Whenever I need to. It's a public garage. Now if you don't mind." She moved to roll up her window.

I snapped a shot of her license plate as she drove away in case I needed it for reference. But since she arrived two hours after the murder, I didn't see how any of that was relevant. Desperate times. However, desperation led to mistakes. Maybe that's how Brad and I missed whatever it was we missed.

On the fourth level, I peered around. Unlike the previous floors, this one had a lot more empty parking spaces. The security cameras were focused on the up and down. A few covered the interior rows, but the only camera that covered the area we were interested in faced away from the vehicles. This would be the ideal spot to commit murder.

I moved along the front wall. Half the spaces were empty. I checked for spent casings, but I didn't find anything. The concrete wall didn't show any chipping or fresh scratches from a tripod.

A bulky SUV and a classic pickup caught my attention. The vehicles were high, the hoods raised almost level with the opening. Could the sniper have been set up on top of a vehicle?

I wasn't sure how he could have made a shot like that. The hoods were too short to support him and the long gun, unless he held it. But precision shots required a stable base.

My phone rang. *Brad.* "Hey, what's up?" I asked.

"The equipment arrived. They want to test the trajectory with laser pointers. Where are you?"

"Level four."

"All right. Stay there. I'll tell Ellie we're ready." Once Brad sent the text, the two of us watched, waiting for the laser sight to indicate where the shooter had been.

"Unlike at home, this time, I'm on top," I said.

Brad snorted. "Which position do you prefer?"

Despite the circumstances, I couldn't stop the blush or keep the sly smile off my face. "I'm not telling. You have to play your cards right if you want to find out."

"I could guess."

"You could." But before he could respond with something playful, I spotted the laser sight. "Tell Ellie I know where the shooter was positioned."

"I'll inform the mobile crime lab. Let's get everything processed ASAP."

# TEN

"I can't believe this," Brad said.

"I can. This guy is good. He killed Ryan Dugrey without anyone noticing. In fact, if our assumption is accurate, he killed Dugrey because he had gotten caught. I'm not surprised we didn't find anything at the garage. If we had, it would have been another body."

Brad looked skyward, fighting not to say whatever was running through his mind. But I'd spent enough time with him to know those thoughts were a string of expletives. "We should have had something. The security cameras should have seen him enter or exit."

"Do you think he had a car?" I asked.

"He must have. Nearby traffic cams didn't spot anyone carrying a suspiciously shaped case in or out of the area."

I reread the notes I'd made concerning the crime tech's observations. "You and I searched high and low. We didn't find any shell casings or anything suspicious. No shoe prints. No discarded binocular caps. Nothing."

"I know, but you heard Ellie. The shot came from that garage."

"Level four. I know." My prior theory resurfaced. "Do you think he could have fired from his vehicle? I noticed a van and truck parked near there, but the hoods weren't long enough to support the shooter and the gun, unless he held it."

"There's no way he fired like that." Brad keyed something into the computer. "What about the bed of a pickup? That would have worked."

"Would it be high enough?"

Brad grabbed the reports, looking for the measurements. Once he found them, he ran a comparison to the numbers in our vehicle database. "A few models ride high enough for that to be the case." He reached for the phone. "I'll have someone check traffic cams for these specific vehicles."

"What about hydraulics and other mods? Bigger tires or a custom suspension system would put the bed higher."

He snapped his fingers and pointed at me. "Good thought."

"I'll run comparisons to the list we have, starting with those four names. If nothing tracks, I'll expand to the hunting clubs and see if any vehicles matching that description were at the wildlife reserve yesterday."

"Did you run the backgrounds yet on the two non-military members from our short list?"

"I was just about to. I guess I'll start with their vehicle registrations."

Before I could get to it, Mac dropped into the chair beside my desk. She looked exhausted, but I refrained from asking when she'd slept last. That would do nothing but earn me a round of glares from her and my partner, and I didn't need that kind of disapproval in my life. If I did, I'd call my mother.

I entered the first name in the computer, Seth Ramsay, and waited for the information to populate. "Should I ask how it's going?" I glanced at her from the corner of my eye while I scanned the screen. *Mazda Miata. 1994.* Not a classic. Maybe a clunker. Either way, not an appropriate vehicle to use to take the shot.

"Probably not," Mac said.

"Brad, how do we know he didn't set his rifle on the opening in the concrete wall? Wouldn't that make the most sense?" I asked.

"No scratches or scrapes on the concrete. No shoeprints nearby."

"Would we even have seen any of that?"

Brad sighed. "I don't know. It depends on a lot of factors, but you saw that garage. The floor was covered in grime.

Between leaked fluids and trash, Ellie swears there would have been some sort of path from his vehicle to that wall."

"Even if he parked in front of it?"

"Especially if he parked in front of it. You saw those wet places. Even you and I left a trail."

"You should have had booties," Mac said, her eyes brightening. "Do you think the killer could have had on booties?"

"Booties wouldn't stop anyone from leaving a trail behind. All they'd prevent is creating identifiable shoeprints," Brad said. "What we need is to find him on the security footage." He stared at her. "Tell me you figured out why what we recovered is useless."

Mac rubbed her palm into her eye before yawning. "The footage from the garage was wiped. The hacker was good but not great. Ramirez and Scofield can handle that."

"Are you sure?" Brad asked.

Mac tried not to chuckle. "They should be fine. I told them once they uncover the hacker's identity or recover the deleted footage, they better pass it along to you."

"Thank you kindly," Brad said.

Mac tipped her imaginary hat in his direction before poking me in the arm. "As far as your earlier requests, I got the names associated with those IPs. Two of the hunting clubs had their accounts set to private. Only members accessed them. The third is a problem. They started running online ads days after Ryan Dugrey posted photos of that spot he found in the wildlife reserve. Hundreds of people accessed the account after clicking on an ad. Conceivably, they all saw his post. Turns out, his best kept secret wasn't a secret."

"Dammit."

"However," she grinned, "I sorted that list based on duration—the time spent on the page. The majority clicked, realized it was for a hunting club, and left. I'd call those bounce backs, even if they technically don't qualify."

"We're not worried about proper tech terms if it leads to a suspect," Brad said.

"Right, so anyone who lingered on the page for a while or visited again is at the top of the list." She indicated the upper portion of the page she printed. "Unless the killer has an instantaneous eidetic memory, which I don't think is a thing but would be really cool and come in handy, then he would have had to memorize the details, take a screenshot, or come back a second time to make sure he could find the place."

"You're the best," I said.

"I try, but it doesn't feel like it." She turned her attention back to Brad. "I still can't track down the gun sale. Everyone I've talked to hasn't been able to lead me to much of anything. Someone must be dealing in MRADs, but all I've found are parts, not the entire weapon, and no suppressors that fit. But buying one of those would be easier and less traceable through official channels, so maybe he acquired the gun a while ago and bought whatever specialty parts he wanted through normal means."

Brad wasn't buying it. "What about hired hits?"

"Like a hitman?" Mac's ponytail whipped back and forth. "Nothing definitive."

"Do you think they know you're working with the police?" I asked. "Maybe that's why no one wants to talk gun sales or contracts with you."

Mac slumped further into the chair. "I don't know. I've been careful. I have the lingo down, but a lot of people on the dark web have plenty to hide. They like to be cautious." A thought crossed her mind, and she shot upright. "I have an idea. I'll be back later."

"What?" I asked, but she had already sprinted across the bullpen and was halfway through the door.

Brad rocked in his chair, watching the door swing a few times before closing. "Hand me that list." He pointed to the printout Mac had given me. After skimming the names, he handed it back.

"That was quick." I picked up the list. Near the middle, not at the very top but closer to where the bounce backs started, I spotted what Brad had seen. "These two guys made the short list."

"Which just got even shorter."

Of the four potential suspects which Brad had determined from his trip to the gun range and the intel the park rangers provided, two had seen the photo Dugrey had posted. One of them, Charles Robard was active military. Brad had already checked into him, but an exemplary record and decorated service didn't prove Robard hadn't returned home on leave with an insatiable thirst for blood. The other name, Jim Parnell, never served. I'd been in the middle of running his background check when Voletek informed us of Ken Yeger's murder.

"Let me see what they drive."

"Start with Robard," Brad insisted. "If the sniper rifle wasn't purchased on the dark web, Robard would have been able to procure one while overseas on a mission." He pulled out the notepad he'd tucked into the top drawer, the one he'd been so vehemently scribbling on while on the phone. "Robard worked classified missions. Given his training and specialty, I can only assume he was overwatch, providing support and cover for..."

"For?" I hated when Brad trailed off like that. Half the time, he was flashing back to something he would have been better off forgetting, and the rest of the time, he realized how farfetched his theory sounded and hoped by going silent I wouldn't pester or tease him about it.

"I don't know. It's not important. Just find his vehicle registration."

I keyed everything in and waited. "He drives a Santa Cruz."

Brad pulled up vehicle details. "That's basically a cross between a pickup and an SUV."

"Would it be high enough?"

"It should be." He scratched his cheek. "What about Parnell?"

"He drives a two door hatchback hybrid."

"That won't work." The lines in Brad's forehead deepened. "Military sniper and trained killer. We know Robard was at the wildlife reserve yesterday and knew about the clearing. We also know he drives a vehicle which would have made taking the shot without physically stepping foot inside the garage possible. Any idea where he was today at noon?"

"No idea, but we could ask him."

Brad drummed his fingers on the desk. "How many

weapons does he have registered in his name?"

I pulled up the details. "Four. No sniper rifles. He has a hunting rifle, two handguns, and a shotgun."

"That we know about." Brad's fingers flew over his keys. "I can't find anything about him online. No social media. No nothing. But that goes with his clandestine military ops."

"Seriously, what were you going to say earlier?"

Brad looked embarrassed, which was something I wasn't used to seeing. "I was going to say he was working with spies."

"Like the CIA?"

"Possibly, or any of the other intelligence agencies."

"Why would you think that?"

"I was a soldier long enough to interpret the double speak and can read between the lines. But I could be wrong."

"You always want our cases to involve spies or ninjas."

Brad laughed. "You're the one who got on the ninja kick that time." But the teasing quickly dissipated. "Robard could be our killer. I say we pay him a visit, but we need to take precautions. If we're right, he's lethal from a distance. We don't want him to see us coming."

"Unless we have hard evidence, it's not the seeing us coming we should worry about. It'd be the walking away that could be problematic." I cross-referenced his name with Ryan Dugrey and Ken Yeger. When nothing popped, I checked to see if I could find any connection between Robard and Smith and Smith Insurance. The firm hadn't given us their entire client list, so I picked up the phone and dialed. "I'm calling about Charles Robard's policy," I said. "I want to make sure the last payment was received."

"Do you have the policy number?" the woman on the other end asked.

"Not handy."

"What's the name again?" she asked.

I spelled it and waited. A moment later, she told me the automatic draft had gone through a few days ago and it should be reflected in my bank account within the next two or three days.

Brad watched me put the phone down. "Is he a client?"

I nodded.

"Shit." He shoved his drawer closed so hard his chair scooted back several inches. Hoping to quell the outburst, he rubbed a hand over his face. "I got it wrong. Dugrey wasn't an accident. He was targeted."

"We don't know that. The scene—"

"Look at the facts, Liv." He scooped up the keys. "I say we have enough to bring Robard in. I'll notify Winston and see if a tac unit will accompany us. I'm not taking any chances."

While Brad put everything in motion, I read everything I could find on Charles Robard. He fit the profile, but he'd never been in trouble. His service was exemplary. If he'd had any disciplinary issues, Brad's military contact would have mentioned it. Was this guy that careful? His spy friends could have taught him the basics of tradecraft, blending in, and appearing nonthreatening. We could be dealing with a sleeper or someone who had gone off the reservation. Maybe a Jason Bourne or Ethan Hunt.

"No more action movies for me," I mumbled.

"We leave in five," Brad said, not bothering to sit as he organized the papers on his desk and grabbed whatever he thought we'd need. "Winston wants us to bring Robard in. We'll have plenty of backup in case things go sideways."

# ELEVEN

"Mr. Robard, this is the police. Open up." Brad stood to the side of the door, eyeing me as we waited to see what would happen. The house was surrounded. Tactical was covering the rear. The man wouldn't be able to sneak away. "Mr. Robard?" Brad knocked again.

Another member of the tactical team stood beside me, holding the battering ram. Despite the circumstances, knocking down a suspect's door wasn't recommended.

"Let me try." I banged against the door. "Charlie, we need to talk to you. Please, sir. We have questions."

Nothing.

"Should we prepare to breach?" The cop beside me hefted the ram higher. Before he could step back, something creaked on the other side of the door.

Brad held up his hand, instructing the other cop to wait. "Mr. Robard?"

The door squealed as the man on the other side pulled it open. He wore nothing but a towel, his skin and hair still dripping. Half of his face was covered in shaving cream. He looked utterly bewildered to find us on the other side.

I filed that thought away, figuring a killer wouldn't be that surprised when the cops came knocking, unless he was overconfident. "Charles Robard?" I asked.

"Yeah." He looked from me to Brad before zeroing in on the battering ram, identifying the officer holding it as the biggest threat. "What's going on?"

"Police," I said. "I'm Detective DeMarco." I held up my badge and identification. "This is my partner. We need you to answer some questions."

"About what?"

"Where were you around noon?"

Robard glanced at me before his eyes drifted back to the battering ram. "Out."

"Out where?" Brad asked.

"What is this about?" Robard asked.

"Sir," I waved off the tactical team member, who took a few steps back and put the battering ram down, but he wasn't going to leave us on the porch with a government-trained assassin, "we need you to come to the station to answer some questions regarding two recent crimes."

He wiped the shaving cream off the side of his face with the back of his hand and rubbed it absently against the towel covering his thigh. "You mean the two men who were killed by a sniper."

Brad took a step closer, getting a better look inside the house. "Yes, sir."

Robard rolled his eyes, snorting derisively. "Figures." He gave us one last look. "I have to get dressed." He turned, whipping off his towel and walking naked toward the bedroom.

"At least we know he's not concealing any weapons," I said.

"You didn't see him from the front. Who knows what he's packing," the tac team member said.

"Liv, wait here." Brad tested the screen door, pulling it open and entering. "Scroggins, you're with me."

The tac team member pushed past me and followed my partner inside the house. I didn't like waiting outside. I wasn't sure why Brad had told me to wait. Did he expect Robard to run, open fire, or give me a lap dance? Usually, thoughts like that would never cross my mind.

While I waited for them to exit, I worried gunfire would erupt at any moment. However, that didn't happen. Instead, the three exited without incident. Scroggins radioed an all-clear to the rest of the team and escorted us and our suspect to the cruiser.

A blue car pulled up as I was opening the back door for Robard. The woman parked in front of us and got out. Automatically, my hand moved to my gun, pushing my jacket out of the way and displaying my credentials.

"What's going on here?" She moved toward us, peering around me to see Robard. "Charlie, what's happening?"

"It's nothing, Julia. These cops have questions. It's no big deal."

"Questions." She cursed. "What the fuck is wrong with you people? This man is a hero. You can't take him."

"Ma'am," I held my hand out to keep her from attempting to intercede, "we just want to talk to him. That's it."

"I don't care. I'm calling a lawyer." She sidestepped but didn't move closer. "Charlie, I'm calling Murph. I'm gonna tell him what's going on. We'll get you out of this."

"Julia, it's fine. I can handle it." Robard moved closer, letting Brad assist him in getting into the back seat.

"Who are you?" Brad asked, shutting the door and turning his attention to the woman.

"Julia Gotti. Charlie's my boyfriend." She glared at us. "I'll make sure you regret this."

Brad didn't bother to acknowledge her. "Liv, let's go."

I stepped backward, unsure what to expect. Once I made it to the passenger's side, I opened the door. I didn't want to turn my back on her. Thankfully, she let out a huff and turned away from us once her call connected.

"Feisty woman." Brad eyed Robard in the rearview. "Clearly, she loves you."

Robard turned to look out the back. "Most of the time, anyway."

While we drove to the precinct, I explained to Robard that he wasn't under arrest, but we had reason to detain him until he answered our questions. Robard wasn't stupid. He knew why we came knocking, but he didn't resist. Again, that struck me oddly.

Once we arrived at the precinct, we brought him to one of the interrogation rooms and settled in. Robard looked around. "I've seen worse."

"Do you spend a lot of time in police interrogations?" I asked.

Robard chuckled. "No, ma'am. This is a first." He eyed Brad. "Did you serve?"

Brad nodded.

"How many tours?"

Robard wanted to bond with my partner. Usually, we tried to bond with the suspect to gain their compliance. I wasn't used to a suspect putting in the work for us. Did he want our sympathy? Did he think that would convince us to let him go?

"Three." Brad settled back in the chair. "When we came knocking, you said you knew what brought us to your door. Why would you think this is about a sniper?"

"I saw the news." Robard smiled. "There aren't many people who can make shots like that. It makes sense you'd track down anyone who could. I'm sure I'm on the short list."

"Do you want to make this easier and tell us why you did it?" I asked.

"I didn't."

"All right." Brad stretched one leg out beside the table but otherwise didn't move. "Since it wasn't you, why don't you tell us where you were at noon today so we can get you out of here?"

"I was out."

"Out where?"

Agitation played across Robard's face. "I don't have to answer that. It's none of your business."

"Were you cheating on Julia?" Brad asked.

Robard set his jaw, shaking his head and staring at the ceiling. "I know what you're trying to do. It won't work."

"You don't have to tell us where you were today," I said. "How about yesterday? Where were you yesterday?"

He licked his bottom lip, his head still shaking. "You know I was there, at the wildlife reserve."

"Were you hunting?" Brad asked.

Robard's cheek twitched. "Not exactly."

"Target practice?" I asked.

"I didn't kill anyone or anything, at least not in the last two days."

"Then tell us where you were today," Brad insisted.

"Where you were yesterday doesn't help your case. In fact, it helps ours, and I don't want to jam you up because of unfortunate circumstances. That is not why we're here."

Robard considered my partner's words.

"Look, you came willingly. That tells me you understand what's going on. Things don't look good. You have the necessary skills, and you were in the wrong place at the wrong time yesterday. Tell us where you were today, give us an alibi, someone who was with you, anything, and I will walk you out of here," Brad insisted.

"It'll make it worse."

"You were there today too," I said. The second murder hadn't hit the news yet, at least I didn't think it had. "It's how you knew there was a second victim."

"I saw the police cars. I heard people talking. I didn't take that shot," Robard said.

Brad glanced at me. My partner was about to bluff. "Officers are searching your place now. You have four guns registered in your name. How many more are they going to find?"

Robard stared at my partner. "I know how this looks, but you got the wrong guy."

"That's your story?"

"That's the truth."

"Where were you today?" I asked. "Were you at Smith and Smith?"

"What if I was?" Robard asked.

"Do you know Ken Yeger?"

"Who is that? Is he one of the victims?"

I didn't like the game Robard was playing. He knew a lot. More than he should. But he insisted he had nothing to do with it, even though everything he said indicated otherwise. "What about Ryan Dugrey? Does that name ring a bell?"

"It does because I heard it on the news last night. He was the man killed at the park."

"How far can you shoot?" Brad asked.

"As far as I have to." Robard stared at him. "What's your point?"

"Don't give me that. You're a sniper. What's your record?"

"I'm sure it's better than yours."

"I'm sure you're right."

Robard arched a challenging eyebrow. "You want my kill stats too?"

"Two people are dead," I said. "This isn't a joke."

"I wasn't joking, ma'am. I didn't kill them. I've killed dozens of people but not them. I follow orders. No more. No less."

"Tell me about your insurance policy," Brad said.

"It's insurance. A little something extra in case things take a turn. I want to know my family is taken care of."

"I bet those premiums are a beast," I said. "Given your military career, I'm surprised you could get coverage."

"Smith and Smith was willing to take me on." Robard stared at me. "What's your point?"

"Did an actuary perform the assessment?"

"I'm sure someone did." Robard sensed this was a trap.

"That's why you're paying through the nose." Brad sat up a little straighter. "I bet that pissed you off. Most guys I served with took the coverage provided or whatever they could get through organizations specifically designed to deal with service members. Smith and Smith doesn't fit the bill. Why did you choose them?"

"Julia insisted. She works there. That's why I was there today. I went to meet her for lunch."

"Why didn't you say that sooner? If you were—" Before Brad could finish his statement, Robard cut him off.

"She was with a client. I left food with the receptionist at the front desk. After that, I took a walk, hoping for some solitude. I don't know where I ended up, but by the time I circled back to pick up my truck, police cars were everywhere."

"Where did you go?" I asked. "Security cams could clear your name."

"There were no cameras. No people. Nothing."

"That's hard to believe. Where did you go?" Brad asked.

"I don't know. I have a tendency to wander. I put on my headphones and tune out the city. If not...I don't know."

Brad scratched his cheek, but he didn't push harder. "We'll have to arrest you unless you can provide evidence to the contrary that you aren't responsible."

"I told you what I can. I didn't do this." Robard looked resigned, not scared or desperate, which was how a lot of wrongly accused usually appeared. "I can't be the only sniper around here."

"Like you said, you're on a short list," I said. "You're a member of a gun club, right?"

"I have a membership to a range. What does that have to do with anything?"

"Don't you have access to military resources for target practice?" Brad asked.

"I try to separate from that when I'm on leave," Robard said.

"Do you know anyone at the gun range who could have made those shots?" Brad asked.

Robard thought for a moment. "Maybe, but I don't know names."

"You're not helping yourself here," I said.

"I'm telling you what I know, ma'am. I can't give you facts I don't possess."

"Do you own an Mk22 MRAD?" Brad asked.

Robard fought to keep the corner of his lip from quirking upward. I wasn't sure if it was a smile or smirk, but it meant something. I just didn't know what. "I'm not answering any more questions. I'd like to go home. Can I do that?" Robard knew we'd arrest him. He wanted us to read him his rights. He wanted a reason to stay quiet and have his attorney present.

"I tried," Brad said. "I really did." He stood. "Charles Robard, you're under arrest for the murders of Ken Yeger and Ryan Dugrey."

After Robard was Mirandized, we dropped him off at intake to get processed. This should have been a win, but it didn't feel like it.

# TWELVE

Julia Gotti didn't live with Charles Robard, which made executing the search warrant that much easier. Inside Robard's home, we found the four weapons registered to him, along with a gun safe filled with high-powered heavy artillery, including an Mk22 and a few boxes of 7.62 NATO rounds.

Ballistics was processing the weapon, hoping to match it to the murders, but given the condition of the bullets and the state the victims had been found in, that would take some time. Meanwhile, the suppressor had yet to be found.

Robard's browser history didn't tell us much. He visited the usual places with a stronger emphasis on porn sites and hunting resources than the average person. However, nothing indicated he was radicalized, stalking his targets, or planning to go on a killing spree. What possibly could have set him off?

"Do you think Julia was having an affair with someone at work?" I asked.

Brad shrugged. "We don't have access to her information, so I don't know for sure, but we have everything on both victims. Ken Yeger had her phone number stored in his contact list, but they rarely spoke. No inappropriate texts or voice messages."

"No dick pics?"

"You're spending too much time with Mac. But no. No sexting either."

"That doesn't mean they weren't having an affair. With

Robard deployed, they wouldn't have had to waste time with those types of things. He could have taken her out whenever he wanted. They could have made plans at work."

"Yeger is married," Brad pointed out. "Based on what was in his phone, he already had one mistress. He wouldn't have had need for another one."

"What do we know about the mistress?" I asked.

Brad pointed toward Voletek's desk. "Ask Jake. He was supposed to run that down."

"She's an exotic dancer," Voletek said before I could open my mouth, "at Daphne's. I'm guessing that's how they met. Yeger always brought her a present when he'd stop by. The relationship sounded transactional. He called her twice a week before his lunch meetings. They hooked up on Wednesdays. She wasn't certain he was married, but she suspected."

"Does she have other boyfriends?" Brad asked.

Voletek's shoulders inched upward. "She didn't say. I didn't push."

"If so, one of them may have wanted to see Yeger dead."

"Did the wife know?" I asked. "If she did, she'd also have reason to want her husband dead."

"I spoke to Carolyn Yeger. She said they had problems. They were in counseling, but their marriage has been over for a long time. He slept in another room. I didn't get the impression there was a lot of love between them. I doubt she would have been jealous enough to want him dead or to hire someone to kill him, but I'm looking into her financials and online activity anyway. So far, I've found nothing that connects her with the suspect you brought in."

"Are you keeping the Yeger case?" Brad asked.

"Until word comes back that the same weapon killed Yeger and Dugrey, I don't have a choice. But as soon as we have proof it's the same killer, it's all yours." Voletek smiled winningly at Brad, who looked like he wanted to slap him.

"More than likely, we'll have to work together on it," I said, hoping to keep the peace. "Yeger is yours. Dugrey is ours. That seems only fair."

Voletek rolled his chair across the walkway and sat beside me. "Does that mean I get to take a crack at the suspect?"

"You can once his lawyer gets here."

"Do you think he'll confess?"

"Not a chance. He's denying everything. But he has no alibi, except I feel like he should."

Brad stopped what he was doing and stared at me. "Do you think we have the wrong guy?"

"No. Maybe. I'm not sure." I hated the look he gave me. "Hear me out. Robard would have had a reason to be in the area. In fact, he may have had a reason to be at the wildlife reserve too. He said he likes to get away for the solitude."

"That's true of a lot of military personnel, so what?"

"If he had legitimate reasons to be near the crime scenes, which is probably why he chose those places to commit the murders, why didn't he spend a few minutes coming up with an alibi? He spent plenty of time meticulously practicing and planning. Whoever fired from the garage made sure not to leave any evidence behind. He even hacked the security cams and deleted the footage, so why not manufacture an alibi?"

Brad considered what I said. "Getting caught in a lie would be worse. When we asked him questions he knew would be damning, he didn't answer, even if he alluded to the response. He knows the burden is on us to prove he's responsible. Lying will make him look bad, especially if this goes to trial."

"You're right."

Brad gave me a confused look. "Why do you sound surprised? I usually am."

"I don't know."

He sighed. "I hate it when you get like this."

Jake rolled back to his desk. "I'm not getting involved in whatever's going on with the two of you. You sort it out yourselves. In fact, I'd be happy to give you the rest of my notes on Yeger, and you can run with it."

"We're not taking your case," Brad insisted, even though we already had.

Now that we had someone in custody, it made research that much easier. I looked into Charles Robard's life before he joined the service and everything I could find on him since. Brad utilized every connection he had to gain access to Robard's service record. But the man hadn't committed any prior criminal acts. Most of what he did was classified or redacted.

"I hate to say it," Brad said, "but sometimes, things get to be too much. Maybe he snapped. Did you find any triggering events?"

"Nothing obvious. No personal losses." Robard was career military. He had a nice nest egg. The house where he lived had belonged to a great aunt who had left it to him a decade earlier. He only stayed there when he was on extended leave, preferring to get off base whenever possible. When he wasn't around to take care of the house, his mother and brother took turns keeping an eye on the property. "Things with Julia seem good. I checked social media. Nothing scandalous to report. I went through the bigger dating sites and apps to see if she was active, but I haven't found any accounts. I passed it off to someone in IT to look into, but I don't think they were having issues."

"I don't either." Brad chewed on his bottom lip while he ticked off points from his list. "Medical records are harder to come by."

"Physical or psychological?"

"Both, but psych evals are the worst."

"Do you think he's dying of something?"

"He wouldn't be active if he was. He'd be on permanent leave or given some other special designation." Brad palmed the baseball and rocked back in his chair. After tossing it into the air a few times, he said, "We need to speak to Julia. Even if she wasn't having an affair, Robard could have seen her and Yeger together and got the wrong idea. If Robard's the jealous type, a friendly interaction could be misconstrued as flirting."

"You mean the way a lot of people look at us," I said.

Brad gave me that sly look again. "Yeah, something like that."

However, Julia Gotti wasn't our biggest fan. She wasn't a suspect or witness. We couldn't force her to cooperate. So I had to do my best to plead our case on Robard's behalf.

"Ms. Gotti, my job is to find Ken Yeger's killer. Your boyfriend admitted to being in the area at the time of the murder. He was also at the wildlife reserve when another man was murdered. We believe these two killings were committed by the same person using a sniper rifle."

"A very specific type of sniper rifle and by someone who is capable of making a perfect shot," Brad said.

"You think that's Charlie."

"He has the skills," Brad said.

"That doesn't make him guilty. That doesn't make him a killer." She shook her head, annoyed that we had shown up at her apartment after dragging her boyfriend from his place.

"We didn't say it did," I said. "In fact, I have my doubts, but circumstances suggest otherwise. We want to clear this up. The fastest way to do that is by getting Charlie's alibi, but he won't provide one. His story was vague, to say the least."

Julia looked uncomfortable. "That doesn't make him guilty. He'd never...he...he's not violent. Not like that. Not here. Not when someone isn't making him do those things."

"Is it possible someone made him kill these two men?" I asked.

Her annoyance turned to rage. "Get the fuck out of my house."

Brad and I held our ground. "You work with the two men who were killed," Brad said. "You connect them to Charlie. We know Ken Yeger was a cheater, possibly a womanizer. Did he ever act inappropriately toward you?"

"No." She found the idea preposterous. "You think Charlie did this to protect me?"

"I'd do anything to protect the woman I love," Brad said. "If someone hurt you, Charlie would have a defense—a reason for behaving as he did."

"He didn't do this."

"What about Ryan Dugrey?" I asked. "How was your relationship with him?"

"Ryan would run numbers for me on occasion, but we didn't interact that often. He was a nice guy. Quiet. Kept to himself a lot."

"He liked to hunt. Did you know that?"

"Everyone knew that."

"According to your coworkers, everyone knew where

Ryan would spend his days off. You'd know his schedule and where he'd be."

She pointed emphatically at the door. "Get out. I had nothing to do with this, and neither did Charlie."

Brad nudged me toward the door, even though I wasn't ready to leave. But the last thing we needed was to have a complaint filed against us. However, something told me it wouldn't matter if we left or not, Julia would be making a phone call before we even got the engine started.

"I'm not saying this is what happened, Ms. Gotti. But this is how it looks and why our boss wants to pursue charges against Charlie. But I think he's wrong. I think Charlie happened to be in the wrong place at the wrong time. All we need to know is where he went after he dropped off your lunch. If we can figure that out, I'm sure there must be a security cam or traffic cam that will prove he isn't the shooter. Please, help us help him."

For the briefest instant, she looked unsure. Something was on the tip of her tongue, some secret she wasn't sure if she should share, but she held back. Instead, her stare turned icy. "Get out. This is harassment."

# THIRTEEN

He lay on his back and stared at the ceiling. Given the excitement, he should have felt something. A sense of danger or fear, but instead, there was an emptiness he hadn't expected. Did he regret his decisions?

The question gnawed at him while he counted the ceiling tiles. It was a good kill. Clean. Precise. He hadn't left anything behind. He'd been careful. It was in and out. He shouldn't have any reason to be concerned. The police didn't have anything on him.

A smile quirked the corners of his mouth. Pride. That's what he felt. Maybe he wasn't empty. That had been a damn good shot. Still, he would have preferred if Ken Yeger had been facing forward. Right between the eyes was a much more dramatic statement. It'd make the whispers and rumors more impactful. After all, that was a powerful saying for a reason, even if some found it tired or cliched.

"Right between the eyes," he repeated it quietly to himself.

The shot at the wildlife reserve ended between the eyes, but the round he used had done too much damage. The ME should be able to determine that, but that would require reconstructing the skull, and since it entered from the back of the target's head, no one would mention it like that either.

The next one would have to be between the eyes, if there was a next one. He'd told himself these targets weren't personal. The first wasn't intentional, but he had no choice.

Today was different. He did the research. He planned. He practiced. It was meant to be. His goal. His purpose. The next one would be too.

There were others. A few more names. More targets to tick off the list, not that he had written these things down anywhere. That would be sloppy. He didn't like sloppy.

Running a hand against his cheek, he felt the scratch of stubble on one side, which made him frown. He needed to clean himself up. In order to pull this off, he had to appear innocent. His mother always said people trusted a man when they could see his face, which is why he wanted to be clean-shaven, to prove he had nothing to hide.

A fresh shave. That would be the first thing he did when he got the chance. But for now, that would have to wait.

The TV across the room showed coverage from the afternoon. The sanitized media didn't display any of the gruesome or gory photos, which was a shame. His handiwork would have had a shock factor. For those who understood the art, who were looking for professionals, the footage would have impressed them. His status as a legend would already be percolating across the darkest recesses of the internet and in certain hidden circles that few dared enter and even fewer knew about. But instead, the news only showed photos of the dead man, Ken Yeger, when he was alive and well.

The reporter didn't mention the skill necessary to deliver that sort of kill shot. All he mentioned were vague details which sounded like a mix of fiction and what they suspected. Sitting up, he paid attention to the screen. Those details could prove important if he found himself in too deep. But he didn't want to lie. That would diminish what he hoped to build, but it could prove necessary if there was no other way out.

*　　*　　*

Lt. Winston sent us home after we updated him on the situation. Our CO hated OT so much you'd think the money was coming directly out of his pocket.

Brad seemed calmer than he'd been since we caught the

case yesterday morning. Damn. It had only been two days and already we had two victims. Usually, cases didn't escalate this quickly.

"You were right," I said, "about the time crunch."

"Yeah." Brad stared out the windshield.

"We did the best we could."

"I know."

Usually, conversation was easier. Brad never made me work this hard, which meant he didn't want to talk. Instead, I turned on the radio, hoping that'd be enough to distract him from his thoughts. I could usually read him pretty well. Tonight, I was getting nothing.

"Do you want to have dinner?" I asked. "I have leftovers, or we could order something."

"Your mom sent me home with a few containers of pot roast the last time she had me over. It's still in my freezer. We could heat that up."

"Yeah, okay."

Once we arrived at our apartment building, we took the stairs up. I stopped at my apartment to drop off my things and change while Brad went one flight up. By the time I let myself into his apartment, he had the food in the oven and plates on the counter.

"Maria told me not to microwave it," he explained.

"It'll dry out the meat."

"And the oven won't?"

"Not according to my mom."

"I'll have to trust the chef on that one." He opened the fridge, took out a pitcher of iced tea, and grabbed a bag of salad mix. "Is this okay?"

"It's fine." Food was the last thing on my mind, even if my stomach wouldn't agree.

We sat through dinner, staring at our plates, our thoughts a million miles away. Finally, Brad said, "At least it's over."

"Yeah." But something nagged at me.

"You don't believe that."

"I don't know."

"All right. Let's talk through it. What's the problem, DeMarco?"

"Lack of alibi."

"Already theorized and explained."

"Lack of motive."

Brad sipped from his glass to buy time. "Maybe. Maybe not. We don't know what was going through Robard's head. You heard what the guy said in the car. He said *most of the time anyway*."

Now I was confused. "What are you talking about?"

"I said Julia must really love him, and that's what he said in response. It was off the cuff. Not something he thought about. It just came out of his mouth."

"You think that means she was cheating?"

"That's irrelevant. All that matters is what Robard thought."

"So he thought she was cheating?"

Brad got up to clear the table. "He was unsure of her conviction to them as a couple. Maybe he felt threatened by the other men in her life and decided to act to make sure she wouldn't cheat."

"Based on everything we know about Ryan Dugrey, I don't think he showed any interest in her or posed a threat."

"Maybe she was interested in him."

"You don't have any evidence to back that up."

Brad returned from the kitchen to grab my plate, even though I wasn't finished. "I still don't think Dugrey was his intended target."

"How can you say that?"

"Circumstances." He waited for me to snag the last carrot with my fork before whisking my dish away.

I chewed and swallowed before following him into the kitchen. "You're not sure about this either."

"Yes, I am."

"You're not, but you want to be."

Brad placed his palms on the edge of the sink and stared into the shiny abyss of the drain. "We found the weapon, the ammo, and what connects him to both victims. Tell me how we could be wrong."

"I'm not sure we're wrong, but I want to know why."

"The only way is to get Robard to talk. His girlfriend won't say a word. Jake spoke to his family, his mother and his brother, but they couldn't believe he'd do anything like this."

"What about his CO and army buddies? They spend the most time with him. They would know him better than anyone. They'd know his frame of mind, what was going through his head, if he was unstable."

Brad turned on the water and started scrubbing the dishes. "They won't talk, not to us."

"Even if it would help him?"

"They know it won't."

"How could they know that? Unless he's guilty. But even if, you'd think they'd do whatever they could to protect him, including covering it up."

He glanced at me as he placed a dish into the drying rack. "We have no idea what they've already covered up, but that would explain how we got to this point."

The pain in his eyes made me shut my mouth. Brad understood things I couldn't. He lived them. No part of me believed he'd cover up the types of atrocities that became national news, but minor things, things that didn't seem like they'd matter, maybe.

"I can hear the wheels turning, Liv. Stop it. This isn't about me."

I dried the dishes and put them away while Brad filled the pan with water and left it to soak. "What about the gun range?"

"I'll see what else I can get out of the owner in the morning."

"Okay." I ran a hand down his arm, but he moved away from my touch. "It's late. Neither of us slept enough last night. So I'm gonna go. Thanks for dinner."

"Yeah, no problem." He walked me to the door.

"I'm downstairs if you need me."

He smiled, but it didn't make it to his eyes. Then he gave me a hug. "I'm fine, just tired." He pecked my cheek and let go, like he'd done a million times before.

"I'll see you in the morning."

# FOURTEEN

Brad left for work before I even got up. He sent me a text saying he wanted to get an early start. Last night when I left, he didn't seem frenzied like he had the previous night. Deep down, he thought we caught the guy. But the unanswered questions bothered him, just like they bothered me.

When I arrived at the precinct, Brad wasn't at his desk. Neither was Jake. "Hey, Lisco," I called, "have you seen Fennel or Voletek?"

"They went to the gun range. They mentioned something about target practice."

"Thanks." I didn't think they'd waste the morning expelling lead unless it served another purpose besides practicing for their requalifications. However, Brad didn't leave me a note or a message. At least he took Jake with him. That made me feel slightly better.

"Oh, um...that tech was looking for you. The bubbly one with the crazy hair."

"Mac?"

"Yeah."

"Thanks." Since Mac was my favorite computer genius and underutilized by the rest of the department due to her age and prior criminal activity as a hacker, I wasn't surprised Lisco didn't know her name. Mac was my secret weapon. Actually, she worked almost exclusively for the intelligence unit, but since my transfer, she'd been doing a lot more with homicide and other departments.

I found Mac in the tech lab, huddled behind her workstation, earbuds in, bopping to the music only she could hear. I tapped her on the shoulder, relieved when she didn't jump out of her skin.

"Good morning." She pulled out the earbud and put it down on the desk before peering toward the door. "Has Brad come back yet?"

"You know where he went?"

"He went to a gun range to find out more about Charles Robard, which is why I was looking for you." She hooked her ankle around the rolling office chair beside her and pulled it out for me. "Take a seat, my dear." She patted the cushion before turning her attention to the screen and minimizing whatever she'd been working on.

"What did you find?"

"It's not what I found. It's what I didn't find."

"What didn't you find?"

"Everything."

"That doesn't sound good."

She ticked off the points I'd made to Brad the night before about Robard's lack of criminal record and other indicators he planned to kill someone. "He doesn't have any social media accounts. He has two e-mail addresses. One for work. One personal. His contacts are friends and family. And to be honest, he doesn't have a lot of friends who aren't in the service. He has maybe twenty in total. A few guys from the neighborhood where he grew up. A couple of buddies from school. And some family friends. Y'know, older people who knew his parents and took an interest. In my family, it'd be aunts and uncles without any blood or marriage ties."

"I gotcha."

Mac clicked something else which brought up a long list of web addresses. "These are the places he visited, including the hunting club's social media page where Ryan Dugrey posted the photo of his favorite spot."

"Right, which is where he set up for target practice and where Dugrey was killed," I said.

"Yeah, maybe."

"Again with the maybe." I wondered if she had the same doubts I did, but I didn't want to voice them. I wanted to know what conclusions Mac had reached on her own.

"Charles Robard went to the page. There's no doubt about it. He lingered. He must have seen the photo," Mac said.

"Okay, so what's with the maybe?"

"Now that we have a suspect, it's easier to trace his activity backward through everything. His prints weren't on anything we found at any of the crime scenes."

"We didn't recover prints," I said.

"Yeah, I know, but I wasn't talking physical prints." But even that obvious fact didn't sound particularly confident. "I traced his movements as best I could. Robard has a pretty fancy cell phone. The kind that gets great reception in places where most people can't get a signal."

"Uh-huh."

"Yeah, well, he either left his phone in the car or he wasn't at that clearing."

"What about yesterday? Where was he yesterday around the time of Yeger's murder?"

Mac glanced around before entering a few things into the dialog box at the speed of light. "He was in the area. I can't get an exact location. There are a few towers. Even if he was in the garage, he could have pinged a different tower a little farther out depending on carrier and the number of users, overload—"

"Mac," I interrupted, "where was he?"

"It looks like he may have been too far south." She brought up a map of the area and drew a big red circle around a few blocks. The garage where the shooter had set up was right at the edge of the circle. "I know. It's not conclusive."

"You don't think he's the killer?" I asked.

"Brad seems certain."

"But you're not."

"I want to see his computer. He could be hiding anything and everything. But from the records I've been able to access thus far, the jury's out."

"What about the girlfriend?"

Mac made a face. "He could do better."

"He could be a killer," I pointed out.

"That doesn't mean he can't do better."

"What's wrong with her? Was she cheating?"

"No, but she didn't exactly say yes when he proposed."

"He proposed?"

"Twice. Some people don't believe in marriage. I get that. But if that was the case, she should have told him. I don't see why he would have gone through the embarrassment or trouble a second time. People usually only ask when they're pretty sure the answer is yes or if they're desperate."

"Was she pregnant?"

"I didn't think about that. I assumed it had to do with his deployments and wanting to be married in case...y'know." She clicked a few keys. "I'll see what I can dig up."

"All right." I stopped halfway to the door. "How do you know he proposed?"

"His mother mentioned it on her social media account both times it happened. She went into details on what he spent on the ring and where he took Julia and everything after that."

"Did Julia see it?"

"No. They aren't friends online. Julia is friends with his brother, but the mother's account is set to private."

"Then how did you—" I shook my head. "Never mind. That's a stupid question."

Mac grinned. "Isn't it?"

After checking with Ellie Simmons, Brad's favorite crime tech, to see if anything new had been processed from either crime scene that would be of use, I returned to my desk.

Lt. Winston spotted me the moment I returned. "Detective DeMarco," he crooked his finger, indicating I should join him in his office, "I'd like to have a word with you."

When I entered the office, I found a man in uniform sitting in front of Winston's desk. Winston gestured at the man. "This is Major O'Neal. He's in charge of Charles Robard's unit."

O'Neal stood and offered me his hand. "Ma'am."

"Sir." Too bad Brad wasn't here. He would have found the routine amusing. Like something out of a 19th century comedy. Maybe I should curtsy. That would cinch it as comedy gold. *Too little sleep,* my internal voice whispered. "We've been trying to get in touch with you."

"I'm aware. I spoke to Detective Fennel yesterday." O'Neal glanced toward Brad's empty desk. "I was told he should be in momentarily."

"Is there something I can do for you in the meantime?" I glanced at Winston, wondering what was going on.

"I thought it'd be best to answer your questions in person, so we can get this cleared up as quickly as possible." O'Neal folded his hands neatly behind his back as if told to stand at ease.

"Sure. Let's start with—"

"Detective DeMarco," Winston cut me off before I could ask my question, "Charles Robard is being released from custody."

"Why?"

Winston's eyes narrowed, but he fought off the glare which was aimed at Major O'Neal. "It turns out our suspect was running drills on base at the time of the murder."

"That's not possible. He was at the garage. We have witnesses. He brought his girlfriend lunch," I said.

"He left right after that," O'Neal said.

I stared at the major. "With all due respect, how do you know he didn't kill Yeger before showing up for drills? And if he had been running drills on base, how come we were able to locate him at his home a few hours later?"

"The training exercise was canceled." O'Neal was lying. It was obvious, but he didn't even care.

"Charles Robard could be dangerous. He's our prime suspect. Every piece of evidence we have links to him."

"It's circumstantial," O'Neal said.

"I'm sorry. Are you his lawyer?"

Winston coughed. Normally, the LT was the first to reprimand, but given that he hadn't shut me down, I couldn't help but wonder if he called me into his office so I would tell off this prick in the military uniform.

"I am not, but Robard is needed back on base. The United States government invested hundreds of thousands of dollars training him. Unless you have hard proof, he's coming with me." O'Neal turned to Winston and pointed to an official looking document on Winston's desk. It had a seal and everything. "We've already discussed this. You can't interfere. If a crime was committed, we will open up our own investigation into the matter."

"You just said Robard was on base for a training exercise. Now you're saying you'll investigate if there is something worth investigating. Don't you find it hard to talk out of both sides of your mouth at the same time?" I asked.

Winston coughed again. "That's enough, Detective."

O'Neal took a step closer. He was a tall man with at least a decade and a half on me. He thought towering over me would have some kind of lasting effect. All it did was ensure I mentally labeled him a bully. As a rule, I didn't like bullies.

"I'm not in basic training. The drill sergeant routine won't intimidate me." I stared at him. "This is the part where you're supposed to say drop and give me fifty."

"DeMarco," Winston snapped, "that is enough."

I glanced at my boss. "Yes, sir." I turned to leave.

This wasn't good. Charles Robard was getting released. He was our prime suspect. Hell, he was our only suspect. Brad was right. I wasn't convinced, but now with a looming cover-up, I couldn't help but think we had the right guy.

"I apologize," Winston said, even though his words sounded far from sincere. "Solving murder cases takes priority around here."

I didn't hear what else he said as I hurried across the bullpen and pushed open the door. This wasn't exactly ethical, but it wasn't an overt rights violation either. I knew how to operate in the grey when necessary. Downstairs, I found Robard waiting to get released. They'd moved him to a temporary holding cell while the paperwork was finalized.

As soon as the officer on duty let him out of the cell, I met him at the desk where he waited to collect his belongings. "Charlie," I faced him, keeping one eye on the door in case O'Neal showed up, "I see you're getting out of here. I guess you were right. I owe you an apology."

Robard fastened his watch while he studied me. "I told you I didn't do it."

"So you used your one phone call on O'Neal?"

"What are you talking about? I didn't call anyone."

"I guess he must have caught the news. Good thing he provided an alibi for you, but all you had to say was you were on your way back to base."

"I wasn't."

"You weren't?" O'Neal hadn't spoken to Robard yet. He didn't know what lie he was supposed to tell, but I assumed he'd agree to anything I said. Maybe Robard wasn't as clever as I suspected. "Oh, that's right. I must have gotten confused. Your truck was parked in that garage because O'Neal picked you up or had someone else pick you up." I gestured wildly. "Whatever he said. It doesn't really matter. All that matters is he explained why the security cam footage we recovered from the deleted hard drives shows your vehicle still parked inside the garage at the time of the shooting. But since only your truck was there and you weren't, we have no reason to hold you." I bumped against him in a friendly gesture, like we were chums sharing a secret. "You couldn't give us your alibi because of something top secret, right? One of those, *I'd tell you, but then I'd have to kill you* kinds of things. God, you should have said that. I eat that stuff up. I always thought it was a creative license in movies, but Brad said that's really how these agencies are."

"Yeah." My prattling confused Robard, which was my intention.

"So when did you get back there to pick up your truck?" I asked.

"I'm not sure. It was after emergency vehicles had already responded to the scene."

"Sometime after the murder?"

"Yeah."

I snapped my fingers. "Brad and I must have missed you by a matter of seconds, maybe minutes. If we'd been a little faster, you could have explained all of this to us at the time, and we wouldn't have made you spend the night in that uncomfortable cell. Again, I apologize for the inconvenience." I held out my hand, and we shook.

"You were just doing your job, Detective DeMarco. No hard feelings."

Spotting O'Neal coming through the opposite doorway, I made myself scarce and booked it out of holding and up the rear staircase. Once upstairs, Winston cornered me before I could enter the bullpen.

"O'Neal's covering for Robard, but everything about that story is a load of bull."

"I know," I said.

Winston's face was pinched, more so than usual. "What are we going to do about it?"

"I'm not sure, but Robard just admitted to me his truck was parked inside the garage where the shooter had been set up."

"I'll make sure the techs know recovering that data or finding additional security cam footage is our priority. In the meantime, dig up whatever you can on Robard. There has to be something or someone who will come forward."

"How can we do this when he's being protected by the United States military?"

"He won't be once we prove he's a danger to society."

# FIFTEEN

By the time Brad and Jake returned, my head was pounding. Winston had locked himself inside his office. The lieutenant was calling every contact he had to find out what was going on and how to fix it.

Brad sat down, leafing through the notes and papers that had accumulated on his desk and the stack that I'd placed on the seam where our two desks joined together. "What did I miss?"

"Robard's been released."

"Why?"

"His CO pulled some strings and made us hand him over. I don't know if they plan to handle this mess in-house or if this is nothing more than a cover-up. My gut says it's the second. Everything will be swept under the rug, like it never happened. You were right. Robard must be our guy. There'd be no reason for any of this otherwise."

"I'm not so sure about that. Even if Robard is innocent, he's still active military. I knew they'd take over jurisdiction. They always do. I figured the lawyers would have been duking it out. Instead, the big gun came to handle it himself." Brad glanced toward the LT's office. "Let me guess. Winston capitulated."

"He called me into his office and let me play bad cop."

"Seriously?"

"Yeah."

"Damn, I missed it."

I filled him in on everything else he missed. "Right now, the techs are desperate to find proof Robard's truck was parked inside that garage at the time of the murder."

"He admitted it to you."

"Yes, but we both know that won't stand up without anything else to support it." I nodded toward the notepad he placed on his desk. "How did it go at the gun range? Did you get us anything useful?"

Brad skimmed his notes before sliding the pad toward me. "I spoke to the owner and everyone who was there this morning. The whole two of them. Robard shows up a couple of times a week whenever he's home, which isn't very often. He buys a box of ammo for his sidearm, goes through that, and then he sets up outside where they have the distance targets. He never brought the Mk22 with him, but he did bring a few different sniper rifles that we have yet to locate. The owner said Robard prefers a bolt action."

"How was his aim?"

"Precise." Brad pointed to something he wrote down on one of the pages. "When I gave the owner a hypothetical, using the details from Yeger's murder, he said Robard would have easily been able to make that shot."

"He's not the only one," Jake said from his desk. "A few of the other shooters were just as precise."

"How many others are we talking? Yesterday, we had four names. How many more do we have now?" I handed Brad back his notes and turned to Jake.

"Two for sure."

"Both active military?" I asked.

"No. Neither is."

"One's retired," Brad said. "He was a gunnery sergeant. He used to be an instructor. I'm not sure if this is true, but he supposedly trained Robard."

"I think they were joking about that," Jake said.

Brad pointed at him. "Weren't you going to run that down?"

"I'm waiting for the details to come back."

"It might be a while. The military isn't playing ball. O'Neal made it clear he has no intention of cooperating with our investigation," I said.

Jake picked up his phone and dialed a number. "All right. I'll do this the other way."

I wasn't going to ask what the other way was. Usually, it was best not to. "What about the other one?"

"He's a gun nut, like a lot of guys around there. He treats the range like a video game. He's always competing for a high score."

"Does he have the skills to back it?"

"I didn't think so, which is why I overlooked him yesterday." Brad shrugged. "But the guy who runs the place disagrees. He says Brewer could have made the shot that killed Yeger."

"You disagree?"

Brad appeared conflicted. "I looked at this guy's targets. When he's on, he's fire. But he's not always on. He's like a baseball player. He could pitch a perfect game, or he could throw nothing but homers. To make two perfect shots with moving targets and real world distractions, I don't see this kid, Brewer, pulling it off."

"So he's all or nothing?"

"He's human, like the rest of us."

"But Robard and this retired guy aren't? What's his name?"

"Balenti," Brad said. "And soldiers aren't allowed to have off days. That's how people get killed."

Jake turned, giving Brad the same look that was on my face. But he didn't say what was on his mind, and neither did I. Brad had heard it a million times. He had a therapist he could talk to if this was too much. Instead, we pushed on.

"How does any of this help us?" I asked. "I thought you were going there to get more details on Robard."

"I figured it was best to learn everything I could about everything and everyone, but you're right. I don't think any of this was helpful. All I know is Robard has the skills, and the owner gave us proof—the targets Robard hit and the security cam footage from his last few practice sessions. Once we find footage of his truck inside the garage, that should be more than enough to take back jurisdiction and arrest him again. We already have Robard's gun." Brad searched the papers, categorizing and filing them into the appropriate order as he went. "Did ballistics come back yet?"

"I haven't seen the reports. In fact, I haven't seen any reports. Nothing. No autopsy or ballistics or anything. I checked with Ellie, but she didn't have anything for us."

"That's because the killer was nowhere near the primary scene," Jake said. "And the secondary scene was wiped."

"The wildlife reserve wasn't," I said. "He didn't dig the slugs out of the trees or anything like that."

"But we don't have footage that proves Robard was in that particular spot at that particular time," Brad said.

"Dammit." Jake slammed the phone down. "They didn't answer." He pressed the speaker button and hit redial. "I thought the park rangers provided us with footage placing Robard in the park."

"He was in the park. He never denied that," Brad said.

"Mac tried her magic with his cell phone, but she said he must have left his phone in the car or something because it never showed him in the vicinity of the clearing," I said.

"I thought cell signals were spotty there," Jake said.

"Robard gets better service than most."

"He would have left his phone or turned it off," Brad said. "He's a pro. He does this for a living. He wouldn't want a beep or buzz to give away his location. He's trained to operate in stealth and remain invisible."

"That would explain deleting the parking garage footage and making sure he didn't leave any physical evidence behind." Jake grabbed the receiver and turned off the speaker when someone finally answered. From the greeting I heard, I suspected he had called his father. The top brass at HQ had lots of contacts in government. Surely, one of them could pull strings and get us access to the intel we needed. I hadn't even thought about it, figuring Brad's previous career would be enough, but my partner always insisted he was a nobody. Jake would make sure we found a somebody.

"Liv," Brad snapped his fingers at me, "the cell data Mac pulled places Robard in the area at the time of the shooting."

"Yeah, but how can we use that when his CO is lying for him? I'm not even sure that would help. Mac wasn't sure the data she scraped placed him inside the garage when the shooting occurred. She said it placed him too far south."

Brad thought about what I said. "Most snipers operate with a spotter."

"Do you think he's working with someone?"

"It's possible, but the setup at the park indicates otherwise." Brad rocked in his chair. "I'm starting to come around to your point of view."

I hoped he wasn't going to tell me he thought Robard was innocent. My resolve had been solidified the moment Robard lied to me after I left Winston's office. "Which is?"

"We need to determine motive. We've been exploring the possibility this is personal."

"Most murders are."

"Yeah, but not for snipers. Not really. That's not the training. It's different for them. They don't get up close with their victims. It's not personal. It's a job."

"Robard's girlfriend connects him to both victims."

Brad's head jerked to the side, almost like a twitch. "It does..."

"Do you think someone hired him to kill Dugrey and Yeger?"

"Just Yeger. Dugrey was an accident. A coincidence."

"Hell of a coincidence," I said.

Brad didn't like this theory any better than I did. "Did Yeger do any work for the government? Maybe he had contracts or something to tie him to government officials."

"He works at an insurance firm. There was no overlap."

Brad brushed his hand over his keyboard, wiping off imaginary dust, before pulling up a business profile on Smith and Smith. "Maybe we're missing something. Maybe Smith and Smith is a front."

"Like they sell insurance by day and train assassins by night?"

He glared at me over his computer screen. "I wasn't thinking anything that dramatic."

"Dramatic? It's the plot for half the shows on TV."

"If you list them, I will never speak to you again." His eyes twinkled, and he turned his attention back to the screen.

"You're only saying that because you made me watch all

of them."

He laughed, that velvety sound that told me everything would be okay. "I'll dig into Smith and Smith to see if there was any reason a hit, sanctioned or not, would have been ordered against Yeger. In the meantime—"

"I will dig through the rest of our suspects in case we made a mistake."

# SIXTEEN

Our suspect list hadn't gotten any larger. Unfortunately, it hadn't gotten any smaller either. I'd already run Seth Ramsay and Jim Parnell's names through the database. Despite being in the park at the time of Dugrey's murder, neither drove a vehicle which sat high enough to have been the vantage point for Yeger's murder.

Ramsay drove a tiny sports car, which Emma liked to refer to as a Barbie car. Barbie drove something larger, but that had been my best friend's choice insult for the pompous know-it-all who had been in her biology and chemistry classes and liked to proudly proclaim he'd been accepted into a prestigious medical school. On graduation day, his tires had been slashed. Emma swore she had nothing to do with it, but to this very day, I still wasn't sure.

Shaking off the wayward thoughts and forcing my mind back on track, I gave Jim Parnell another look. He drove a hatchback. The rear could be raised, exposing the back. It sat higher than a regular car, but to steady his aim, he would have had to pull out the back seats and place some kind of sturdy surface in the cargo area to rest the sniper rifle.

After jotting down my theory at the top of the page, I circled it and moved on to the other name from our previous list of four. Brad had already pulled whatever he could on the other serviceman. That hadn't led anywhere, which is how we ended up with Charles Robard.

Robard checked every box. Right vehicle. Right place.

Right time. And he had ties to the victims, if we were playing by the rules of six degrees of separation. Robard had to be our killer.

I called the lab again. Ballistics were inconclusive. Maybe those rounds came from the Mk22 we found in Robard's house. Maybe they didn't. His vehicle had been parked in the garage, but whoever hacked into the security feed and deleted the footage made it nearly impossible to recover. Right now, all the techs had was footage of Robard entering the garage. He didn't park on the first level. He circled up the ramp. Footage from the fourth floor hadn't been recovered yet, but I was convinced it would show him parked at that wall.

If he backed into the space, he could have left the tailgate up and steadied the long gun on that. Once he fired the shot, he could have easily driven away. Or he could have hung around a little while longer to bask in the glory of his kill, escaping moments before Brad and I arrived.

"Do you think he was watching us?" I asked.

Brad looked up from the million open windows on his screen and the mountain of pages he'd printed. "Who?"

"The sniper."

"By the time we got to the crime scene, it was three hours after the fact. The sniper would have been long gone by then."

I turned. "Did you go inside the garage, Jake?"

Voletek rubbed his eyes. "No. I didn't know what I was seeing. The reports were all over the place. Patrol insisted the kill came from close range. It wasn't until after I left that I realized what had happened."

"Sure. Drop it in our laps," Brad mumbled.

I kicked him under the desk. Normally, he was nicer to Jake. They were friends. Prior partners. Ribbing wasn't uncommon, but this felt different, almost like when we first started in homicide and Brad failed to introduce us. Maybe Emma was right. Maybe Brad was jealous.

Turning my attention to the two newest names on our suspect list, I pulled up everything I could on Aaron Brewer. He, like the other men I'd looked into, was in his twenties. He didn't own a car. He worked retail. A lot of retail. He'd covered everything from gas stations to discount stores to high-end department stores. Currently, he worked in an electronics and appliance store.

He had a juvie record. Nothing too bad. Tagging and illegal trespass. One count of underage drinking and one count of joyriding. The records weren't sealed. He'd served a lot of community service, but all charges had been misdemeanors. He didn't have any felony convictions looming over his head.

I checked his social media accounts. He was incredibly active online. Lots of video game websites and live streams. He even had a live video posted at the time of Dugrey's murder.

After marking him off the list, I looked into Balenti. He was the oldest, coming in at forty-seven. According to what Jake and Brad had been told, Balenti was physically capable of everything. He stayed in shape. He worked out.

I checked into his online activity, but I couldn't find anything to tie him to Dugrey's posts or any of the hunting clubs. Perhaps the killer stumbled upon that clearing on his own.

Deciding that meant I couldn't rule Balenti out, I ran his vehicle registration. Mike Balenti drove a classic Mustang. The car didn't fit, but maybe we were quick to jump to those conclusions. People could rent all sorts of vehicles. Or they could steal them. Again, I wondered if we had been too quick to judge.

I detoured from my research into Mike Balenti and checked to see what vehicles had been reported stolen lately. I skimmed the list, finding too many to count, and that was assuming whatever vehicle had been stolen had come from the city. Since that wasn't going to get me anywhere, I went back to my research into Balenti, which felt just as pointless.

"I don't know," I said when I couldn't take the research any longer. "No one looks good for it except Robard."

"Told you." Brad didn't even look up. "But we had to check."

"Why do you think Yeger was targeted?" That had been Brad's job, but I didn't think he'd had any better luck than I did.

He leaned back to stretch. "Smith and Smith appears to be on the up and up. Yeger didn't have a great marriage, but things never turned violent. No money troubles to report either."

"Even though he's been having an ongoing affair with a stripper?"

"Exotic dancer. He made decent money. Enough to take care of his wife and mistress."

"What about his health? Did he have an exorbitant insurance policy?"

Brad chuckled. "Nothing like that showed up in his financials. Did you find anything, Jake?"

"The autopsy should tell us more, but assuming he was in decent shape, nothing indicates his wife wanted him dead. She didn't care enough about him to bother to divorce him, so I doubt she'd kill him. His girlfriend doesn't seem too torn up about it either. She must have other johns...customers...boyfriends. What term would you like me to use, princess?"

That time, the princess was aimed at my partner. "Okay, boys, what is going on with the two of you? Did someone not get invited to a sleepover or birthday party?" I asked.

"Leave it alone, Liv." Brad's eyes told me I shouldn't have opened this can of worms.

Jake snorted. "It's nothing important. This guy has decided he can't trust me, not with personal stuff anyway. Even though last time he didn't tell us things, we all ended up in a heap. Do you remember how that went?"

Brad shook his head and went back to work. He didn't want to fight with Jake. Usually, this was where I'd do the fighting for him, but something told me I shouldn't.

"All right, so the mistress didn't want Yeger dead. His wife didn't want him dead. Barring the possibility he had some incurable disease that would make him want to off himself, do we have any idea why he was targeted?"

"He was murdered outside his office building. His coworker was killed the day before. Those two points indicate this has to do with Smith and Smith, which could mean more employees will be targeted." Jake peered in Brad's direction, but Brad didn't look up.

"Okay." Reaching across the desk, I snagged the stapled pages on top. "Smith and Smith is operating in the black. They've shown a moderate level of growth over the last five years. The IRS hasn't flagged them. Neither has the SEC." I keyed some things into my computer. "I'm not seeing any recent scandals or news stories. The last thing I'm seeing is from six years ago." I clicked the link. "A man died from a drug overdose. Smith and Smith refused to pay out, saying it was suicide. The family filed suit. The insurance company refused to settle. The judge ruled in favor of Smith and Smith." I brought up the court transcripts. "Yeger was the agent on record."

"Send me the details," Jake said. "Who died?"

"Ramon Danes." I e-mailed him the link and related filings and continued reading. "Danes had a history of drug abuse. He had a criminal record." I checked the police database, finding a long list of charges which abruptly stopped when Danes was released from prison due to overcrowding. While reform was the goal, I didn't think someone who never showed an interest in working the program had suddenly decided to change his tune.

"How could someone like that get life insurance?" Brad asked.

"I don't know."

"Hang on. I think I found something." Jake leaned closer to his monitor. "Okay, so Danes' folks opened the policy when he was a baby. Smith and Smith had some sort of weird gimmick going to start the policy at birth. Lower premiums and the policy would reach maturity sooner, which meant the holder could borrow against it, if he so desired, or he could hold on to it and no longer pay premiums by the time he was forty-five. Somewhere around there."

"That's creepy," Brad said.

"My mother would say it's bad luck," I added.

"Then your aunt would have to spit." Brad winked at me, knowing how oddly superstitious that side of the family was.

"You've been to too many family events with me."

"Whose fault is that?"

Jake laughed. "Should I be relieved we didn't work

together long enough for that to happen to me, Liv? Or should I be offended?"

"Both," Brad said.

Jake nodded. "Noted."

"Did Danes ever borrow against the policy? Is that why they wouldn't pay out?" I asked.

"No. It never reached maturity. He wouldn't have been able to do it beforehand," Jake said.

"But they didn't pay out upon his death either, probably since Smith and Smith had a lot to lose given how low the premiums were and how many more decades they expected to receive payment." I checked the details. "Someone in Danes' family would have had a reason to want Yeger dead, but this case was closed six years ago. Why would anyone wait that long to exact revenge?"

"I'll look into his relatives. See if anyone else was incarcerated and recently released." Jake tapped furiously on his keyboard and mouse, as if playing a drum solo.

While he did that, I looked into the details of the case. Danes had been in his early-twenties when he died. By now, he would have been in his early thirties since he died a few years before the case made it to court. Danes never paid any of the premiums. His parents had set up a trust with an automatic draft. Ramon Danes came from money, but unfortunately, his addiction had destroyed his life and all the opportunities he would have had. Danes' family could have paid someone to murder Yeger, but why would they have waited so long to do it? And what would be the point? They didn't need the money.

Danes' record wasn't what I expected from an affluent family. It was what I'd expect to see from someone who didn't have many choices in life. "His parents cut him off. He didn't live at home. His LKA was in a crappy apartment building on the wrong side of town." I looked into a few more things. He died almost ten years ago under suspicious circumstances. Four years later, the Danes family took Smith and Smith to court.

The more I dug, the more suspicious the situation became. Ramon Danes didn't get out of prison and turn over a new leaf. Someone turned him into a snitch. He was working as a police informant, which explained the early release but not why anyone would want to murder Ken Yeger.

Details on such matters remained classified. But I knew how to read between the lines on reports and what red flags to look for. Most detectives did. The detective on record had retired three years ago, but the lieutenant who signed off on the paperwork was someone I knew very well. Vince DeMarco, my father.

# SEVENTEEN

"Is it just you tonight?" Dad asked.

I thought that'd be best. Dad would tell me things he wouldn't say in front of Brad, not that I thought he had anything to hide, but if there was something he didn't want getting out, he'd be more forthcoming this way. "Yep, it's just me."

Dad rested his forearms on the counter. "All right. Tell me what you want from your old man."

"First, stop calling yourself an old man."

Dad laughed. "Great, we're in complete agreement." He peered through the doorway. "You may want to hurry it up. Your mom's gonna be home any minute, and you know she hates it when we talk shop."

"Do you remember the Ramon Danes case?"

"Kid died of an OD."

"That's the official version."

"I take it you don't believe that."

"Who was running Danes?"

My dad rubbed his face and turned to open the fridge. For some reason, we always ended up having these kinds of conversations in the kitchen. In fact, almost all important conversations happened in the kitchen. I wasn't sure if that was unique to my family, Italian families, or if everyone did the same thing. "What makes you think he was an informant?"

"Wasn't he? I can go through every discrepancy and odd

occurrence if you want, but I figured you could save us both some time."

"That's why you didn't invite your partner to dinner." Dad took out a covered casserole dish, placed it on the counter, and turned on the oven. "Honey, tell me what this is about. What's going on?"

"Two men were murdered in the past seventy-two hours. We're looking at a sniper. The circumstances surrounding the murders are murky. Our prime suspect was sprung from custody via military intervention."

"What does any of that have to do with Ramon Danes?"

I explained everything about the case and the victims. "Brad thinks someone hired a sniper to kill Yeger. We have yet to find a reason why someone would want him dead or why they'd be willing to hire someone to do the deed for them, so I went back to what connects the two victims."

"That would be where they work, which led to everything else." He put the casserole in the oven, even though it hadn't preheated yet, and set the timer. "Come with me."

I followed my father into the basement where he kept records from his time on the job. He grabbed a box and placed it on the table before opening it and leafing through the folders inside. "Y'know, things are digital now. Maybe you really are an old man."

"Well, if you don't want this old man's help, Olive—"

"I didn't say that. But digitizing these would be faster."

A moment later, he pulled out a folder. "I'd say that was fast enough." He opened it and laid it flat on the table in front of me. "The kid was twenty-four when he died. The homicide investigation didn't turn up anything conclusive, but it never sat right with me. I did some digging but not too much. Narcotics was working on a complex sting operation. They had their sights set on some pretty big fish. Everyone in the department was told to back off."

"Even a gung-ho lieutenant?"

"That was right before I made captain. I didn't want to rock the boat too much. Now, I'm thinking I should have." He pushed the folder closer. "You're right. Danes was informing for someone in narco. Homicide figured Danes' dealer or someone in the cartel had found out Danes snitched and offed him, but the evidence didn't support that theory."

"Danes got an early release from prison. Do you know how or why?"

"That was need to know. I assumed he got dirt on his cellmate, who was working the drug trade inside the prison, but again, I don't know for sure."

I read my father's neatly handwritten notes. Each letter precisely formed in black ink. He had lots of theories, but nothing to support them. Instead, everything indicated Danes died of an overdose.

"Do you think he killed himself?"

My dad shrugged. "I don't know. He supposedly got clean. The random drug testing showed he was, but if someone in narco was running him, lines can easily get blurred."

"You think someone cut corners or altered the reports?"

"I'm not saying that." He pointed a finger at my face. "You know how much I abhor corruption, but I also know how things work. If that happened, and again, I'm not saying it did, there must have been a damn good reason. But I don't think Danes ODed on purpose. Accidents happen. Mistakes are made. Drugs are laced with all sorts of lethal shit."

"No one found him in time."

"I wasn't there. I didn't work the scene. All I did was sign off on the reports. The detective on record should know more. He was a homicide detective, told to report to the scene of a suspicious death. That's how the 9-1-1 call came in, that there was a dead man at that address." He pointed to the details he'd written in his personal set of notes. "I didn't note anything else. From what I recall, no calls had come in prior to that. There were no reports of fighting or weapons being brandished or discharged."

"If Danes was informing, why wasn't his handler keeping tabs on him?"

"He wouldn't bother unless there was reason to believe danger was imminent or if Danes was actively working to gain intel."

I read my father's notes one more time. "Dad, I hate to ask, but I don't know what else to do."

"You never ask for favors."

"Rarely," I corrected. The nepotism thing bothered me, even though that had nothing to do with how I got the job. Unlike Voletek, I didn't like using family connections to get what I wanted, but two people were dead. Brad and I had nothing to go on. We owed it to Yeger and Dugrey to figure out why this happened to them.

My dad sighed. "All right. I'll make some calls and see if I can get you the name of Danes' handler." He closed the folder and put it back in the box. "Y'know, I was subpoenaed to provide testimony in that civil trial between Danes' parents and the insurance firm. The only questions they asked had to do with the manner of Danes' death and whether the police department believed foul play was involved. I told them what was in the report. The evidence was inconclusive. It was the truth, but the judge sided with the insurance firm and said Danes intentionally harmed himself. That verdict never sat right with me."

"Did it remind you of Emma's dad? The insurance paid out in that case. I don't see why they wouldn't have paid out in this situation."

"His insurance policy was different. It didn't have the same limitations. Tragedy is tragedy. Money won't fix it, but it makes it easier for the mourners to get back on their feet. I was surprised the judge ruled with the insurance company. My best guess is he figured the Danes family didn't need the cash and just wanted to have someone to blame. The PD couldn't provide them with a villain, so they went after the insurance company instead."

I wondered if the insurance company labeling Ramon Danes an addict had anything to do with the recent murders. Still, six years was a long time to wait to get revenge. "Do you remember the judge?"

"Overholdt, I think."

I committed that to memory just in case. As we headed up the stairs, I asked, "Do you think we're reading this situation wrong?"

"I don't know, honey. This could have nothing to do with Smith and Smith. It could have everything to do with Yeger. Maybe Brad's right. Maybe Dugrey was an accident. Your best bet is seeing if someone paid Robard. If not, you still need to come up with a motive. That's where I'd focus my attention."

"We tried. I guess we can try harder. We won't know until we know, which is why we have to look everywhere."

He chuckled as we returned to the kitchen. "I told you a thousand times being a detective isn't easy. Solving crimes isn't as fun as they make it look on TV."

"I know that."

"So, do you really think we're looking at a government cover-up?"

"Only to the extent that the military is covering for Robard."

"I hate to say it, but are you sure he's responsible?"

"That's what the evidence suggests, but I can't wrap my head around why he'd do it. Sure, his girlfriend works at that firm. But there didn't appear to be any cheating or impropriety going on."

"What about sexism in the workplace? Was she skipped over for promotions because of these two men?"

"They didn't work in the same department, and she doesn't work in the same department as either of them." I climbed back onto the stool. "However, if Robard's a hired gun, the motive would be financial. That's easier to explain."

"You still have to figure out who wanted Yeger dead. Either way, you have to come up with a motive. Do you think the girlfriend connected Robard to whoever wanted Yeger dead?"

"We haven't considered that. But we haven't found any suspicious activity, financial or otherwise, in Robard's accounts." I tapped on the counter. "Unless the money and communications went through Julia."

"It'd be worth checking," Dad said.

"In that case, let's say Robard is working as a contract killer. Why the lies and the cover-up? Wouldn't Major O'Neal want Robard stopped?"

"Imagine the fallout if an active member of the United States military is moonlighting as a contract killer or is using those skills to eliminate every man who ever smiled at his girlfriend. That wouldn't be good for Uncle Sam's reputation, and it'd open up a can of worms that would trigger all sorts of backlash."

"I guess."

Dad took a seat beside me. "Remember, this is the job. You do what you can, the best way you can. Not every case gets solved. I have boxes downstairs to prove it."

# EIGHTEEN

The energy coursed through him. It had fizzled for a while, but it was back. He had a couple more names to mark off his list. The police were actively investigating. He'd been keeping an eye on the news, but they weren't sharing many details. Instead, they were hoping members of the public would come forward. What they didn't realize was no one had any idea what he was doing, so they couldn't be expected to report him.

He continued his walk. To any onlooker, he looked like a man out to stretch his legs and take in the sights. They wouldn't realize he was conducting recon, determining the best location to set up for his next shot.

The park would be the best place to set up. This shot would be more challenging. He wouldn't have the advantage of height. In fact, this would be more of a straight-shot. He'd be nearly level with the target, possibly slightly lower. Given the distance and gravity's pull, he didn't like that.

He paid attention as he walked the paths. The ground wasn't entirely flat, but he'd have to be somewhere with cover. People would be out during the day. Even now, after the sun had set hours ago, people were still out. The city never slept, and committing another act midday would mean it'd be downright crowded.

That would add to the challenge, so he needed a good vantage point. Something with a clear shot. Traffic would make that harder. Vendors, pedestrians, signs, all those things would be out and in his way.

The trees may work. He'd have to find the right one to provide cover and strong enough to support him. It'd also have to be positioned in the right place.

That didn't feel right. He wasn't Tarzan. Climbing trees felt childish. He'd need somewhere better to set up. Somewhere no one would see him.

The metal bleachers caught his eye. He'd have to make sure no little leagues or intramural teams were playing soccer in the afternoon, but kids would be in school at that time, unless they came out on their lunch break. If so, the small metal bleachers may be occupied.

However, after circling the area a few more times, he decided to check them out. They only went four rows high and about twenty seats wide. The back was covered, but he found an opening in the side. Beneath the bleachers, he found a few crack pipes, condom wrappers, empty pill bottles, and two needles. Luckily, no one was presently using the spot.

Edging toward the far end, he peered through the opening between the seats. From here, he could make a direct shot. The seat in front of him could steady his rifle. He'd have to do something to adjust for the curve of the seat, but that'd be an easy fix. The architects had placed the bleachers up on what he assumed was a manmade hill. The ground was slightly elevated here, allowing spectators a better view of the soccer field. If he could find something to prop himself up a little higher, he'd be able to see over everything.

Pulling the pen from his pocket, he wrote down the numbers from his binoculars, recording distance and angle and did some quick calculations. This was doable. It would all depend on outside factors. If the situation became too complicated, if factors beyond his control came into play, he'd wait. Snipers had to be patient. He couldn't be the exception. But now that he had a taste of infamy, he wanted more.

*   *   *

Before leaving my parents' house, I sent a text to Brad, letting him know everything I'd found or failed to find. Today felt like a waste. We'd run ourselves in circles, made an arrest, and were forced to release the man we arrested. It had been a crazy seventy-two hours.

Once I got home, I poured myself a glass of wine from the open bottle in the fridge and took a healthy sip. The thought of calling in sick had never been so appealing, but it was rare I played hooky. Usually, Emma was to blame. But I wouldn't be able to use her as an excuse if I didn't go to work in the morning. Plus, I couldn't do that to Brad.

A knock sounded at my door. "Liv?"

"You know I'm here. You heard me come home and you have a key."

Slowly, Brad turned the knob and let himself inside. "I didn't want to barge in. You could have been entertaining. Plus, you always knock, and you didn't give me a key to make myself at home. You gave it to me in case of emergencies or in the event you locked yourself out."

"As if picking the locks is something neither of us is capable of doing."

He looked around, eyeing the wine glass beside me. "Should I leave you alone? You seem—"

"Distraught."

"I was going to say drunk."

"I'm not drunk. You've seen me drunk."

"Twice. Once was fun. The other time, you were kind of mean, like you are right now."

"I'm sorry."

"I get it. I don't like this either." He took a seat beside me and poured a glass for himself. "I thought Vince would have had more for us."

"Dad had tons of notes, but it wasn't his case. He'll try to get us more by the morning."

"More?"

"He's going to call in some favors. If it doesn't pan, there's no point in mentioning it."

Brad smirked and sipped the wine. "Except you already mentioned it to me before you went to meet him for dinner."

"Pretend I didn't."

"Okay, so where are we on the girlfriend angle?"

"I spoke to Mac. She already did a deep dive and didn't find anything suspicious. No strange calls. No weird internet activity. No unexplained cash transfers."

"Robard's military. He may be aware of what triggers red flags. They could be doing everything below the radar. We should assume whoever wanted Yeger dead is local. It could be someone who met Julia at work. The party responsible could have had an appointment. It'd look like legitimate business."

"What did he do? Give her an envelope full of cash which she handed over to Robard?"

"That wouldn't be so farfetched."

"We didn't find cash at his place. A team executed a search warrant. They checked everywhere."

"It could be at her place or in a storage unit, safe deposit box, or somewhere on base."

"How do we find that out? The military shut us down. They won't let us search, and they sure as shit aren't going to help us. The last thing they'd want is for us to find evidence against Robard." I let out an exasperated sigh. "This is insane. Why would they want a killer in their midst?"

"Some guys go private when they get out. Security. Paramilitary. Face it, men with Robard's skills are highly sought after. It doesn't mean he'd pursue it, but he could. The last few days could have been a taste or a test."

"Of things to come? Ugh. That makes it so much worse." I put my head in my hands, fearing this would be that one case I'd never clear off my desk, the one that would always haunt me. I wasn't sure why, but I knew it would.

"Hey," Brad reached into his pocket and pulled out a coin which he placed in front of me, "penny for your thoughts."

I slid the coin off the counter and put it in my pocket. "No refunds."

"C'mon, Liv. Talk to me. What's wrong?"

"Isn't it obvious?"

He brushed my hair behind my shoulder. "Can we table the case for a second?"

"How about for the rest of the night?"

He didn't answer, but I took his expression to suggest whatever he was about to say had nothing to do with work. "I'm sorry I put us in a weird place."

I looked around. "We're at my island counter. It's not that weird."

"That isn't what I meant."

"I know, but I didn't think we were in a weird place. Are we in a weird place?"

"Aren't we?" He swiveled around so he could rest his back against the counter and face me directly. "A few nights ago, we were in this little bubble. Then we go to work, and the bubble goes away. We come off shift, but now everything's weird. I didn't think this through. We shouldn't have."

"We haven't." Shaking my head, I didn't want to put too fine a point on things. Honestly, this wasn't about sex. Or was it? I didn't know. I couldn't figure out work. How was I supposed to figure this out? "We're us. Bubble. No bubble. I'm following your lead. You seemed like you wanted some space, so I'm giving it to you."

"You never follow my lead."

"That's not true."

"Okay, fine. You sometimes follow my lead, unless you think you have a better plan." He cocked his head to the side, his brown eyes studying every inch of my face. "What happens if I kiss you right now?"

"I would say try it and find out, but that sounds a little threatening. So I'll save you the drama. I'd kiss you back."

He cupped his hand against my face, but he didn't move closer. "Normally, this is how I cope with a bad day. I don't want that to be how things are with us. I don't want this to be a band-aid for getting my ass kicked on the job." He dropped his hand and got off the stool. "The worst days were always the ones where I'd call Carrie or Donna or..."

"Whichever blonde you were seeing that week."

"They aren't always blonde."

"Is that the problem? Should I dye my hair?"

The question surprised him, and he laughed. When he tried to stop, he only laughed harder, which made me laugh. "No, Liv," he choked out, managing to sober, "you are beautiful no matter what. The first time I saw you, I thought you were the sexiest woman to ever wear a badge. You broke my heart when you told me you'd never date a cop. It never mattered if you were undercover with fire red hair or jet black hair or that weird mohawk thing you had that time. It's never changed the way I feel about you."

"It could. Things change. For the record, you weren't too shabby that first day either. White dress shirt. No tie. Dark jeans. If it hadn't been for the lack of tie, I would have been even more frightened by your filing system than I already was, but I figured anyone who didn't bother to be completely buttoned up couldn't be that bad."

He snorted. "I spilled coffee on my tie earlier that day. That's why I took it off."

"Well, thank god. If that hadn't happened, I would have gone straight to Cap and asked for a new partner."

"He would have given you one too."

"Probably."

Brad let out the breath he'd been holding. "How do we do this? When I'm not obsessing about the case, I've been thinking about you...us...the other night."

"What do you want to do?"

"I want to kiss you."

"So do it."

"It won't stop there, and this can't be another way I forget about a bad day."

"Why not? It's how a lot of cops forget about bad days." It wasn't how I chose to cope, but I wasn't like most people. Even Brad had told me on several occasions to go out and have some fun and blow off steam. But I wasn't wired that way. Too many trust issues and horror stories, and that was just from observing Emma's dating life.

"Because I love you. Shit." Spinning, he pressed both palms into his eyes before running his hands through his hair. "I shouldn't have said that. God, you must think I'm a lunatic."

"You are, but I love you too."

"No, not like that. I just...I'm going to shut up."

Getting up, I gripped both his biceps, forcing him to face me. "I know. Me too."

The grin pulled at his lips, and then he kissed me. After

that it was a frenzy, limbs tangling and clothing flying. Nothing had ever felt so intense or so right. My heart raced, our breath shallow and gasping whenever we surfaced long enough for air. My brain shut off, my body moving on instinct and desire. The only thought that managed to pop into my head was Emma was right.

# NINETEEN

My phone dinged. Lazily, I reached for it. When I couldn't quite grasp it from my spot against Brad's chest, he reached out and snagged it for me.

"Is it work?" he asked.

"No, it's my dad."

"Am I supposed to sneak out the window?"

I laughed and smacked his pec. "We're two consenting adults. My father would respect that."

"You're his little girl, Liv. I can't imagine a world where he wouldn't threaten my life if I hurt you."

"Then don't hurt me." I met Brad's eyes before reading the text from my dad. "He got us the name. Detective Tony Vale. You ever hear of him?"

"No. Maybe he transferred out."

"I don't know. This was ten years ago."

"He may have retired." Brad took the phone and put it back on the nightstand. "Before we switch back to DeMarco and Fennel, I want to ask you something."

"Let me guess. You want to go steady."

"Even though I would never say it in such an antiquated way, yes, I would like to go steady." He nuzzled against me, brushing his nose against mine before giving me a gentle kiss. "But what I was going to ask is if you're okay. Last night was intense. I know it's been a while for me. Longer for you. I just wanted to make sure we're good. Everything's good?"

"You mean fantastic."

He kissed me again, his fingers running along my collarbone. "I'm glad we're on the same page." Something flitted behind his eyes. "God, you're amazing."

"The neighbors may have heard you mention that once or twice."

He dropped his head back to the pillow, grinning. "Oh well."

I pulled myself up and grabbed my phone to see if I had any other messages. Despite everything, we had to get back to work, which meant I had to file this away into a neat little box for later. "We should get going."

"Yeah." He traced a finger down my spine. "We wouldn't want anyone to get the wrong idea. Jake's already giving me enough grief."

I got out of bed, pulling a t-shirt over my head before turning to face Brad. "About what?"

"He thinks I'm hiding something from him."

"You are."

"Not the point, Liv."

"Actually, it kind of is." I sighed. "Look, if you want—"

"No. This is ours. I promised you this wouldn't blow back on your career. That's always been your biggest concern. I will not derail you like that. Jake doesn't need to know about this. It's none of his business. In fact, it's no one's business."

"Okay, but I don't want to be your dirty little secret."

Brad grinned. "That's tantalizing."

"Stop." I threw his shirt at him. "Get dressed. I'm kicking you out. Go upstairs and get ready for work."

"Yes, ma'am." He got dressed and headed for the front door. "It's your turn to drive."

"I'll meet you at the car."

"Copy. I'll bring the coffee."

"It better be coffee," I called after him. "You pull that tea trick on me again, and I will look for another partner."

Brad was waiting in the lobby for me. He held out a travel cup, a sly grin on his face. "Good morning, Detective DeMarco. How did you sleep?"

Rolling my eyes, I took the cup from his hand and gave it a tentative sip. "At least you're not trying to poison me."

He didn't say anything as he pushed the door open,

holding it for me to go through. I unlocked the car and slid behind the wheel. Despite work being what it was, last night left Brad a little giddy. It left me giddy too, but I was working on acting normally. My partner hadn't stopped smiling.

"Brad."

"Hmm?"

"Stop that."

"What?"

"Being happy. We work homicide. You hate homicide. People are dead. Now is not the time to smile."

"Right. You're right." He cocked his head to the side. "Except, it's only us right now. And don't you usually try to cheer me up when we're at work? People might get suspicious if you're telling me to be miserable."

"I'm not telling you to be miserable."

"It sounds like you are."

"Brad."

"I know." After taking a sip from his cup, he rubbed his eyes. "What's our gameplan? We know Ramon Danes was working as Vale's CI. However, we still don't know if any of this has anything to do with the sniper's two recent kills. Do we know if Vale or Danes or any of those people connect to Robard or Julia?"

"Not that I know of, but it's worth exploring, unless something else has surfaced in the last twelve hours." I glanced at him. "Do you have a better idea?"

"Who was the judge on that case?"

"Overholdt."

"Barring the break we need, we should speak to him too."

"You really don't think the crime lab or our computer whizzes came up with anything?"

"I'm trying to be optimistic, but I don't see that helping. Even if we find footage of Robard holding the weapon, that may not be enough. The military could say he had it with him, that they were moving the weapons as part of a training exercise."

"You can't be serious?"

"We need to know why Robard did it."

"Maybe we should focus on his girlfriend's interactions with the victims. Maybe there was an office party we don't know about. Maybe Robard attended, words were exchanged, and things got heated, but he had to wait until he was stateside again to exact revenge."

"Revenge is a dish best served cold."

"I can't believe you just said that."

Brad shrugged. "You lined it up. I had to knock it down."

When we got to the precinct, we hoped to divide and conquer. Brad checked with the crime lab. I checked with the computer whizzes, specifically Mac.

Since our evidence was flimsy, Mac had taken a few creative licenses to get access to the intel I wanted. Technically, none of that would have been admissible, but I liked to know ahead of time if it was worth it to pursue gaining access through legal means. From everything she glimpsed into Julia Gotti, we were barking up the wrong tree.

"There's nothing here. Nothing on her phone. Her e-mails. Her accounts. She wasn't having an affair. She didn't engage in any suspicious online communications," Mac said.

"What about an encrypted app?"

Mac rolled her eyes. "Please. Do I look like an amateur?"

"Nothing dark web either?"

"Nope." She clicked the mouse and pointed at a second monitor. "Nothing with Robard either. Though, most of his activities are monitored by the U.S. government when he's on base."

"Tell me you didn't hack into their system."

"No. I don't want to have my internet rights taken away for the rest of my life. I also have a lot of stuff that wouldn't fit neatly into an eight by ten cell."

"Good. I don't want you getting in trouble. And I definitely don't want you getting caught."

"I know." She clicked the mouse a few more times and directed my attention back to the first screen. "The footage from the garage was recovered. I'm not sure if this is helpful or harmful."

"Let me see what we have."

She played it from the beginning. Robard's truck entered the garage. He circled up the ramp, parked on the second floor, walked down the stairs, and left. He returned twenty minutes after the shooting took place. He didn't hang around. He didn't go to any other level. He went back to his truck and left.

"That's it?"

"I'm checking everything again to make sure the recovered footage wasn't replaced."

"You think the hacker replaced it and then deleted it?"

"I'll admit, it's not likely, but it would be rather ingenious."

"But if that's not what happened, then Robard isn't our shooter. For one thing, he was parked on the wrong level. For another, he wasn't in the garage at the time of the shooting. He couldn't have taken that shot."

"Maybe. Maybe not."

I turned to her. "The footage shows him leaving."

"I wouldn't be so sure. There is one entrance not covered by cameras. It's meant for people to use in the event of an emergency. It's too small for any vehicles. Robard could have reentered the garage on foot via that exit, stuck to the blind spots, went up to the fourth floor, and took the shot."

"We see him leaving his truck with takeout bags. We don't see him with anything large enough to be a sniper rifle. So where did he stash the gun?"

"Don't most snipers have accomplices?"

"You mean spotters?"

"In this case, aren't they the same thing?"

I considered what she said, more perplexed than I had been. "Maybe."

"Yeah, well, that person could have had the sniper rifle. All he or she would have had to do is wait for a pro-shooter like Robard to show up and bada bing, bada boom, emphasis on the boom."

The last thing we needed was more unsubstantiated conjecture. "Where would he have taken the shot? The crime techs determined no one had set up on the concrete wall. We would have seen evidence of their presence."

"I don't know. Maybe they were careful. Or maybe his accomplice spotter buddy provided a vehicle with a vantage point."

"Okay, fine. Any idea who this person may be or what he drove since we just ruled out Robard's truck?"

She handed me a printout. "That's every car that entered or exited during our projected window. I took the liberty of reviewing the footage of every vehicle that parked on the fourth floor. Again, we have blind spots, so it's impossible to say for certain where everyone parked and who may have been in a space against that wall at the time of the shooting."

"Play it for me." I watched the screen. Two pickups, six SUVs, and three vans parked on that level. Any one of them would have provided ample space for a sniper to set up. "Did you run their plates?"

"Most." She handed me another list. "Nothing telling here."

Grabbing a highlighter off her desk, I marked the plates and vehicle registration information for the pickups and SUVs, pausing when I couldn't find the details on the vans. "Why are we missing their tags?"

"All three vans were from different services. Groceries, mobile dog grooming, and prescription drugs. The grocery plates checked out. They were registered to the store. The dog grooming and pharmacy delivery have been harder to ascertain." She showed me the footage. "The pharmacy's vehicle is new. It has temp plates. I called, but no one has gotten back to me yet."

"What about the dog groomer?"

"No answer."

I pointed at the image frozen on the screen. "Why didn't you run the plate number?"

"I tried."

"What happened?"

"I only have a partial." She showed me the footage. "None of the permutations I checked link to a dog groomer. But I haven't checked every possibility yet." She indicated the program running in the background. "Hopefully, we'll hit on it soon."

I studied the image again, but the stickers in the corners said the tags weren't expired. "Try narrowing it by the registration renewals. That may make it easier to identify."

"Good call, Liv. I can't believe I didn't think of that." She picked up her oversized cup and gave it a shake. "The caffeine is failing me."

Given Mac's superior intellect, I was always surprised whenever she missed something. She entered a few things into the computer and frowned at the screen.

"Well, that makes no sense," she said.

"What?"

"The only possibility it's spitting out is a vehicle registered to Evelyn Rennie, permanent resident of Shady Oaks Retirement Home."

"I take it she doesn't run a dog grooming business."

"No. She's eighty-four and retired. She drives to church and that's about it." Mac stared at the screen. "This must be a glitch. Someone must have entered something wrong in the DMV database."

"What kind of car does Evelyn drive?"

"A four-door sedan."

"This is a red flag." I jotted down Evelyn Rennie's information. "I bet those are stolen plates." The shooter wanted to cover his tracks. And given the footage I'd seen, I was having a hard time believing it was Robard, even if he had parked in the garage.

"Okay." She didn't argue, but she didn't quite understand why I said that. "How does this connect to Robard?"

"It may not."

"But he's your only suspect."

"Unfortunately, we don't always get it right." I pointed at the plate. "I need everything on this. I'll send uniforms to Shady Oaks to speak to Mrs. Rennie and check things out."

She wrote down the information and handed me the sheet. "I'm sorry, Liv."

I shook away her apology. "No one's perfect. But this will break Brad's heart. He likes to think of you as his little robot buddy. Now he'll be forced to accept the fact you're human.

# TWENTY

After leaving Mac, I grabbed a hold of my partner and headed to Shady Oaks to find out what was going on with Evelyn Rennie's car. When we arrived, we found the vehicle in question. The plates weren't missing. But they didn't belong to her vehicle. They belonged to a delivery van registered to a flower shop.

"I'll send someone to the shop to check it out," I said.

Brad peered around the parking lot. Half the spots were empty. There wasn't a lot of in and out. "I'll see if anyone inside can shed some light on the situation. I'll meet you in there."

We reconvened at the front desk. Management hadn't noticed anyone suspicious lurking about. The residents received visitors regularly, at least some of them did. Others had groceries and food delivered, and there were always a handful of volunteers showing up for one reason or another. The place wasn't bustling, but it was far from quiet.

"No one reported seeing anything odd?" Brad asked.

"No."

"Do you have security cams covering the parking lot?" Brad pointed to the area where Rennie's car was parked.

"A few."

"Great. We need the footage."

The man working the desk hesitated. "The residents are entitled to their privacy, as are their guests."

"Evelyn Rennie's plates don't match her vehicle. They were found on a vehicle we believe was used in the commission of a serious crime." Brad's eyes narrowed. "A homicide to be precise. So are you going to help us? Or are you going to give me a reason to think you may be involved? Accessory to murder is a serious charge."

The man behind the desk let out an aggravated sigh. "Fine. I'll get you copies."

"Thanks." Brad jerked his head toward a hallway. "You said Evelyn Rennie's in room 107?"

"That's right."

"I'll see what she has to say," I said. "Meet me once you get everything we need."

Brad winked. "You got it."

My conversation with Evelyn Rennie didn't take long. She hadn't used the car since Sunday, when she went to church and out to lunch. She returned to Shady Oaks a little after three that afternoon and hadn't ventured out since.

"Did you notice anything odd about your car? Any signs of damage?"

The woman looked bewildered. "No. Are you suggesting someone tried to steal it? It has anti-theft whatever." She waved her hand as if she couldn't come up with the proper term or didn't care enough to concern herself with it.

"Do you know what your license plate number is?"

She stared at me like I was trying to trip her up. "Yes." She rattled off the number. "Do you want me to tell you today's date or name the presidents in order?"

"No, ma'am. That won't be necessary. I'm only interested in whoever switched the plates on your vehicle. Did you happen to notice if you had the proper plates when you used the car last?"

"I didn't look. I always park in the same spot. I get in. I get out. It never occurred to me to pay attention to such things. I'm sure I would have noticed if there wasn't a plate, but there was."

I nodded, making a note of that. "Whoever did this must have figured as much. Does anyone else have access to your car?"

"Access? It's parked outside. Tons of people could walk

right past it."

"Does anyone else have a key? Perhaps you let someone borrow your car or use it when you aren't?"

"No. I'm the only one who drives it."

"No spare keys? No relatives with access?"

"No."

I held up my palms, realizing from her tone that was a sore subject. "What about pets?"

"Pets?" She stared at me like I was crazy.

"Your plates were found on a dog grooming van. I wondered if there was any overlap."

She shook her head. "They don't allow animals here, except service animals."

"Okay. Thank you for your time." I turned to leave, finding Brad waiting in the doorway. I wondered how long he'd been standing there.

"Wait," she said, "what happens now? Do I have to file a police report or come to the station or anything to get this sorted out? What about my insurance?"

"We don't believe your vehicle was damaged. However, you are more than welcome to file a report. Everything you said will be placed in a file." I handed her my card. "If you have any questions, feel free to call."

"What about my plates? When do I get them back? I can't go anywhere without a license plate."

"We'll make sure temporary plates are issued," Brad said, swooping in and offering her his winning smile. "Don't worry. I'll make sure to have our best officer handle this. If not, I'll do it myself."

Her face brightened and she reached out to shake his hand. "Thank you so very much."

"It's my pleasure." Brad jerked his head toward the door. "We've taken up enough of your time. You have yourself a nice day. We're sorry to have bothered you so early in the morning with all this nonsense."

Once we were on our way back to the precinct, I shook my head. "You can't help it, can you? You don't even know when you're doing it."

"Doing what?"

"Charming the pants off little old ladies."

"I wouldn't call you old."

"Forget what I said about charming."

He laughed. "I call that polite professionalism."

"I call it practically pornographic."

He rubbed a hand over his mouth. "You're still thinking about last night."

"Brad. Stop."

Shaking it off, he flipped through my notes. "I'll go back through our suspects' profiles and see if anyone has any ties or connections to Shady Oaks. Taking plates from a car parked there seems a little off the beaten path unless the unsub was in the area." He rubbed at his cheek. "I don't recall Robard having any relatives besides his mother and brother."

"Do you still think he's responsible?" I'd already told him everything Mac had said. "He left the garage. His vehicle couldn't have been where he set up to take the shot. More than likely, the dog grooming van is where the sniper set up."

"Which is why we came all this way to look into the plates."

I nodded.

"Still, Mac said he could have snuck back inside. He could be working with someone."

"Who? O'Neal?"

Brad gave me a look, a cross between confusion and admiration. Either he thought I was brilliant or a total idiot. "That would be something."

Once we got back to our desks, I found Officer Roberts waiting.

"The flower shop's been closed for a while," Officer Roberts said. "Looks like they had a major plumbing problem. No one was around to question."

"Did you see any delivery vans?"

"Two."

"Did you check the plates?"

"Yeah, they matched. Even had valid registration stickers and everything."

I pulled up DMV records. "According to this, that flower shop has three delivery vans, not two."

"Right. Because it couldn't possibly be used for anything other than delivering flowers."

"Do we know where the third van is now?"

Roberts shrugged. "You want me to issue a BOLO?"

"Yes."

"Okay." He gave me another look and walked away, muttering to himself.

Roberts never liked me, but he had saved my life. If it hadn't been for him, I would have bled out on the floor of a liquor store. So I'd given him a free pass when it came to our interactions.

Beside me, Brad bristled. "I have half a mind to say something to that guy."

"Don't."

"I have before. Clearly, it didn't take."

"Let it go. It's fine."

"It's not. He's screwing with you and impeding our investigation."

"Brad."

He held up his hands in surrender. "Yeah, okay. Whatever you want," he paused, "princess."

"Oh, don't you dare."

He went to update the LT on our progress. It wasn't much, but we had reason to believe the dog grooming van may have belonged to the closed flower shop. It would explain the plates we found on Evelyn Rennie's car, and it would also explain why the dog grooming company denied having a van in the first place. According to what they had told Mac, they didn't offer mobile services.

I examined a still image recovered from the parking garage's deleted footage. The van didn't have anything on it to indicate it belonged to a florist, but the exterior was super shiny and clean, as if someone had used sheets and decals to recover it so it wouldn't be recognized. It was easier and faster than painting.

When Brad returned, I shared my theory with him.

"That could be. We'll need to get security footage from the flower shop. Whoever did this must have gotten spotted somewhere." He eyed the USB we'd received from Shady Oaks. "I'll drop this off with Mac on our way out. I gave it a quick scan, but didn't see anyone. I hope she'll have better luck."

He collected a few files and adjusted the hem of his jacket to cover his holster. Once he was situated, we headed out to meet with former detective Tony Vale.

# TWENTY-ONE

Vale retired nine years ago, which explained why we didn't know him. I hadn't started yet, and he wasn't one of my dad's work buddies. So we weren't sure what to expect, but we'd find out soon enough.

"Do you think we're completely off the mark?" Brad asked. "First, we thought Robard. But between the recovered footage from the garage and what we discovered with the dog grooming van or flower delivery van, whatever it is, I'm not sure what to think. Maybe we have everything wrong, including Yeger being killed because of his work at Smith and Smith."

"Hopefully, Vale can shed some light on this."

Brad flipped through his notepad. "Julia Gotti connects Robard to both victims. It makes sense it would be him or that this has to do with the insurance company, unless Dugrey getting killed was entirely coincidental, which is what I originally thought." He ran a hand through his hair. "Dammit. I am so twisted around on this."

"All right, let's talk it out."

"I don't think there's anything left to say. This is a hell of a clusterfuck."

"Fine, I'll riff off the Robard angle since you just laid that out. Mac said Robard could have returned to the garage without getting spotted. Either he had the rifle stashed nearby and picked it up after dropping lunch off for Julia, or someone else brought it to him." I chewed on my bottom lip while I drove through downtown traffic. "Could we be looking at an accomplice?"

"Possibly, but the setup at the wildlife reserve indicates the shooter is working alone." Brad turned in his seat. "You never liked Robard as a suspect. Admit it. You don't think he has anything to do with this."

"I don't know. O'Neal lied. Robard lied. They must have a reason. Why would they do that if Robard wasn't involved?"

"I don't know. There could be a million reasons. Before that happened, what was the sticking point for you?"

"Robard thought he and Julia were having lunch. She had a last minute meeting, which is why he dropped off the food and left. If that's true, our timeline doesn't work. He would have needed time to set up and prep. Also, I checked, but Yeger wasn't the reason Julia Gotti missed lunch. So we can't argue killing Yeger was a heat of the moment thing."

"Agreed. Yeger's murder was not a rash decision. It was a planned and carefully executed hit." Brad considered what I said. "Sometimes, I hate it when you're right. But Robard checked all the boxes. It makes sense why we'd think it's him. He was at both crime scenes. He has the necessary skills, no alibi, and ties to the victims."

"That's not always enough. However, I don't understand why he lied and why he can't provide us with his alibi or why someone with a lot of clout forced us to release him."

"Robard may know who the killer is. Snipers train together. Maybe he has suspicions but doesn't want to share them until he's sure, unless he's been instructed to allow the MPs to handle this on base. They could conduct their own investigation and follow through with their own proceedings."

"A civilian was killed. Two civilians. We aren't at war. This is local. We should have jurisdiction." I handed Brad my phone. "Has ADA Winters left any messages?"

"Nope. Nothing."

"Usually, Winters is more on the ball."

"Maybe he has a new favorite detective to pursue since you're otherwise occupied."

I glared at Brad. "Logan and I were never romantically involved."

"He asked you out. You've had dinner several times."

"Working dinners." I turned to him. "Do you want to play this game? I can guarantee you'll lose."

"I'm teasing, Liv. Y'know, like we always do." He gave me a confused look. "Is that off limits now?"

"It's always off limits." I winked at him. Maybe juggling our multi-faceted relationship wouldn't be as easy as I thought. My mental storage boxes had a lot of overlap when it came to Brad. And our friendship box and relationship box shared some of the same things.

"That's what you told Winters," he said.

I smiled. "Damn straight."

"Robard should talk to us. That would make this a lot easier."

"I agree. Why don't you tell him that?"

"I would, but we have no way to gain access to him. Patrols are monitoring his place, but I'm guessing he hasn't been allowed off base since he was released from custody."

"We're keeping an eye on his girlfriend too, but she looks clean. Mac couldn't find anything." I parked at a meter a block and a half from Tony Vale's current place of employment. "Let's hope Vale has some insights to offer."

"It can't hurt. If nothing else, he may know why someone would be targeting Smith and Smith employees, if that's even what's going on here."

"What else could it be? We've looked into Yeger. He wasn't a saint, but he wasn't evil incarnate. As far as we know, no one had reason to want him dead."

"Could these be random hits? Could we be looking at a serial killer? Maybe his victims fit a profile."

"Don't say that."

"Well, if this isn't about a personal vendetta or seeking revenge on Smith and Smith, I don't know what else it could be." Brad shrugged as we fell into step beside one another. "My head's spinning in every direction, and it's not all because of you."

"Stop that," I hissed.

He turned, as if studying something across the street so his lips were closer to my ear. "This is a little harder than I thought it'd be."

"You said that last night."

He let out that laugh that always made me happy. "I'm serious, Liv. It's like I can't remember where the line is. We always teased, but now most of that feels inappropriate. Have I been harassing you these last two years and failed to realize it?"

"That would imply your comments were unwanted." I nudged him in the ribs. "Only about half of them were, but we've always been about the playful ribbing. It's not like the things the other guys say to me or about me."

Brad let out a growl.

"See, that's another of those things. You always did that."

"I'm your partner. I don't like it when anyone disrespects you."

"I know, but now, there's additional context. That's where things get muddy and the confusion comes in. I know it's making me second-guess things."

"Like letting me remind Roberts to be nice to you?"

"Roberts gets a pass."

Brad looked like he wanted to argue, but I pulled the heavy glass door to the office building open. "Detective DeMarco." I flashed my badge at the man behind the reception desk. "I have an appointment with Tony Vale."

"The security guard?"

I nodded.

"One second." The man pressed a button on his earpiece. "Vale, your eleven o'clock is here." He pointed to a door labeled security. "He's right through there. Someone will buzz you in."

Brad followed me across the lobby to the indicated door. I gave the handle a tug, but it didn't budge. Before I could knock, a buzzer sounded and the lock released. The light changed from red to green.

Inside, the room was massive. A large bullpen was filled with desks, all facing forward. Each one had a computer. The wall at the front of the room was covered in monitors. Three offices lined the other walls. One on each side.

Tony Vale met us at the door. Instead of the cheap suit favored by most public servants, Vale had on something that would have set me back a month's salary. Maybe two. He held out his hand and introduced himself.

"DeMarco," he said as he led us toward the nearest office. General operations was stamped on the brass plate at the center of the otherwise glass door. "Is your pop on the job?"

"He was," I said. "He's retired now."

"Lot of that going around. It happens to the best of us." Vale took a seat behind his desk, which looked like it should belong to a CEO or investment banker. He glanced from me to Brad. "It'll happen to the two of you one of these days, if you're lucky. Just remember, it's not as bad as it seems. It's a hell of a lot better than you'd think. Don't forget that."

"We'll try not to," I said.

Vale pushed a keyboard aside and adjusted in his chair. "What can I do for you?"

"We need information on Ramon Danes. Do you remember him?"

Vale opened his mouth and cocked his head to the side. "I haven't heard that name in quite a while. Kid fell off the wagon. It was a shame really. He was young. Maybe he could have turned it around. Y'never know."

"You were running him," Brad said. "He was your informant."

Vale smirked. "Kid's dead. His intel didn't pan. I've been out of narco for a while. I don't see what use I can be to you."

"After his death, his family sued Smith and Smith."

"A law firm?"

"An insurance company," Brad said. "Danes had life insurance, but the company didn't want to pay out."

"Right. I remember something about that. I could never figure out why they'd give life insurance to an addict. Someone must have screwed up. It's no wonder they didn't pay. If you ask me, the family didn't need the cash anyway. The entire point of that was to make Ramon out to be something he wasn't. They wanted to place him on a pedestal. Instead, the opposition dragged him through the mud. Instead of being a tragedy, they made him look like a lowlife convict junkie."

"Was he?" Brad asked.

"Ramon tried to turn it around, but he was a screwup. Why does any of that matter?"

"Two people were murdered. They both worked at Smith and Smith. We're looking for anyone who might hold a grudge against the insurance company."

"You can't seriously believe that's connected to a dead CI from ten years ago."

"The civil case was handled six years ago," I said.

"Ramon's been in the ground for ten. If someone wanted revenge, they wouldn't have waited so long."

"Perhaps the person who wanted revenge was incarcerated or out of the country," I suggested. "Was Ramon Danes close to anyone? Maybe someone involved with the cartels?"

Vale rubbed his mouth for a second. "What would they want with two suits?"

Vale wouldn't help us. I already knew it. "I don't know, but we're looking into anyone and everyone who may have a beef with Smith and Smith, particularly the two dead employees."

Vale squinted. "I only heard about the one on the news. Who else got popped?"

"An actuary."

"How?"

"Same way," Brad said. "A sniper took him out."

"You think little Ramon Danes had gotten in so good with the cartel that they sent a sicario six years later to get revenge on the insurance company for not giving his rich parents more money? I'd love to see the evidence trail on that." Vale rolled his eyes and shook his head. "Do you have anything at all to support that theory?"

Brad bristled. "Most killers aren't precision shooters. Even fewer have sniper training."

"Okay." Vale leaned back in his chair. "Seriously, what does this have to do with Ramon? He's old news. Over and done with. Caput. Capeesh?"

"He was your informant. Did he ever give you anything valuable?" I asked.

"You're barking up the wrong tree, lady. You're not even in the same universe."

Before I said something I'd regret, Brad took over. "Ramon Danes got an early release supposedly due to overcrowding, but it's because he snitched. He was your CI. You needed the intel he provided to build your case against the cartel. That must mean he had connections. Was he close to anyone who may have been incarcerated for say the last ten years, who may have gotten out and—"

"And what?" Vale asked. "Wants to wipe out the insurance people who didn't pay up when Ramon died? That's the worst theory ever. When I was on the force, homicide detectives were topnotch. Now, well, I guess name recognition goes a long way."

I wasn't sure which of us would correct Vale first. Maybe Brad and I should play rock, paper, scissors to decide. But before we could tell him where to shove his pension, the desk phone rang.

Vale held up his finger, which I wanted to break, and spoke on the phone. "Yeah, okay. I'll get right on that." He put the phone down. "Duty calls." He took two embossed business cards from the fancy holder on his desk and held them out to us. "You come up with some better questions or need a real detective to think up a more plausible theory, give me a call."

Brad dragged me out of the office before I lunged for Vale's throat. It wasn't worth it. The reason it bothered me so much was because Vale was right. This theory may have been our worst, but it was the only major issue we'd found by researching Smith and Smith.

"Hey, Detectives," Vale called after us, "more than likely, whoever popped those guys was recently denied a claim. You got the right idea, but you're a decade too early."

# TWENTY-TWO

"Should we even bother with Judge Overholdt?" I asked.

Brad gave me the side eye. "Vale got in your head."

"He's right, isn't he? Our theory is about as far flung as it gets."

"Not necessarily. *Danes v. Smith and Smith Insurance* is the only recent civil proceeding in the last decade that the court ruled in favor of the insurance firm. In fact, there weren't really any other cases. You spoke to upper management and the head honchos at Smith and Smith. They didn't mention any issues arising. No disgruntled employees. No vindictive customers, current or former."

"They did say people were upset from time to time." I thought back to the conversations I had when Ryan Dugrey was our only victim. "None of it sounded serious. Not serious enough for anyone to remember specifics or give me a name."

"Right." Brad looked pointedly at me. "And when Jake investigated, he asked the same questions plus some and didn't get anything either."

"That doesn't mean there's nothing to find. Smith and Smith could have all sorts of secrets and dirt they're keeping a lid on."

"They could." Brad ran a hand through his hair while he waited for me to come around to his way of thinking. "Isn't that what led to the research into the company and the court case?"

I parked the car and turned in my seat. "Stop being so damn rational."

"One of us has to be."

I scoped out our surroundings. The area around the courthouse was always congested, but there were several empty spaces on account of lunch. Judge Overholdt didn't order in and eat in his chambers like most of his colleagues. He preferred to get out of the robes and enjoy a leisurely lunch somewhere with a wine list. When asked about it, he said he liked to clear his head between cases or while letting the facts and arguments from the ongoing trial sink in. I always wondered if it was so he'd have a nice buzz going when things continued, but no one had ever reported him being drunk at work. Though, it would explain most of his rulings.

After checking the time, I reached for my phone. I didn't have any messages. "Did you receive any notifications?"

Brad checked his phone. "Nothing." He stared out the windshield. From here, we could see the courthouse steps. We'd intercept Judge Overholdt before he got too far. Based on the time, he should be coming out the door at any moment. "What are we going to do, Liv? Assuming Robard's not our guy, this psycho gunman is still out there. He could be anywhere."

I shot a text to Officer Roberts. *Any updates on locating the van?*

Roberts' reply made my phone buzz. *Not yet.*

*What about checking into the owners? Pull security footage. DOT feeds. Whatever.*

Again, my phone buzzed. *I never would have thought of that.*

Even though the tone of text messages was open to interpretation, I could read the sarcasm loud and clear. "We still don't have anything on the van with the suspicious plates."

"We have the name of the flower shop. We'll swing by after we speak to Overholdt."

"The place is closed."

"I know, Liv." Brad reached for the door handle. "That doesn't mean the van wasn't parked somewhere nearby.

Maybe someone saw something. It's in a commercial neighborhood. The chances are good someone noticed a strange guy poking around the closed shop or wondered what happened when the van suddenly went missing."

"We should speak to the owners. I don't know why Roberts hasn't done that yet."

"You didn't want me to say anything to him."

"Feel free to tell him that. In fact, I insist."

Brad snorted and pulled out his phone. "Okay." He made a call, placed the request, and joined me on the sidewalk. "Before we speak to Judge Overholdt, I'll see if the court clerks can pull records from the trial. They may have some intel we haven't seen concerning people in attendance or threats that were made."

"You think someone threatened the judge?"

"Not necessarily, but people spout out a lot of stuff when things aren't going their way. Once the judge ruled in favor of Smith and Smith, a discontented party may have lashed out. A bailiff or someone could have escorted him from the courtroom."

"Here's to hoping." We approached the looming courthouse. A coffee truck was parked near the front steps. "If this was about Danes or something Smith and Smith did, do you think the killer's done now that Yeger is dead?"

"I hope so." But Brad's expression told me he wasn't sure. "Either way, we need to get this guy. My money's on contract killer, which means he could resurface at any time. I don't want more weeks like this one."

"We're grasping at straws."

"I know." He checked his watch. "Samara said Overholdt has a full docket today. She said he might be a few minutes late heading out. That gives us a few extra minutes to grab coffee."

"Samara?"

"The court clerk."

I snorted, resisting the urge to roll my eyes. "How long did you date?"

"We only went out a couple of times. I wouldn't say we dated."

"Was she blonde?"

"I don't see—"

"They're always blonde." I shook my head before he could protest. "It doesn't matter. I've spent the last two years observing from the sidelines. None of this comes as a shock." Even if it made me wonder why he had any interest in me when clearly I was not his type. It must have been from all the long hours, the nights and days spent together, and the danger we faced and things we survived.

"So coffee?"

"Are you sure we have time?"

Brad held out his wrist so I could see his watch. "We're early. We have ten minutes, and that's if things are running on schedule. It could be longer." He nodded to the food truck. "It's my treat."

I eyed the photos on the side, which showed various treats, none of which were grain-free. Emma had ruined all of that for me with her nutrition lectures and documentaries. But a part of me really wanted a donut, even though I hadn't had one since childhood. "Do you think cop food would make us better at our jobs?"

"What are you thinking?"

I pointed to the picture of the chocolate glazed donut.

"If you want it, get it. I won't tell."

"Do you want one?"

I'd never seen him look more concerned and confused. "Are you feeling okay, Liv? You're not pregnant, are you?"

I slapped his arm hard enough that I may have left a mark. "Don't even put that out there. There were precautions. Lots of precautions. Tons of precautions."

"Okay, easy." He held up one hand while he backed away and rubbed his arm with the other hand. "It was a joke."

"That is the least funny thing you've ever said."

"I'm sorry. Take it easy." He glanced at the people in line in front of us, but like most people, they were oblivious to what was going on around them. "I've never once heard you say you wanted a donut. Never. And you know I don't eat overly processed, chemical-laden things if I can help it. I'd say that's a preservative-filled death trap."

"With chocolate frosting."

The concerned look on Brad's face remained. "Do you

want one?"

"No, but Jake swears by the pastries in the break room, which are nothing more than stale donuts, and at this point, I'm willing to try just about anything. Also, I'd really like some chocolate."

Brad tried not to laugh as he put a comforting arm around my shoulders. "On our way to the flower shop, we'll make a quick stop and pick up the organic dark chocolate you like. Will that help?"

"Probably not."

When we reached the window, he placed our order, fished out the money, and handed me a cup once it was ready. "Y'know, we usually take turns being pessimistic. I already called dibs on this case. You're supposed to insist we'll identify this guy and stop him. You aren't supposed to go off the deep end by suggesting we follow Voletek's example by eating like him."

"My optimism melted away after spending the morning with Roberts and Vale." I took a sip, finding the coffee watered down and burnt. Somehow, that seemed fitting. "Overholdt will probably tell us the same thing Vale did. I'm not sure what the point of us being here is."

"We check things out. It's what we do. It's how we gather evidence. I can almost guarantee Judge Overholdt isn't going to tell us the same thing Vale did. Instead, he'll say he doesn't remember or he can't discuss the case." Brad made a face and put the lid back on his cup as we headed up the courthouse steps. "That's what this job is, Detective DeMarco. And regardless of what anyone says, you're a damn good detective. Do not let Roberts or Vale get in your head."

"They aren't." But they were. If anything, I felt guilty for last night. We shouldn't have wasted so much time. We should have stayed on topic, focused on the case and finding evidence. That may have been why Brad had been so hesitant or resistant. Sure, he blew off steam with his previous female companions, but that last night he spent with Carrie had wrecked him. It nearly destroyed him to learn I'd been attacked while he'd been otherwise occupied. And that had led down a rabbit hole with more twists than I cared to recount.

Now, I understood a little better how he felt. Maybe our time together should have been spent stopping a killer. But that's not how this job worked. We clocked in. We clocked out. It'd consume us if we let it, and then we'd drown.

Sure, homicide detectives worked more than most, and we were never really off the clock, just like every other cop in the city, but we couldn't live our lives with the job being everything. At least that's what I was trying to remind myself until the door to the courthouse opened and Judge Overholdt stepped out in his Brioni suit. He made it three steps before his brain splashed on the brick behind him.

# TWENTY-THREE

"Everyone get down," Brad shouted, yanking me against him and forcing me behind the food truck.

People scurried. I didn't think I heard the shot before the bullet went through the judge's head, but I couldn't be certain. It didn't boom, like I would have expected. Instead, it barely rumbled, almost like far off thunder. Maybe I hadn't heard it at all. That could have been a car.

The man working inside the food truck had dropped to the ground. The rest of the customers were huddled nearby or had fled despite Brad's warning. I didn't blame them. Getting picked off from a distance wasn't the way I'd want to go.

I tried to peer around the side, hoping to spot the shooter, but Brad jerked me backward, his chest heaving. "We need eyes on the shooter," I insisted.

"You poke your head out, and it'll be your brains I'm mopping up."

"Do you know where he is?" I reached for my phone, hitting the button for dispatch.

"No."

Nodding, I updated everyone on the situation. "Shots fired. Active shooter. We're looking at a sniper." I gave them our location and pertinent details. "Let's form a perimeter. Ten blocks out." Despite my orders, I knew we'd never box in the killer. He was too far away and had too much of a head start. "Roll ambulances to my location, and notify the

raced through my mind as I calculated the likelihood the man I was pursuing was the killer while my legs carried me as quickly as they could. The wind whipped through my hair. For the briefest moment, I lost sight of him in the crowd. Then he emerged, closer to the steps.

"Police. Freeze," I screamed before he could descend the stairs. Every person on the street turned to look at me. I aimed, gasping. "Put the briefcase on the ground and show me your hands."

Brad stopped beside me, scanning the crowd. No one moved. A few people pulled out their phones and started recording.

The man with the backward baseball cap did as I instructed. "What's going on?" he asked.

"Hands behind your head." Brad approached him, slapped on the cuffs, and patted him down. "What's in the case?"

"I'd rather not—"

Brad spun him against the wall, forcing him to keep his back to me. "Open it, Liv."

I holstered my weapon and flipped open the latches. Carefully, I lifted the lid. Inside were separate compartments each containing plastic bags filled with water and brightly colored fish. There were six in total.

I felt around the inside of the case, but there was nothing inside but the fish. No rifle. No suppressor. No ammunition.

"We're sorry, sir." Brad removed the handcuffs and let the guy go.

My partner said something else, but I didn't hear him. I felt eyes on me. Someone was watching.

Looking around, I realized everyone was watching, but that's not what I felt. A guy to my right moved closer, shoving his phone in my face while he recorded. I batted it away, hoping to find the source of my unease.

At the end of the street, a similarly dressed man with an almost identical case watched us from where he waited in line to board a local bus. "Brad, I got him." I didn't wait for his response before I took off down the street.

Brad caught up to me almost instantly and took the lead. By the time we made it to the bus stop, the bus had pulled away. Brad continued to chase after it, shouting, "Police. Stop." But the driver didn't see my partner's badge or hear his pleas.

Repeating the bus number while I dialed, I notified dispatch that we had reason to believe our suspect had boarded the bus. Units would pull it over as soon as they could. With the perimeter being established, that should be easy. But I feared the bastard would jump off at the next stop and disappear again.

Brad trudged back toward me, catching his breath and glancing uneasily around. "Are you sure that was our shooter?"

"I think so."

He nodded, huffing. "How?"

"It was the case, but there's something about him. Something familiar. But it wasn't just that. It was the way he was watching us. He was so damn smug. It was as if he were taunting us."

Brad stared down the street, in the direction from which we had come. Some of the people had cleared away. A few remained, their phones aimed at us. The man we had temporarily detained glared at us with disgust.

This was bad. Between the video footage and cuffing the wrong guy, our heads would be on the chopping block. The thought brought back the original crime scene. We had to get back there. We didn't secure the scene. We didn't do much of anything. Winston was going to have our asses. Teflon or not, I was screwed.

# TWENTY-FOUR

Brad and I stood in front of Lt. Winston's desk. The three-ring circus at the courthouse involved everything from a growing crowd of reporters, nosy onlookers, concerned citizens, and every idiot who liked to post videos on the internet. Detective Jake Voletek had taken over the scene when Brad and I were summoned back to HQ.

"This has gone viral." Winston gestured at his computer screen. "It'll be on the six o'clock news. In fact, I'm half-expecting it to turn into a national news story."

"I hope they got my good side."

Winston's eyes shot to me. "What was that, Detective DeMarco?"

"Nothing, sir." I stood a little straighter, hearing Brad's silent warning to keep my mouth shut. However, when it came to dealing with Winston, neither of us had been particularly adept at that feat.

"You're lucky patrol stopped the bus and brought in the man you suspect of shooting Judge Overholdt. If it weren't for that, this would be an even bigger PR nightmare." Winston let out a long sigh through his pursed lips, causing an unintentional whistle. "A dead judge on the courthouse steps is massive. It explains why two homicide detectives behaved so erratically. The media officer will be able to spin this to our advantage and paint the two of you in a much better light. That is the only reason you're not getting written up or suspended. Do you understand that?"

"We didn't do anything wrong, sir." Brad held his ground. "We were exploring a theory, which may explain why Judge Overholdt was killed."

"Since you thought he'd be targeted, why didn't you warn him?" the LT asked.

"We didn't have anything to back it or any reason to believe anyone else would be targeted," Brad said. "You've seen the evidence from the two previous crime scenes. Nothing connected. DeMarco and I thought members of the insurance firm were the targets. We thought the judge may have been able to tell us if anyone had been irate or threatening after the ruling."

Winston didn't act like he heard a word my partner said. "All right. Your guy is waiting in the box. He hasn't asked for an attorney yet. See what you can get out of him before he comes to his senses."

"What was in the briefcase?" I hadn't seen the reports. "Did patrol recover the sniper rifle?"

"No." Winston gave me a hard look. "Are you sure you got the right guy? You were wrong once. Another false arrest will make the department look even worse. It'll make us look incompetent."

"We have reason to believe—"

Winston waved me off before I could finish. "Get to it and get me something concrete. Providing the public with good news and a clear villain will help us control the narrative and rewrite your earlier blunder."

"Yes, sir." Brad pulled open the office door and waited for me to go through. He knew better than to let me linger in the LT's office. I was bound to say something glib, which would get me in deeper, and neither of us wanted that.

We headed to the interrogation room in silence. My thoughts on the crime scene, the judge murdered the moment he stepped outside. Maybe Winston was right. Maybe we should have realized the connection.

"Don't do that," Brad warned.

I looked at him as we approached the interrogation room door. "Do what?"

"You know what you're doing. You're rethinking everything. Don't do that. It won't help matters. It won't bring Overholdt back. We screwed up. The best we can do is move forward."

"Did we screw up?"

Brad met my eyes. "I don't know." He pulled open the door, bringing our conversation to a halt.

The man seated at the table had his palms flat against the surface. He looked at us as we entered, a smile tugging at his lips. Suspects didn't usually behave like that. In fact, only the truly deranged ever appeared giddy, which is the one word that came to mind the second I got a look at this guy.

"Finally." He offered his hand to shake. "I was wondering what was taking so long."

Brad and I ignored the gesture before dropping into the seats on the other side of the table. I stared at the guy. His ID said his name was Trevor Wenchel, but I had spent a lot of time researching potential suspects. This guy was a dead ringer for Jim Parnell. Unfortunately, Parnell didn't have a record, which meant his prints weren't in the system. And until now, Trevor Wenchel didn't have a record either, which meant I had no way of proving this was the same guy. Sure, his hair was different. So were his glasses. But he looked like the ID photo I'd seen. This case already had too many coincidences. I didn't believe Wenchel was Parnell's doppelganger.

Brad made the introductions while I leafed through the file. The case the officers confiscated contained a flute, broken down into several different sections. The shiny metal had been photographed, but no bullets or gun pieces had been discovered inside. Lt. Winston wouldn't like this. I wasn't a fan either.

"Detective DeMarco," Wenchel let my name roll around on his tongue, "I was told you're the reason I'm here. May I ask why?"

"What were you doing in the park?"

"I don't see why that's relevant."

"A crime occurred. You were in the vicinity. The sooner we figure out the reason you were there, the sooner we can let you go."

Wenchel held the smile. "I was practicing."

"Practicing what?"

"The flute." He cocked his head to the side. "Officers confiscated the case when they took me off the bus. Didn't you look inside?" He nodded at the folder I held in front of me. "I'd imagine those details should be included in there."

"Can anyone corroborate your story?" Brad asked.

"I'd say the half dozen people who told me to take a hike could probably help you with that. Unfortunately, I didn't get any names. No one offered me a card or my shot at being first chair for the philharmonic."

"What kind of car do you drive?" I asked.

Wenchel quirked an eyebrow. "That's a strange question to ask."

"I'm curious."

"I don't have a car."

Beside me, Brad tensed. He suspected I was on to something, but he didn't know what. He hadn't seen the photos of our potentials.

"Are you sure you don't have a hatchback registered in your name?"

"No." Wenchel appeared confused. "My name isn't that uncommon. Maybe you have me confused with someone else."

"That must be it." I closed the folder, so he couldn't see any of the details, before placing it on the table. "Did you see anyone suspicious while you were at the park?"

"Have you seen the crazies out there? I'm going to need a little more than suspicious."

"Did you see anyone carrying a gun?" I asked.

Wenchel gave the question careful consideration before shaking his head. "Not that I recall. I wasn't paying too much attention."

"Where's your sheet music?" Brad asked.

The suspect shrugged. "I didn't know that was a requirement."

"I'd think if you were practicing, you'd have sheet music."

"I like to play around, compose my own pieces, or practice classics from memory."

"What were you playing today?" I asked.

"Are you familiar with *Peter and the Wolf*?"

"Vaguely."

"I was playing the flute's part."

Brad snorted, covering it with a sniffle. "Where exactly were you set up?"

Wenchel described the place in such vague terms it'd be impossible to pinpoint without forcing him to show us the exact spot.

"Could you see the courthouse?" I asked.

"I could. It's big, which makes it hard to miss, but I was rather far away."

"Did you hear a gunshot?"

"I don't recall."

"Why did you flee the park when you did?" Brad asked.

"Flee?" Wenchel chuckled. "I wasn't fleeing. I was hurrying to catch my bus. When the music takes hold, I lose all sense of time. I didn't want to wait for the next one." He looked around the room. "Given where I ended up, I'm guessing I should have waited."

"All right, Jim, let me see if we have this right." I picked up the folder again, as if planning to read from it.

"My name's Trevor," he said, but his eyes suggested otherwise. "Why did you call me Jim?"

"My apologies. It's been a long day." But I'd bet my badge Trevor Wenchel wasn't his real name.

"That's not a problem. From what I heard and saw, you've been making quite a few mistakes today. Haven't you, Detective DeMarco?"

"Sir," Brad interrupted, "walk us through your day."

Wenchel kept his eyes on me, but he detailed the time he left his house, his trip to the coffee shop, a stop at the newsstand, and how long he waited for the bus. The only details he couldn't provide involved exactly where he was in the park.

"You're sure you didn't hear a gunshot or see anyone suspicious?" Brad asked.

"Come to think of it, there was a guy in a dark hooded jacket who went past. He had something with him. I'm not sure what it was. A bag of some sort. He looked like an athlete. I figured he was going to meet up with friends to play field hockey or something." Wenchel pointed to the blank legal pad and pen in the middle of the table. "Do you want me to write that down for you?"

"Sure." Brad slid the paper closer.

"Excuse me for a moment." I left the room and returned to my desk.

The first thing I did was pull up Jim Parnell's ID photo. That had to be the same guy. He had the same nose and the same chin. Afraid I may be losing my mind, I sent the two ID photos to Mac and dialed her extension.

"I need you to run a comparison on the photos I sent. Tell me we're looking at the same guy."

"Une momento."

I didn't bother mentioning she was butchering several languages at once. Instead, I pulled up Parnell's home address and snapped my fingers at an officer walking by. Brad would say this was why people who didn't know me didn't like me. But I didn't want to confuse Mac with my ramblings. She had a tendency to get distracted, and I needed this now.

"What do you want, DeMarco?" he asked.

Covering the mouthpiece, I said, "I need to know where this guy is. Can someone perform a wellness check?"

"Do you want me to put a rush on it?"

"Please and thank you."

The officer nodded, keying his radio as he stepped away.

Mac came back on the line. "Well, I can't say with a hundred percent certainty it's the same man, but they share a lot of the same features. The glasses and differing hairstyles make it difficult to determine cheek and forehead dimensions, but his nose and chin match. His ears too."

"Is it the same man?"

"The computer says the likelihood of an identical match is seventy-eight percent."

"What do you think?"

"Give me another second." She clicked furiously a few times. "I'd say yes. I did some quick photoshopping, changed his hair color, and added glasses."

"Can we prove it?"

"Not with this."

"All right." I hated giving her more to do, but this was the break we'd been waiting for. Everything else could wait if the killer was in custody. But if I was wrong, again, and this turned into another Robard situation, the killer would have even longer to plan his next strike. "As soon as you can, perform a deep dive on Jim Parnell. If everything's solid, do the same with Trevor Wenchel."

"No problem, Liv. Are you thinking we have an identical cousins situation going on?"

Thoughts of a serial killer I'd tangled with came to mind, but that was an entirely different situation.

"Y'know, like Patty Duke playing two parts," Mac explained.

"Right. Yeah, that's exactly what I'm thinking."

"All right. I'm on it."

I printed a photo of Parnell, shoved it into an empty folder, and returned to the interrogation room.

Brad had gotten up to pace while Wenchel meticulously wrote notes about his day on the blank sheet of paper, spending an inordinate amount of time carefully forming each letter. The smug grin on Wenchel's face got a little bigger when I returned. This was a game to him. He acted like he already won, which worried me. We had him in custody. What trick did he have up his sleeve?

I joined my partner near the back of the room and handed him the folder. Silently, he opened it, examining the sheets that I'd paperclipped to the covers. He studied the photo of Jim Parnell before looking in Trevor Wenchel's direction. Nodding, he handed me back the folder. At least my partner and I were in agreement.

"All right, there you go. A day in the life of struggling musician Trevor Wenchel." He placed the pen down and slid the legal pad to the middle of the table. "Am I free to go now?"

"Free to go?" This guy had to be joking.

"Easy, Liv." Brad reached for the legal pad. "Let's see if this cleared everything up for us." He skimmed the notes Wenchel had made. "You don't deny you were at the park at the time of the shooting."

"I don't know anything about a shooting, but I was there all afternoon. You saw me leave."

Brad rested his hips on the table beside Wenchel, as if

they were pals sharing office gossip at their cubicles. "Tell us again about the guy playing field hockey."

"I never saw him play field hockey. I just assumed given the bag and his clothes and build."

Brad dragged the pen down the side of the legal pad. "You provided a decent description. I'd like you to sit with a sketch artist."

Wenchel turned to look in my direction, but I remained impassive. This was Brad's show. I was purely here in a support position. "I don't know how much help I can be. I didn't get a good look at him. He crossed near me. But I'll try."

"Sit tight. We'll send a sketch artist in as soon as we can."

# TWENTY-FIVE

We needed to buy time. That was the name of the game. However, Trevor Wenchel was getting antsy. He hadn't provided the sketch artist with anything viable, not that I thought he would. It wasn't like he could describe himself to the guy.

Uniforms were still canvassing the area while CSU determined the spot where the shot had been fired. It had originated at the park, near some bleachers in a closed off section that was currently undergoing maintenance after a storm downed several large trees. Unfortunately, the security cameras in that area had also been taken out by fallen trees and the storm.

Detective Jake Voletek returned, looking harried and overwhelmed, which was precisely how I felt. "The news people are out in droves. I spoke to a few witnesses. No one saw where the shot originated. They didn't even remember hearing it."

"The silencer," I said.

Voletek flipped through the pages on his desk. "Most likely, or it had to do with the distance the bullet traveled. That shot wasn't quite record-breaking, but it was damn close. Only the best of the best could pull that off. The guy was practically firing into the future, at least that's how the ESU snipers I spoke to described it." He picked up the Robard file. "Any idea where this guy was when Overholdt went down?"

"We haven't checked," I said. "I assume he's still on base."

Voletek pulled out his chair and took a seat. "The ME said the bullet went into Overholdt's third eye. Dead center. I'm not sure the guys we looked at from the gun range could even pull that off."

"What about Jim Parnell?" Brad asked.

"Didn't you rule him out for Yeger's murder?" Voletek dug through his notes to see what he had on Parnell. "Shit. You don't think there's an entire group of highly trained snipers working together, do you? Is this some kind of shadow military operation thing?"

Brad put down the phone. "From what I was told, Robard is still on base. He's been on base since he was picked up from police custody."

"Uniformed officers at his place and his girlfriend's place can't contradict it," I said, even though that didn't mean Robard hadn't slipped away and found somewhere else to hang out. I'd have Mac ping his phone when she had a free minute, just to make sure.

"Courthouse cameras are useless," Voletek continued. "DOT and security feeds in and around the park are our best bets, except you guys made an arrest. So where are we on that?"

Brad looked at me before jerking his head toward Voletek. Great, I got to be the bearer of bad news.

"We're working on it. I recognized him at the park. Not only was he acting suspiciously, but I'd seen him before."

"That's good. Why hasn't he been properly processed and booked yet?"

"Winston wanted to make certain we didn't fuck up again," Brad said, "especially since there's a kicker."

"What kicker?" Voletek asked.

I sighed. "The man we arrested claims his name is Trevor Wenchel. He has a state issued ID to prove it. Preliminary checks confirm the details. The only problem with that is I'd say his alter ego's name is Jim Parnell. As I'm sure you remember, I already ran everything on Jim Parnell. He's legit too."

"That's fucked up. What are we thinking? Identity theft?

Falsified records?"

"Mac's in the midst of a deep dive. Whatever's off about this, she'll find." I had to believe that. "In the meantime, we sent uniformed officers to show Trevor Wenchel's photo to the guys at the gun range. Most of them identified Wenchel as Jim Parnell, but not everyone did."

"What about family?" Voletek asked. "His own mother should be able to tell us if this guy is her son."

"Jim Parnell has no family. His last known relative died eight months ago," Brad said.

"According to Wenchel, he grew up in the system. He bounced from group home to group home. We've verified a kid with that name stayed at the houses he mentioned, but we haven't been able to get in touch with anyone who remembers him or who has been in contact with him recently."

"What about phone records?" Voletek asked.

I glared in the direction of Winston's office. "We haven't had much luck. Fishing expeditions will not be tolerated."

Voletek chuckled. "Have you seen the video? It went viral."

"Winston mentioned it, but no, I haven't seen it." Dread filled me.

Voletek pulled out his phone and clicked a few times before showing me the recording of Brad and I detaining the man with the suitcase full of fish. The content creator had paired it with a catchy jingle from a frozen fish product and put some blaringly obvious text about the police going on a fishing expedition. To add to it, he even superimposed stickers of fishermen's hats on top of our heads. "Three million views and counting."

"Fuck." I rubbed a hand down my face.

Brad took the phone and watched the footage play. "Liv, with all that undercover work you've done, this isn't good."

"I'm not the only one." I eyed Brad before picking up my phone. "I have to warn a few informants who may be compromised because of this."

"Yeah, me too." Brad grabbed his phone and a notebook he kept hidden away in his locked drawer.

None of my prior cases remained open, but that didn't

mean there wouldn't be fallout. This was why I always did my best to stay out of the press. On occasion, it had been unavoidable, but none of those stories had ever hit this big. It was always something I worried about, even though every precaution had been taken and protocols remained in place for these types of situations. Things would be different and so much worse if any of those undercover ops were still in play or if I was still working undercover. But it never hurt to make some calls.

Thirty minutes later, I was back on track. By then, Voletek had caught himself up and was pestering Mac for any insight she could share. He spoke to the officer I had sent to track down Jim Parnell, but the man hadn't been located. I was pretty sure that was because he was sitting inside our interrogation room, but without viable prints or DNA, that would be hard to prove.

"What about dental records?" I asked.

Voletek pointed at me. "You may be on to something. Officer Beck, see what you can find."

"Yes, sir." The uniformed cop disappeared behind a computer terminal.

"Have you tried tax records?" I asked, nearly out of ideas.

"Parnell and Wenchel have separate filings. Separate social security numbers. Separate everything." Voletek tapped his pen a few times on the pad. "However, Wenchel's tax records are spotty. He filed this past year. Prior to that, he filed five years ago."

"And the IRS is okay with that?"

"Wenchel doesn't have any W-2s or 1099s to contradict any of that. For his vocation, he has musician listed."

"How does he afford rent?" I scooted closer so I could see the information on Voletek's screen.

"He has a place now, but the last address on file belonged to one of those mailbox places."

"So Wenchel is Parnell's alter ego, the false identity."

"Liv, I'm on board with everything you've said. I've seen the photos. It looks convincing, but holding both these ID photos up to a jury and asking them to believe that's the same man may be harder to prove."

"Wow, that's confidence, Jake. You're already taking this

to trial."

"You get my point." He glanced toward Winston's office. "We're delaying the inevitable, but Wenchel asked for a lawyer. He's tired of waiting. We keep insisting he hang around, which is why he wants counsel. He doesn't think he has any reason to stay, and once his attorney gets here, we'll have to cut him loose unless we can prove he's involved."

"He's more than involved. He's the shooter."

"Where's the gun?" Voletek gestured emphatically with his hands. "Tell me where to look, Liv. Tell me where he hid it. You and Brad saw him board the bus with his flute case. Patrol pulled the bus over. They escorted him off the bus, and they grabbed the same black case you saw. So where'd he hide the gun? Did he have another bag? A jacket? Did he throw it out the window without anyone noticing?"

"Maybe he left it behind."

"A weapon like that, there's no way. Whoever took today's shot," he held up his hand before I could voice an objection, "is highly skilled. That weapon allows him to be that skilled. He wouldn't ditch it."

"Are you telling me we got the wrong guy?"

Voletek looked away. "We have to consider every possibility. We were convinced Robard was responsible. Even after his CO forced us to release him, we stuck with that theory. Now we have another theory, which is just as good as our last, except that doesn't make it right."

"Have you spoken to him?" I asked. "Have you seen Wenchel's face? He thinks he's won."

"Are you sure? Maybe he's excited to be assisting. He could be one of those who gets a thrill out of being close to the action. He's an artist, musician, creative, whatever you want to call him, which means he's a people pleaser who craves attention."

"Since when do we profile?"

"We always profile. Tell me what part of that you disagree with."

"He's not a musician."

"I spoke to several witnesses who had been at the park at the time of the shooting. They remember a man playing a musical instrument very badly."

"That doesn't mean it was Wenchel. There are always a bunch of lousy performers at the park."

"What are you thinking? He's impersonating someone else to make himself look innocent?"

"I don't know, but we can't be wrong again."

Voletek considered my words. "Here's the rub of it. Now that Judge Overholdt has been added to our victim list, that indicates this has everything to do with that court case, which means your partner was right. Ryan Dugrey was never an intended target. However, he may have been a source for the killer to gain additional intel on his target, Yeger, since they worked together. The clearing where he liked to go could have been an added bonus."

"Jim Parnell knew about that spot. He checks all the boxes."

"Like Robard did?"

"Ugh."

"Liv, I'm not being nasty. I'm working this the way I see fit. Winston wants me to take over the case. Yeger was mine. More than likely, this has to do with that court case. Our killer wants everyone to pay for what happened to Danes. That means Overholdt's murder is related. The LT made me primary. I'm sorry."

"I don't care," Brad said, sneaking up behind us. "You can have it. I never wanted it."

"Are you okay?" I tilted my head back to see Brad.

He nodded. "We'll do whatever you want, Jake, whatever needs to be done. But this has to stop."

"In that case, start knocking on doors. Since we know a lot more about Jim Parnell, find his friends, his coworkers, his neighbors. See what they can tell you. Show them the photo of Wenchel and see if they recognize him. And find out where Parnell is. If we can't find him, that'll get us one step closer to figuring out if Trevor Wenchel is responsible."

# TWENTY-SIX

It took hours, but we finally found someone who could help. According to Parnell's boss, the owner of the comic book store where Jim Parnell worked, Parnell was on vacation. He'd taken off two weeks and had gone on a camping trip to decompress. When asked about Parnell's outdoor habits, we hit another dead end. His boss didn't know much. He didn't even know Parnell owned a weapon.

We'd already spoken to Parnell's neighbors, a follow-up to the wellness check patrol had performed, but no one had seen Parnell in the last five days. His hatchback remained parked in his assigned space. According to his neighbors, he had gotten into a van the morning he left.

"We can pull traffic cam footage from the area and see what we get on the van." I looked around.

"The flower shop isn't far from the comic book store where Parnell works. If he is our guy, he could have noticed the shop was closed due to a leak and decided to steal the van."

"Are we sure that's the van our shooter used?"

Brad indicated his phone. "Officers picked up footage from outside the flower shop. A week ago, someone dressed entirely in black snuck around back and drove off in one of the three vans. Mac and Ellie agree. That's the vehicle our shooter must have used. It makes the most sense."

"What about the two other vans?" I didn't want to be wrong again. Everything from here on out had to be solid.

"They ruled out the other two vans, and the reconstructed footage from the garage indicates that the dog grooming van, which is the same make and model as the flower shop van, only with different decals, was parked against the wall where the shot had been taken."

"How do they explain the decals?"

"They're stickers, Liv. Anyone can purchase them or have them custom-made. It'd be the easiest and fastest way to disguise the stolen vehicle."

"I'm glad our techs have you on speed dial."

Brad bumped against me. "Jealous?"

"No."

He didn't like my tone. "For the record, I don't like this any more than you do. But progress is progress, even if it's leading us around the long way."

"Any idea what happened to that van?"

"A BOLO's been issued. Someone will find it."

"Do you think the sniper's still using it?"

"That depends."

"On what?"

Brad stared into the distance. "Wenchel took the bus."

"Are you siding with Jake now? Do you think we arrested the wrong man?"

"I'll admit, we may have been quick to jump to conclusions with Robard, but Wenchel and Parnell look the same. The likelihood we're looking at two different people is unfathomable. Wenchel has to be Parnell, or vice versa. That's the only thing that makes sense."

"Wenchel grew up in foster care," I said. "According to Child Services, he was dropped off at a firehouse. No questions. No family. No history. Maybe he had an identical twin brother no one knew about."

Brad considered what I said. "That's a little farfetched, even for you."

"Hey."

He chuckled. "Sure, I guess it's possible. Daytime soaps love using that plot device."

"When do you watch daytime soaps?"

"I don't. It's what I've heard."

"Uh-huh. Which one's your favorite?"

He gave me a sideways look. "Barring the possibility Wenchel and Parnell are the same man or they're twins, we should consider the only other feasible possibility. They're related."

I checked my phone. "We weren't able to locate Parnell's dental records."

"Even if we did, it's not like we're hoping to identify his body. Those wouldn't be turned over without a warrant, and Winston wouldn't even allow us to entertain the possibility without some sort of proof."

"Voletek was looking into it. He's golden. He may get away with it."

"You're golden too."

"Not anymore." Thoughts of that viral video came to mind. "It turns out I was gold-plated, and it started to peel."

We got back to the car and stared out the windshield, unsure what our next destination should be.

"Here's a theory," Brad said. "Jim Parnell has been planning this for a while. I don't know why or for how long. As far as we know, he has no known connection to our victims. He could be a hitman for hire."

"He works in a comic book store."

"Not to stereotype, but those cliches were established for a reason."

"What?"

"The guys who are into comic books tend to fall into certain categories. Intelligent being one of them. Unhinged being another."

"Lots of people read comic books. I read comic books."

"Sure," Brad shrugged, "I have a stack beneath my bed too. But I'm not talking about the average reader. I'm talking about that smaller subsect. Y'know, the stereotypical dweeb. The guys who spend a lot of time on the dark web looking up some pretty nasty things. Y'know, the angry loners who were rejected by the prom queen and never got over it, who have several different plans for taking over the world, who have plotted revenge on their bullies for twenty-plus years."

"No more *Big Bang Theory* for you."

"You get my point, Liv. Parnell worked there. Even if he deviated from the cliché, he would have been around someone who fit the bill. Let's say one of those people learned of his shooting acumen and made him an offer."

"Maybe we should go back to the comic book shop and get a list of customers."

"I tried, but the owner wouldn't hand over those details. Like most comic shops and bookstores, the place is barely scraping by. Everything's digital now. The few people who enjoy reading, regardless of the format or material, are finding other things to do with their free time given all the other forms of entertainment readily available for consumption."

"Wow."

"What?"

"You're a closeted nerd."

"I prefer the term geek. Plus, you like geeks. Mac's one of your favorite people. And don't get me started on Emma. She's the queen of all things factual and boring."

"Great, so I'm the dumb friend."

"Well, I didn't want to say anything," he teased.

"You do like bimbos."

He pointed a finger in my face, the joking aside. "We will have a conversation about that at some point, but I'm tabling it for now. Identifying the sniper is more important. I think we need to retrace the shooter's steps from today. With any luck, we'll find the gun."

"Where do you want to look? Patrol's searched every square inch of the park."

"There has to be something they missed." He started the engine and headed back the way we came. "When you first spotted our suspect, you saw him putting things in a case."

"Yeah, the black case."

"You didn't see anything else?"

"No."

"But you knew it was him?"

"I can't explain it."

"His behavior tipped you. After he caught your attention, you must have realized he looked like Parnell. That's why we went after him."

"But he slipped us. It's how we got him confused with that weirdo with the fish."

The thought hit both of us at the same time. "That's when he realized he was caught and dumped the gun." Brad drove toward the street where everything went down. It ran perpendicular to the courthouse.

Parnell must have been in the lead. He blended into the crowd, hoping to duck us, which was how we got him confused with the other man. But once we grabbed him, everyone took notice. In the ensuing chaos, Parnell would have had to ditch any incriminating evidence and hurry to the bus stop. Was his priority losing the gun, or did he hope to hide it somewhere safe so he could return for it later?

Brad and I got out of the car and searched every nook and cranny. The street had plenty of doorways and trash bins, but I didn't spot any suspicious black cases. We looked around, seeing a few ladders that led to fire escapes. Even if Wenchel or Parnell, whatever his name was, had stowed his weapon above our heads, he couldn't have climbed that high. It would have taken too long.

I went up another fire escape to check the higher levels we couldn't see from the ground while Brad pulled up the video from earlier. The one that had gone viral wasn't the only one circulating. Several other bystanders had filmed us and posted online.

"Do you see anything?" Brad called up to me.

"Negative." I stopped outside a window, wondering if the sniper could have an accomplice or friend. Someone who would hold his case for him and wouldn't open it or ask questions. "What did you say about a spotter?"

"What?"

"The other day, you said snipers usually have spotters with them."

Brad offered me a hand as I neared the bottom. "We didn't think our guy had that, given the way his practice area was set up."

"What about an unwilling participant?" I explained my theory while Brad checked different parts of the street.

"Neither Parnell nor Wenchel have much in the way of family. Friends didn't seem like a priority. Based on the feedback I received from the gun range, Parnell kept to himself. The only time he spoke to others was to brag about a shot he took. He always wanted the external validation. The proverbial pat on the back." Brad pointed to the bus stop on the corner. "Let's check over there."

After twenty minutes of searching, we weren't any closer to locating the weapon. "Maybe I have it wrong." Defeat didn't look good on me, particularly when dealing with an open homicide investigation involving multiple victims. I stared up at the sky and cursed. Thankfully, no one decided to film it.

"You're not wrong, Liv." Brad removed a latex glove from his inner pocket and used it to pick something up from the crevice between the sidewalk and the catch basin. He held it up. "I'd say that's a 7.62 NATO round."

# TWENTY-SEVEN

The bullet suggested the sniper had fled in that direction. But it didn't prove Trevor Wenchel was the sniper. The casing didn't have any prints or identifying marks. Unlike some brazen individuals who liked to carve things into the tip of the bullet, this one remained pristine.

"It has to be Wenchel's," I said.

Voletek rolled it around inside the evidence bag. "I'll get you a piece of masking tape and a sharpie. Then I'll walk away for ten minutes. When I come back and I find it says *Property of T. Wenchel* on it, I'll assume the lab overlooked it."

I laughed, and Jake winked at me. "If only it were that simple. Unfortunately, I'm not in the business of falsifying evidence. I hope you aren't either."

He sighed. "No. I want to make sure we get the right guy and that whatever we get on him will stick like superglue." Voletek pointed to the clock. "Didn't you say you were calling it a night?"

I glanced at my partner who'd been staring at the murder board, rearranging notes and studying the crime scene photos for the last hour. "Brad, are you ready to call it quits?"

"Go on ahead."

"We carpooled, remember? I'm that annoying neighbor who lives beneath you."

A sharp jerk of his ribcage indicated he found that

amusing, but he didn't turn. He wouldn't risk giving away our secret over something as innocuous as sharing a ride to work. After all, we'd been doing that ever since we became partners. It'd be weird if we stopped now.

"Go home," he said. "I'll get another ride."

"Are you sure?"

"Yeah, you have that thing with Emma tomorrow. Don't you need to prepare for that?"

"Prepare? It's dress shopping. What's to prepare?"

"It's Emma," he reminded me, "and you're her maid of honor."

Jake snorted. "Brad's not wrong."

"Would anyone like to go in my place? I'd be more than happy to pull a double. Hell, a triple even, especially if it means getting this guy."

Lt. Winston coughed, making me cringe. He was standing right behind me. "I know that was a joke, DeMarco, but the city isn't paying you extra so you can avoid your personal life. Go home. You've done more than enough with this case. It's time Voletek handles it."

I didn't bother pointing out Brad had been primary and that I'd been assisting. Winston knew those details. But Brad hadn't made the bad call. I did. "Yes, sir."

Without turning, I hit the power on my computer and grabbed my purse from the bottom drawer. Once I had my things, I snagged the keys and went downstairs to the car. After waiting five minutes, I pulled out of the spot. Brad was a big boy. He could get home on his own.

By the time I let myself into my apartment, my phone was ringing. It was my dad. How he knew I was home worried me. Did he have my place bugged? Did he know what Brad and I had done the night before? Cringing at the thought and irritated that no matter how old I got the adolescent fear had yet to vanish, I answered with a friendly, "Hey, Dad. What's up?"

"Olive, are you okay?"

"Yes. Why? What did you hear?" Was my head really on the chopping block at work?

"Not hear so much as see."

"The video."

My dad did his best to make light of it. "It's not that big of a deal. It's kind of funny. If you had to be recorded, that's not a terrible way for it to happen. You and your partner followed protocol."

"It's bad, isn't it?"

"Honey, it'll blow over, not before you turn into the punchline of every joke for the next few months, but it'll get better after that. I promise."

"Winston reassigned the case."

"It's his unit." Even now, my dad remained diplomatic. "Did you get reprimanded? If so, you should reach out to the union."

"He didn't take any official action. No formal write-ups. Nothing I had to sign or anything."

"He doesn't want the bad press. The department's coming under a lot of pressure. The public is getting nervous. A dead hunter at the wildlife reserve is one thing. But a businessman getting taken out in front of his office and a judge on the court steps means no one is safe. Those who are taking notice are starting to panic. They think they could be dealing with a serial killer sniper."

"Three makes it serial." I hadn't really given that much thought, but technically, the term would be accurate. "Brad thinks we may be looking at a contract hitter."

"What do you think?"

"I don't know. I wish I did. We searched everywhere. We found a bullet, but no gun."

"I thought a suspect was in custody."

"Yeah, but he's claiming he's innocent." I took a seat at my island counter, wishing I was at my parents' house, having this conversation in their kitchen so Dad could sneak out the hidden tub of ice cream that no one knew about that we'd eat on those rare occasions that life had kicked us in the teeth. It was our secret, and it always made everything better, even if it gave me a tummy ache.

Dad laughed. "No? Really? A suspect claiming you got the wrong guy? What is this world coming to?"

"It's more than that. We have no way to prove he's involved." I told Dad about Jim Parnell and Trevor Wenchel. "Without DNA or prints, I don't know how we prove they're the same man."

"What about utility bills? Phone records? It's expensive to live two lives, not to mention complicated. He must have screwed up somewhere. Maybe he called a contact using the wrong phone or picked up groceries from the wrong market while dressed as the other version of himself."

"You're grasping."

"No, Olive, I'm reminding you what being a detective entails."

I hated it when he used that tone. I hated it even more that he was right. "I'm not sure what kind of access we have. Winston's afraid of blowback after the fish debacle."

"That's why he reassigned the case. Who's running the investigation now?"

"Voletek."

Dad thought for a moment. "Okay. Follow his lead. If he veers too far off course, offer a few friendly hints to correct him. You worked with him while Brad was on sick leave, so he shouldn't be opposed to your input."

"He's not."

"Great." Dad adopted that encouraging tone. "See, I told you everything would be okay."

"If you thought that, you wouldn't have called."

"That's not true. I'm your dad. I like to check in on my only daughter from time to time and remind you how much I love you. Also, your mom wanted me to remind you that Emma has an entire day planned. After the dress shopping and whatever else you ladies are doing, we'll go out to dinner as a family."

"The four of us?" I asked.

"Well, your mom's planning it, so I'd say five at a minimum."

"Five?"

"Dino."

"Right."

"She'll probably invite the rest of Emma's bridesmaids to join and whoever they're bringing to the wedding."

"Great." I hated big events, and with the DeMarcos, everything was a big production.

In the background, I could hear my mom. A moment

later, my dad said, "You should invite Brad, so you don't feel like a third wheel."

"Gee, thanks, Dad."

"Sorry, honey, that was a direct quote from your mother."

I rolled my eyes. "I know. Don't even bother. I know how the rest of that sentence went. She doesn't understand why I don't have a date of my own."

"For the record, I didn't say any of that."

"I know. Tell Mom I love her. I love you too. I'll see you guys tomorrow."

"Good night, Liv. Try not to worry. Things will work out. You'll see."

After hanging up, I stared at my phone, wondering if Dad meant with work or with my personal life. Regardless, I wasn't feeling particularly optimistic on either front, which was weird since Brad and I had an amazing night. The memory of it sent shivers through me. But I'd come around to his way of thinking, and I wasn't sure how we could handle balancing both or if we should try. Maybe it was too much. The last thing I needed to lose was my partner, but Brad was more than that. He was my person.

I spent the next few minutes searching my closet for something to wear tomorrow. Dress shopping would entail more than just Emma searching for the perfect wedding dress. It also meant she'd be picking out what her bridesmaids would wear. So far, Emma had changed her color choices seventeen times. Secretly, I hoped she'd let us wear whatever we wanted, but I knew that'd never happen, particularly since my mother was in her corner, encouraging every wedding fantasy dream she had for me.

Once I found a decent dress to wear, something informal that would be easy to take on and off so I could try on the million ugly designs she'd want me to model, I wandered back into the main room of my apartment and went back to work. When we first caught the case, I hadn't realized how troubling it would become. But Brad knew from the get-go. I had hoped he was wrong, but he wasn't. I was.

When I heard footsteps above my head, I realized he was home. Not that much time had passed. Not enough for me to have made significant progress, anyway. I waited, wondering if he'd knock on my door once he put his things down.

Did I want him to knock on my door? "Dammit." That answer was complicated. Too complicated. This was why people were cautioned to be careful what they wished for. I wanted this. And now that we were here, I didn't know what to do about it. A part of me wanted to march upstairs, knock on his door, throw him against the wall, and have my way with him. That part was due largely to Emma's influence, I suspected. The saner, more practical part, thought it'd be best to stick with our original plan. Slow, like molasses. However, given the circumstances and current case, I wondered if backing off entirely would be for the best. Or would that freak out Brad now that he had come around to the idea? "Dammit." I could say it a million times, but it did nothing to help with the predicament.

While I worked myself into a tizzy, the footsteps from above stopped. A moment later, someone knocked on my door. Taking a deep breath, I smoothed my hair back and headed for the door.

"Hey, I wasn't sure you'd—"

Brad pushed past me. "I told you Liv would still be up and working on this." He gave me an apologetic look. "Jake gave me a ride home. We thought you'd want in on this."

"Yeah, of course." I shook off my confusion, relieved Brad shut me up before I said something stupid.

"Do you have any of those snacks left?" Jake asked as he put copies of some files on my counter and opened my fridge.

"There's not much, but help yourself."

"Thanks." He pulled out a few containers and put them down before grabbing a hard cider. "Anyone else?"

"I'm good."

"Me too." Brad took a seat beside me, his knee rubbing against the side of my thigh as he swiveled on the stool. The contact sent chills through me. Based on his reaction, he had the same memory of the previous night.

"Did you come to any brilliant conclusions after Winston sent me home?" I asked.

Jake cracked open the bottle and took a long swig.

"Wenchel got cut loose."

"No."

He nodded before taking another sip. "Yep. He got smart, lawyered up, and given everything else surrounding the circumstances in which he was taken into custody, the brass decided it'd be best to cut our losses and let him go until we had more evidence or a stronger case against him."

"No," I repeated.

"Surveillance units are keeping an eye on him. They're providing hourly updates." Brad indicated his phone. "In the event Wenchel isn't responsible, we'll know soon enough."

"You think there will be another murder?" I asked.

Brad looked uneasy, but he refrained from going to the fridge and opening his own hard cider. Instead, he stared at the countertop. "This guy isn't done. He took out the guy who sold Danes the policy and the judge who ruled in favor of the insurance company. There has to be other targets he'd want to eliminate."

"You don't think these were contracted hits? That had been our assumption since we could only tangentially link the suspects to our victims."

"It doesn't matter either way," Jake said. "Whoever wanted Judge Overholdt and Ken Yeger dead will want more people dead." He flipped through the copy of the file and found the notes he'd made. "This is from the court case. I made a list of every named party, including witnesses and members of the court."

"What about the jury?" I asked.

"It didn't get that far," Brad reminded me.

I skimmed the sheet. "Do we have any idea who was present in the courtroom? I'm assuming if the victims are being chosen due to this case, the person responsible must have been there."

"We don't have any footage. No sign-in sheets. No nothing. All I have are the official filings and transcripts." Jake placed them in front of me. "I checked with a few bailiffs I know, but this case is too old. They have no idea who was there and who wasn't."

"Apparently, time doesn't heal all wounds," Brad said.

Jake met my eyes. "I was hoping your dad could help us

out. I know it wasn't a criminal case. But the police records were subpoenaed. He testified as to what they contained. If he's anything like my pops, I'm hoping he has his own set of records he could review. Maybe he remembers a few bangers sitting in the peanut galley or some sicario making notes on his phone."

"I already asked, but none of that panned."

"I told you what Liv said." Brad reached for a celery stick. "It's why we started our day the way we did."

"I know, which is what led to Judge Overholdt and the courthouse." Jake gave me big puppy dog eyes. "Your dad's intel was good. Those must have been the high points, but maybe there was something else, something smaller, less obvious, that he didn't mention or you overlooked."

"Maybe." But I didn't think so. Dad and I had gone through all of it. However, it wouldn't hurt to do it again. Pulling out my phone, I pressed the speaker button and called home. "Hey, Dad, I'm here with Fennel and Voletek. They have a few questions for you. Would you mind helping us out?"

# TWENTY-EIGHT

Brad moved closer. "I thought he'd never leave."

"You brought him home."

"He gave me a ride."

"I would have given you a ride."

"Liv. Behave."

"I didn't mean that." I smacked his arm, a stray thought wisp finding its way to the gutter, but I shook it off. "Do you think any of that was useful?" I looked down at the lists we made, the profiles we ran, and the details we'd been fleshing out. "I went over the same thing with my dad last night, but none of it seemed promising."

Brad looked at the list. "There has to be something here."

"None of it connects to Wenchel or Parnell or Robard for that matter."

He slumped onto the couch. "We need to ID the sniper. Barring that, we're doing the next best thing, hoping to determine his next target. My money's on Tony Vale. He had ties to Danes. If I wanted revenge for what happened to Danes, Vale would be the first person I blamed." Officers were keeping an eye on the retired detective, but given that our killer liked to strike from a distance, I wasn't sure it would matter. We had tried to warn Vale to take precautions, but he dismissed the warnings. Instead, I had to hope Wenchel was the killer since we had him in our sights.

"What if they're random?"

Brad gave me the side eye as I tidied the kitchen. "Our victims have a connection."

"Not all three."

"Dugrey wasn't a target."

"Oh my gosh. How many times are you going to flip-flop on that point?"

Brad sighed. "You're right. We don't know if he was targeted. But nothing connects him to Judge Overholdt."

"Are we sure?"

"Fuck." He reached for my computer. "The divorce proceedings."

"I don't know." I'd only been playing devil's advocate. I didn't know if he connected to the judge. "We could ask his ex or current wife."

"They could have crossed paths when it came to the adoption stuff too."

"Brad," I took a seat beside him, "we'll figure this out."

"Before someone else dies?"

That question landed like a punch to the gut. "You don't think Wenchel's responsible?"

"I'm not counting on anything at this point." After accessing court records involving Ryan Dugrey and finding nothing of use, he pushed the laptop aside. "The sniper was there. We were on him. That bullet didn't end up near that bus stop by accident."

"But we don't know where the gun is."

"There's the rub."

Picking up the laptop, I brought up an area map and marked off every building we passed while in pursuit. The distance between the park and bus stop wasn't far. However, a few of those buildings were residential, holding dozens of possibilities. It'd take all night, but I was willing to run down every name.

Hours passed before I looked up from the screen. Brad was working on something too, but his stern expression said he hadn't made any progress either. "I don't know. I'm not even sure what I'm seeing anymore," I said.

He looked at me, rubbing his eyes. "Liv, it's late. You have early morning plans."

"That doesn't matter. Emma will understand."

"What Emma are you thinking of because the one I'm thinking of will hold this over your head for the next decade."

"No, she won't. Not when it's this important."

"At least take a break." Brad nudged a pillow toward me, along with the television remote. "Your eyes are so red. Have you even blinked in the last three hours?" He put down his notes and phone. "We need fresh eyes."

"You said we didn't have time." But this was a job. It wasn't a nine to five, something we could clock in and out on. Sure, there were always a few individuals who treated it that way. Some were career patrol who thought of this as a good way to get a pension and benefits, but they didn't care about the work. The others had burnt out, having seen too much and becoming disheartened that whatever we did could never be enough. "But you're right. We can't let this consume us." I slid down in my seat, letting my head rest against the back of the couch. "Ever since we arrived at the wildlife reserve, this has been consuming you."

"I know. I'm sorry."

"Don't be sorry." I pulled my legs up and turned onto my side, so I could see him better. "Do you want to talk about it? About what happened over there?"

"Not with you."

"Okay."

"Liv, I...it's nothing personal."

"I know." I shook it off. "I was just offering. I worry about you, you know."

He smiled, settling on the couch beside me and putting his arm around me before pressing his lips to my forehead. It wasn't romantic. It was just us. "What are we doing?"

"If I had a dollar for every time either of us asked that question, I'd have millions by now."

"We haven't said it that much."

"In our heads."

"What have I told you about reading my mind?"

"It's only fair. You do it to me all the time."

"I hope you weren't doing it during those few quiet moments we had before everything went haywire. My thoughts weren't exactly PG-13." He snickered. "Yours weren't either."

"Hey." I slapped the back of my hand against his chest. "Who said you could read my mind?"

"Which brings me back to my previous question. Last night was something beyond my wildest dreams, but maybe we should walk it back. Today wasn't easy."

I pulled away from him and sat up, so we could face one another. "Do you think we were distracted? Do you think that's why Judge Overholdt—"

"No. Do you think that's why we didn't see what was coming?"

I shook my head. "You heard what Jake said. The shot was basically fired into the future. We had no way of knowing what was going to happen or that Overholdt was the shooter's next target, not with the intel we possessed."

"Good. I'm glad we're on the same page."

"Are we?" I didn't want to ask the next question, but I'd been playing the same game with myself ever since arriving home. Maybe if Brad said it out loud, it would make more sense to me. "Why do you think we should walk this back?"

"Don't make me say it, Liv."

"Say what?"

"Since the moment we met at the car this morning, the only thing I wanted to do was pick up where we left off last night. I know that sounds like a distraction, but that's not how I mean it. It's more like the only thing I want to do is kiss you."

"But you haven't."

"We both know where that will lead. It's too soon. We have too much to sort out, with this case, with us, with how to proceed. Last night, you said you were sure, but you're not. I'm not. It's how I'll hide from this," he gestured to our notes, "and try to push it out of my mind for a few hours. And I don't want to use you like that. That's now what I want this to be about." He laughed. "Admit it, DeMarco, neither of us has any fucking clue what to do with this now that we're in it."

A fit of giggles overtook me, possibly on account of the late hour or because hearing him say it made me realize just how ridiculous the situation was. Once I started laughing,

Brad did too. Eventually, our guffaws fizzled to occasional snickers as I snuggled against his side and turned on the TV. Like it or not, we were still DeMarco and Fennel, and we were done for the night.

Text messages from Emma woke me before my alarm did. Opening my eyes, I wondered how I ended up in my bed when the last place I remembered being was on the couch, but then I spotted Brad beside me. He kept his eyes closed, but he scowled.

"You're not fooling anyone." I reached over him and grabbed my phone, which he had thought to bring with him and plug in after carrying me to bed. Nothing had happened. We slept beside each other, which Emma would still consider sleeping together, but we hadn't. Not last night, anyway. "Why didn't you go home?"

He grunted and rolled over, ignoring me as he tried to go back to sleep.

Emma had sent the day's itinerary, a reminder that I needed to get up, and a list of things she wanted me to pick up before meeting her at the house. A moment later, she sent a follow-up text with the dress shop's address and the outfit she expected me to wear, as if she didn't trust me to pick out something appropriate for a day of drinking and dress shopping. After replying to her text, I debated if I could squeeze in another twenty minutes of sleep before getting up, but given the coffee and breakfast run, along with the fun little gift bags she wanted me to grab, twenty more minutes of sleep would make me late. My mother would never let me hear the end of it, even if Emma forgave me.

Grabbing the outfit Emma had selected, I went into the bathroom to shower and get ready. Luckily, undercover work had made me an expert at quick costume changes. By the time I got out, I expected Brad to have left. Instead, he remained a motionless lump.

"Brad," I dug through the closet for shoes, "I have to go. Lock up before you leave."

"Uh-huh."

"What are you and Jake planning on doing today?"

"Knock on doors. Reinterview the victim's relatives. See if any of what your dad said last night leads to any possibilities." Blindly, he reached for his phone, opening one eye and entering his unlock code to check his messages. "Patrol still has eyes on Wenchel. Let's hope he's the shooter. As long as we can keep him in our sights, he can't hurt anyone else."

"All right. You know how to reach me."

"Yep."

I went to my dresser and flipped open the jewelry box, searching for earrings and a necklace. I didn't wear a lot of jewelry on account of the job, but since this was a special event, Emma and my mother both had certain expectations concerning how I should look. It'd be easier to appease them than face the alternative. When I turned around, Brad was watching me.

"You look nice."

I gave my reflection one last look. The makeup barely covered the dark circles and bags. All the hours at the computer had left my eyes red. "I look tired."

"You are tired."

I filled my purse with everything I'd need for a day with Emma, along with my badge and gun in case work called. "Don't forget you're invited to dinner. I'll text you the time and place. It's your call, but you know you're always welcome to join us. You're family."

"Thanks, Liv."

"I mean it."

He grabbed my arm and pulled me toward the bed and kissed me. "Okay."

# TWENTY-NINE

"You're late," my mother said the moment I entered the kitchen. She gave me one look. "Olive, you know today's important. Why couldn't you make this your priority?"

I put the bags on the counter. Too bad I hadn't dragged Brad out of bed and forced him to join me. At least then my mother would be too busy doting on him to scold me. After all, it was his fault I was late this morning. "I'm only a few minutes behind schedule. I had to make some extra stops to get everything Emma wanted." I looked around. "Speaking of, where is she?"

"It's her day. She's taking time to primp and prepare."

"She's only looking at dresses. She's not getting married yet."

"Olive."

Why did I even bother? Shaking it off, I grabbed a mug from the cabinet and poured myself a cup of coffee. "Where's Dad?"

"Your father is not going to get you out of this."

"I just asked where he was." Gunnie was missing too, which meant Dad must have taken the dog for a walk, or he used it as an excuse to escape the craziness.

Muttering to herself, my mother finished setting the table and getting everything ready for breakfast. She set four places. We were having breakfast as a family before beginning our fun-filled day.

Once Emma arrived, my mom stopped picking on me and

focused her attention on Emma. Unfortunately, Dad and I didn't get a chance to talk. We'd done a lot of it last night. All he asked was if there had been a break in the case, and since I hadn't heard a word from anyone, I had to assume we didn't have any new leads. Then again, I wasn't even sure I was still on the case. Lt. Winston basically reassigned me the previous day.

"Hey," Emma nudged me as we loaded everything into the back of the car, "you look tired."

"Uh-huh."

She gave me a sideways glance. "Did Bradley keep you up late?"

"Brad and Jake."

She gave me an evil grin. "Damn. Explain to me again why I'm getting married."

"I have no idea." I leaned in closer, so my mom wouldn't hear. "I think you've lost your mind."

She gave my arm a playful shove. "Threesomes make you extra smart-alecky, I see."

I snorted, rolling my eyes. "See all the fun you're missing out on?"

"Seriously, Liv," the way she scrutinized me made me wonder if she had a sixth sense about what had happened with Brad, "you don't seem like yourself. Is everything okay?"

"Not really, but we're not talking about that today. Today is about you and finding your perfect fairytale dress and glass slipper."

"Ugh, not Cinderella. The last thing I want to do is scrub floors and hem clothes."

"Yeah, but that's how you'll know Dino's your Prince Charming, and you'll go off and live happily ever after in your castle in the sky."

"You mean my apartment?"

"Unless you move into his apartment." I loaded the last bag into the trunk and closed the lid. "Have you discussed where you plan to live once you get married?"

"We keep going back and forth. Right now, we're thinking of looking for another place, so if that's the case, you could always move back into our old place."

"It's a two bedroom, Em. I can't afford that, not without a roommate."

She gave me another sideways look. "I'm sure you could find someone who'd want to move in with you."

"Now I know you've been spending too much time with Mom."

"It's wedding dress day. I get to be as sappy as I want."

"Fine, but while you're being sappy, I'll be spending my nights with two sexy detectives."

"Oh, so now you think they're sexy. Did you tell Bradley that?"

I played it cool. "I didn't have to tell him. He knows. Jake does too. You should see the matching tattoos they got. Mm-mm good."

She rolled her eyes. "I know you too well to believe there's any dirty connotation to that, so you can't make me jealous."

We got into the car, where my mom was already waiting for us. She was on the phone with someone from the dress shop, verifying our plans and arrival time while simultaneously tapping on the tablet on her lap. In another life, my mother would have made an excellent party planner. She loved this stuff, everything from coordinating linens to making sure everyone and everything was exactly where it was supposed to be.

Emma leaned forward. "Everyone is meeting us there. We figured we'd finish up at the first shop, have lunch, and move on to the next shop."

My mom gave her a thumbs up.

I turned to make sure Emma was ready to go and put the car in drive. Out of the three of us, I was the only one who'd remain sober, which automatically made me today's designated driver. However, if I got called in, Dad would have to swoop in and take over. Hopefully, he and Gunnie didn't have any other long walks planned.

The day went about as well as could be expected. The rest of Emma's bridesmaids, three women she worked with, two of which had gone to college with us, and Mac, met us at the first of what would turn into a bridal shop crawl. The champagne never stopped flowing while Emma tried on dress after dress, stopping periodically to force one or all of us to try on whatever caught her eye.

By the time we were almost finished, her bridal party was exhausted. I had lost track of how many bottles of champagne had been consumed. According to Mac's last count, they were up to six glasses each. Given how long we'd been at this, it wasn't terrible. But it would explain why everyone looked like they needed a nap. Maybe now my mother would stop giving me such a hard time. I was the most awake of the bunch.

"Liv?" Emma called from behind the dressing room door. "Can you come in here?"

"I'll be right there." I glanced at Mac who had been on her phone for the last forty minutes. "Is something going on at work?"

She shrugged. "It's hard to say."

"Did Jake make a break?"

"Now you're rhyming." She checked the time. "I need to head out."

"You're not driving."

"I called for a rideshare." She jerked her chin toward the door. "Can you apologize to Emma for me?"

"I will, as long as you tell my mom you have to go. Word of advice, don't mention it's for work."

"Maria is not as terrible as you made her out to be."

"Don't get me wrong, I love my mom. But she's worse."

Mac laughed, rolling her eyes. "All right. I'm out of here."

"If you need me or they need me, call. I'm serious."

Mac nodded and started her goodbye tour while I ducked into the changing room where Emma was waiting. She wore a strapless white dress with light blue trim that somehow made the white sparkle like freshly fallen snow.

"You're beautiful. I think this is the one." I beamed at her through our reflections in the mirror.

"You really think so?"

"I do."

Those words triggered something in Emma, and she choked down some air. "Oh god. What am I doing? Look at me. I have lost my mind."

"Em—"

"No, you said it yourself. You said it earlier. I'm crazy. I must be. Marriage. What could I possibly be thinking? You've met Dino. He's okay, I guess."

"You're crazy about him. The two of you are disgustingly cute when you're together."

She half-smiled despite her panic. "But his family. They're awful. His mother is just so...and his sister. That whole family is baby obsessed. It's like they're opening a factory. A baby-making factory."

"Em, that's something you and Dino can discuss."

"I don't want kids, Liv. Not now. Maybe not ever."

"Does Dino know?"

"Yes."

"Is he okay with that?"

"Yeah."

"Okay, so what's the problem?"

She turned to face me. Tears in her eyes, but the panic was gone. "I'm getting married."

I forced myself not to laugh. "Yes, you are."

"Everything's going to change."

"It'll be okay. You want this, remember? You've always wanted this. That's why you kissed all those psychotic frogs. I already had the talk with Dino. He knows they'll never find his body if he does anything to hurt you. But if you want to pull the plug, you know I will absolutely one hundred percent be your getaway driver."

"Aww, Liv." She hugged me, tears falling from her eyes. "I love you."

"I love you too." I waited a few minutes for her to stop crying before I said, "Does that mean I should get the engine warmed up?"

"No. I just lost it for a second. I'm okay now."

"Too much champagne?"

"Too much taffeta." She spun, wiping her eyes and staring at her reflection in the mirror. "You're right though. This is the dress."

"Great. I'll let them know."

After that, things wrapped up quickly. The rest of her bridesmaids made some calls to their significant others with details concerning the restaurant and where to meet. My mother was in her glory, thrilled to spend more time with the rest of the bridal party. Unlike me, Emma kept her work life separate from our family, so my mom didn't know Emma's other friends very well. This would give her a chance to pry into their lives, which got me off the hook.

As we broke up and headed toward the car, Emma linked her arm with mine. "Is Bradley joining us for dinner?"

"I invited him, but I haven't heard a word." In fact, I hadn't heard a word from anyone at work. Given the situation, the lack of communication worried me, especially since Mac had to cut our day short.

"Call him. Tell him I want him there."

"Seriously?" I pressed the back of my hand to her forehead. "Are you feeling okay? I didn't think you had that much champagne, but you must be drunk."

She batted my hand away. "You dealt with my meltdown. It's time you deal with your own."

"What are you talking about?"

"I know what happened with the two of you."

How could she possibly know? "What?"

"I saw the video. I wasn't going to bring it up, but you've been checking your phone a lot and I heard you talking to Mac. It's okay. You spent the day making me feel special. It's time you get back to work. If you don't, I'm afraid the stress of pretending not to care about work will kill you."

"Are you sure?"

She nodded. "Dino's meeting us there. Once he shows up, you know what it's going to be like. Call Brad and tell him to get his ass to the restaurant or I'll make his life a living hell. In fact, forget that. I'll tell him myself." She pulled out her phone and dialed.

I tried to pay attention to her conversation, hoping she wouldn't freak him out the way she freaked me out which would lead to him spilling the beans. But my best friend behaved herself for once. In the meantime, my mom gave me a hug before we got into the car.

"I'm proud of you," she said.

"Thanks, Mom." Now I had proof everyone had been overserved.

When I arrived at the restaurant, I found my dad and Brad waiting at the bar. They were discussing the case. Dino hadn't shown up yet, which may have been for the best given the conversation. The rest of the bridal party wandered in a few minutes later.

The hostess escorted the eleven of us to a private room in the back, placed menus on the table, and went to grab waters while we got situated. Dino arrived a moment later, looking lost and a little overwhelmed. But once he spotted Emma, he relaxed. They really were perfect for one another.

"Hey," Brad pulled out my chair so I could sit, "how was your day?"

"Don't ask." I looked from him to my father. "What's going on?"

"Vince was right. Wenchel couldn't keep things straight. We're waiting for verification, but Jim Parnell and Trevor Wenchel both suffer from asthma. They have the same prescription. Uniforms went through Wenchel's garbage this morning when he took it out and found Jim Parnell's empty inhaler. Jake tracked down the pharmacy. Parnell and Wenchel use the same one. He's parsing the security footage now from the last few times either man made a pick-up. We're hoping he may not have been wearing the proper disguise. Once we get that, we should have enough for a search warrant, and we're hoping that'll lead to everything else."

"That's amazing," I said.

"It's all thanks to the captain here."

My dad grinned. "This job is about the grind. Never stop digging. Remember that."

"Yes, sir." Brad practically saluted.

# *THIRTY*

We ate quickly. My mind on everything Brad had said. Did Trevor Wenchel know he'd been caught? Two questions remained. Why did he kill those people, and where did he ditch the gun?

"Dad," I said, drawing his attention away from the lump of berry sorbet on his plate, "do you remember Trevor Wenchel or Jim Parnell from any of the files?"

He wiped his mouth. "After I hung up with the three of you last night, I went digging through everything, but I didn't find a thing."

"He wasn't listed on any of the court records either," Brad said. "As far as we can tell, he had nothing to do with Ramon Danes or the resulting court case."

"What about any ties or connections to Dugrey or Yeger?" I asked.

"You already looked, Liv. You didn't miss anything. Jake checked, and then I checked." Brad wiped his mouth. "Parnell doesn't connect to Smith and Smith either."

I tapped my fingers against the table. "What about any ties to Charles Robard?"

Brad cocked an eyebrow up. "Besides the gun range?"

"Yeah, besides that."

"Not that I noticed. We weren't exactly looking for that though."

"What are you thinking, honey?" Dad asked.

"I don't know. But Jim Parnell didn't have any formal training. He never served in the military. He didn't try out for the police academy. He has no known firearms training to speak of, yet he's proven himself to be an excellent sniper. How does that happen?"

"What do you know about his family life?" Dad asked. "He could have been taught from a young age. A parent or relative could have been military or a gun enthusiast. Militia. Prepper. Something like that."

I thought about the details I'd pulled, but they were limited. "I don't know. It's possible, I guess."

"We don't know much about the suspect," Brad said. "We don't even know his real name. What I want to know is how he obtained two legit identities."

The creases on my father's forehead deepened. "You said Wenchel grew up in the system. Look into school IDs. Yearbook photos. Things like that. My guess would be no one paid too much attention to him. He would have gotten a valid ID once he turned eighteen, possibly sooner if he got a driver's license or permit. But kids like that end up on the fringe. A lot fall through the cracks. Wenchel must have crossed paths with Parnell at some point, and Parnell assumed his identity."

"Do you think Parnell killed the real Trevor Wenchel?" I asked.

"It's possible, honey. But there's no reason to speculate at this point. Wenchel could be living on the streets somewhere while Parnell impersonates him."

"Until this year, Wenchel hadn't filed taxes in five years. Trevor Wenchel could be dead, an unidentified John Doe who got tossed into an unmarked grave." Brad took the pen out of his pocket and reached for the stack of unused napkins. "We'll see what we can find in case Wenchel was Parnell's first kill, but where do you think they would have crossed paths?"

"If Wenchel's homeless, it could have been anywhere," I said. "He may have liked to hang out near the comic book store or Parnell's apartment."

"Or on any of the streets, bus stations, or subway stops along the way," my dad added.

Brad jotted down more notes.

"The thing is, if Parnell assumed Wenchel's identity, he's been planning this for a while," I said. "Any idea why?"

"You said Parnell doesn't have a record," my father said.

"None that we found."

"Are you sure Jim Parnell is his real name?"

"Do you think the guy is collecting identities?" I asked.

"It's possible," my dad said.

"That would mean he's done this before. He could be a contract killer with any number of cover IDs he could burn through." Brad checked his phone again, sent a few texts, and put the device back on the table.

My mom glanced in our direction, but she refrained from chastising us for breaking away into our own little group. It was better that no one else knew what our conversation was about. It wasn't appropriate for wedding dress shopping day.

"Do you have this guy's photo handy?" Dad asked.

Brad showed him, but my father didn't react. "Mac hasn't been able to substantiate any of the rumors she's heard circulating on the dark web. We still don't know how Jim Parnell got his hands on that rifle or the suppressor."

"Or where he picked up his skills. Or why he chose those targets." I started ticking off everything we didn't know on my fingers, but Brad grabbed my hand and forced it back to the table, giving it a gentle squeeze before letting go. It was a good thing he stopped me since I would have run out of fingers before too long.

Dad rocked back in his chair, reaching for the spoon and scooping up the melted sorbet. "The guy doesn't look like much. He'd be easy to underestimate. He has asthma and works in a comic book store. Those used to be the kinds of traits schoolyard bullies would home in on. No one would think of him as a predator. A guy like that is easy pickings."

"Do you think that's what turned him into a deadly sniper?" I asked.

"People do a lot of things for a lot of different reasons. It's possible, but this may be a chicken and egg situation. The asthma is immutable, but maybe the rest," Dad indicated Brad's phone, "is part of a disguise he puts on to blend in. That's how the most prolific serial killers got away with murder as long as they did."

"You don't think his motivation is monetary?" I asked.

Dad shrugged. "Given what little we know about this guy, there's no way to tell for sure."

"We should look for old cases," Brad said.

I watched my dad, but he would have recalled a sniper picking people off. "I'll call the FBI and have them broaden the search. If this guy was operating locally, we would have heard about it before now."

"Could this be his first?" Brad asked.

"I don't know." I looked to my dad, but he didn't have an answer. Instead, he ate more of his sorbet and stared at the table. He had some thoughts, but he wasn't sharing them. I wasn't sure if that's because they weren't pertinent or because he wanted to look into things before getting our hopes up. Either way, I wondered what I was missing. "If it is, why Yeger and Overholdt? Why now?"

"What about upcoming trials?" Dad asked. "Do you know what cases Judge Overholdt was scheduled to preside over?"

Brad picked up his phone and tapped on the screen. "I'll find out."

"Smith and Smith wasn't being sued. Any issues were being negotiated and settled. There were no filings, at least none that Jake or I found." I waited for Brad to pull up the docket and Overholdt's schedule for the coming weeks. "Does anything stand out?"

Brad scanned the listings, shook his head, and handed me his phone. I didn't see anything either, so I handed it to my father. He had the most experience, and Vale's accusations continued to haunt me. Was the retired detective correct? Were we really that far off the mark?

"Nothing's jumping out at me." Dad handed Brad back his phone. "Is there anything else that connects your victims besides that court case?"

"Dugrey and Yeger worked together," I said. "But Dugrey didn't have any connections to Overholdt."

My dad finished his sorbet and wiped his mouth. "In that case, a hired hit makes the most sense unless you're looking at a random act of violence."

"These don't feel random," I said.

"Dugrey felt random," Brad corrected. "He showed up at the wrong place at the wrong time."

"But it was his place," I said.

"The sniper wasn't expecting him to be there."

"Which would mean he didn't know Dugrey's schedule."

"That fits with everything we know about Parnell, seeing as how they didn't overlap. We found the gun range when we started looking for a sniper, not while we were retracing Dugrey's steps."

I considered what Brad said. "That would mean Parnell using that clearing for target practice really was a coincidence."

Brad didn't look convinced, but he sent a text to Jake. A moment later, his phone dinged. I read the text over his shoulder. The techs finished with the security cam footage from outside the flower shop. The man who stole the van remained disguised. His build matched Parnell, but it wasn't definitive. However, patrol finally located the van. It had been left in a parking garage on the other side of the city. The plates had been changed again, which made it harder to identify, but the dog grooming decals remained. However, the VIN matched the registration for the flower shop, which gave it away. Upon closer inspection, officers had peeled back the temporary decals, revealing the original paint and logo underneath that matched the florist.

"How long until they finish processing the van?" I indicated the message on the phone.

Brad scrolled to the bottom. "Soon, I hope."

We updated my dad while a million thoughts ran through my mind.

"Go," Dad jerked his chin toward the door, "see what you can dig up. I'm sure Detective Voletek could use all the help he can get. I'll smooth things over with your mother."

"Are you sure?"

My dad nodded. "Be careful, sweetheart." He turned to Brad. "You too." His look lingered for a moment, and I wondered if my dad had noticed the hand squeeze. Something told me he had, but that didn't mean anything. Brad and I were always a little affectionate. I was just paranoid.

# THIRTY-ONE

Lt. Winston didn't say anything to me when I showed up at the precinct. I was surprised since he hated authorizing OT. But this case was gaining publicity. He wouldn't want the bad press.

Detective Jake Voletek was buried behind a mountain of paperwork. He had a system. If he wanted help, he'd ask for it. Instead, I took a seat and pulled up everything on the case.

Forensics had finished with the van. The inside tested positive for gunshot residue, but they didn't find the weapon, bullets, or casings. The front windshield had recently been removed and modified. The glass had a few minor scratches on the exterior side. Little handles had been installed on the interior, which made it easier to pop the windshield in and out.

I pointed those out to Brad while I looked up the flower shop owner's phone number. Brad leaned over my chair, examining the photos on my screen. I nearly rested my head against his chest before I thought better of it. Maybe I had a contact high from all the champagne Emma and her merry bridesmaids had consumed.

The forensics unit didn't find anything else inside. They found a few random fibers, possibly some hair, but the vehicle had been wiped. No prints.

"This is Detective DeMarco," I identified myself when the van's owner answered. "I have a few questions about your stolen van." As I suspected, the owner hadn't made any modifications to the front windshield and didn't know what I was talking about. The only custom work he had done was the paint job. Everything else had been factory specifications.

After hanging up, I brought up a copy of the surveillance footage from when the thief had stolen the van from behind the closed shop. I watched it, finding it to be everything Brad had said and nothing more.

"That could be Wenchel...Parnell," Brad corrected, squeezing the bridge of his nose, "or it could be any other thin, young man."

"It could be you," I said.

Brad gave me a sideways look. "I have more meat on my bones than that."

"If you say so."

He gave me a strange look. Today had left me in a weird mood.

"Anyway," he said, "I don't see how this is going to help us. The guy's covered. We can't see his face. He's wearing gloves. There is no visible skin. We can't even see his hair."

"What about the footage from Shady Oaks?"

"Jake," Brad called, "has that been uploaded yet?"

Jake pointed to my computer, never looking up. "It should be there. If it's not, call IT and tell them to get to it. I was told everything was added to the servers. We want high visibility. All hands."

While I entered the case number and waited for the search to spit out the intel I needed, I glanced toward the LT's office. "How does Winston feel about that?"

"He's chomping at the bit to hold a press conference announcing homicide's victory." Jake turned to look at me. "You realize that's why he reassigned the case. He wants to trot me out like a show pony and applaud my legacy detective status. It would have been you if that video hadn't gone viral."

"I don't care about politics. I didn't become a detective because I was looking to get promoted."

"Neither did I. Still," Jake looked apologetic, "credit should go where it's due."

I shook it away. "Mention Brad. He's done the work. It's his case."

My partner looked uncomfortable. Too many people died for him to want credit for this. "Let's make sure we get enough evidence to stop this guy before we start celebrating."

After watching the footage from Shady Oaks, I couldn't help but wonder if Jim Parnell was that good or if he'd gotten lucky. "Did Mac see this?"

"Every tech did. They've all taken a stab at it and the footage from the flower shop, but they can't get a clear shot of the thief. No reflective surfaces. No weird angles. Nothing useful to make an ID," Jake said.

"How's it coming with the pharmacy footage?" Brad asked. "Surely, that's our kicker."

Jake held up his palms. "The guy always wore a hat, regardless of who he wanted to be."

"Same hat?" I crossed my fingers.

"Maybe. It's a plain black cap."

"We need to search their apartments. His apartments. Whatever. Where are you on obtaining a warrant?" Brad asked.

"I'm still working on it." Jake sighed. "It'd be a lot easier to convince a judge if someone from the pharmacy said Parnell and Wenchel were the same guy. Right now, we have someone else's prescription in Wenchel's trash. That's not conclusive. It doesn't give us much to go on."

"What about prints?" I asked.

"Why would we bother dusting it?"

"Why wouldn't you?" I got up and headed for the stairs. We didn't have either man's prints in the system, not officially. But Wenchel had been taken into custody. He touched things. We'd gotten his prints. If his prints matched what was on Parnell's inhaler, that might be enough to sway a judge, particularly one who may have worked alongside Overholdt.

I understood the judge's hesitation to grant our search warrant. No one wanted to appear vindictive or biased due to recent events. Judges were supposed to be impartial. But no one could be after seeing a colleague's brains splattered on the front steps of the courthouse, which was why they were overcompensating to make up for it. In the meantime, the killer was biding his time, possibly planning another hit once the heat died down.

"Hey, Ellie," I called, spotting her examining something on the table in the lab, "I need a favor."

"What is it?" She glanced behind me, smiling at Brad who must have followed me down the stairs. "Afraid I wouldn't grant your partner a wish, Brown Eyes?"

Brad snickered. "I know you better than that."

Ellie took off her gloves, tossed them into a bin, and reached for a new set. "What is it?"

"We need you to print Jim Parnell's inhaler and compare it to Wenchel's prints." I nodded toward the evidence bags piled up at another workstation.

"The inhaler was in his garbage," she said. "I'm sure it and all the other trash have the same set of prints on them."

"That's the point. We need solid evidence like that to convince a judge to sign off on our search warrant."

She pointed a finger at me. "I knew I liked you."

Brad and I waited while Ellie dusted the inhaler and a few other items that had been recovered from the trash. Once the prints were scanned in, she ran a comparison, finding they matched.

"They're not perfect. Everything's a bit smudged."

"But the computer's sure?" I asked.

"The computer's sure enough." She handed me the printout. "Go get this asshole."

Brad winked at her. "We couldn't do it without you."

"Aww shucks. You know how to make a girl blush." She returned his wink. "Is there anything else I can do for you?"

"We'll let you know." Brad followed me up the stairs and back to Jake's desk. "There. Now make the call."

Jake picked up the phone before looking at the results. "I can't believe I overlooked that."

"Happens," I said.

After some back and forth, we got the go-ahead on the search warrant. Jake grabbed his jacket. "I'll take Wenchel's place. He's there now, but the uniforms will keep him company while I conduct a search. The two of you should head to Parnell's apartment. It should be quiet. Dig through everything. We need to prove something's going on here. If the only thing we can get him for is identity theft, so be it. It'll be enough to open up even more doors and something is bound to shake loose on the string of shootings." Jake gave us a final look. "Be careful."

"You too."

Brad palmed his keys. "I'll drive. It's late and you had a busy day."

"Haven't you been working all day?" I asked.

"It's my turn."

I held up my palms. "Fine. I have no problem being chauffeured around."

On the way to Parnell's, I filled him in on my day with Emma and all the dress shopping glory. "Did Mac get in trouble for coming into work a little less than sober?"

"I don't think anyone noticed. She's been banging away at the keyboard since she arrived. I think she's on to something."

"What?"

"She hasn't said much, but she's hoping to track down who hired a hitman to take out Yeger and Overholdt."

"So we don't think Parnell is acting alone? On his own accord?"

"I don't know, Liv." He glanced at me. "I hate this case."

"Don't you hate them all?"

"Yes, but sometimes, it makes sense in a sick, demented way. Crimes of passion, jealousy, money, those are easy to determine. This isn't any of that."

"It could be money."

"If it is, it hasn't hit any bank accounts."

"That we know about. Who knows how many more identities Parnell has up his sleeve? He could collect them like trading cards."

"Do you think he killed Trevor Wenchel?"

"I don't know."

Brad nodded, his eyes focused on the road. "Wenchel could have been his first. The five year gap in his tax records could indicate how long he's been dead. I asked some of the guys who work cold cases to look into missing persons reports in case there's something to that."

"Why would Parnell kill Wenchel and sit on his identity for five years?"

"Maybe he wasn't sitting on it. Maybe he's been doing this for a while."

"We've both said there haven't been any recent victims who fit Parnell's MO."

"Maybe he wasn't acting locally. I spoke to the Feds. They've been researching our request. There have been several murders over the years. None of them were high profile, so they never gained news coverage. It was always one here or there. Hard to track. Hard to trace."

"They were all long-distance kills?"

"More or less. The skill level varied. But even if a few are attributable to Parnell, then he could have been active for a while. It'd explain how he could pay for two apartments, especially on a comic book salesman's salary."

"Okay, but if he was using Wenchel's ID to travel, can't we trace that?"

"The Feds are working on it, but there aren't a lot of national databases when it comes to traveling domestically. With artillery like that, I doubt he ever flew."

"He has a car, or he could have stolen one since he seems to be particularly clever and skilled when it comes to that."

"Right," Brad checked the mirrors and switched lanes, circling Parnell's apartment building before parking close to the front door, "which would mean he didn't rent a car or take out insurance either."

"That leaves us with what? Hotel accommodations? Vacation rentals? Things of that nature?"

"Pretty much."

I sighed. "Y'know, I'm glad the Feds are running that down for us. It'd take forever, especially since we have no way of knowing how he paid."

"I can almost guarantee he used cash."

"We're never going to pin anything on this guy, are we?"

Brad gestured to the apartment building. "I guess we're about to find out."

# THIRTY-TWO

The police were on to him. He had seen it in Detective DeMarco's eyes. She knew or suspected. And she didn't seem like the type who would give up, even though she'd smiled at him and tried to play it off. But she'd shown him her true colors. He didn't believe anything she did was an accidental slip or friendly blunder.

The police had been forced to release him. They didn't have a choice, but ever since, they'd been watching, waiting for him to slip up. Waiting for him to lead them to a damning piece of evidence. They didn't have the gun. Without that, they had nothing.

He hadn't retrieved his rifle yet. If it wasn't so valuable, he would have tossed it, but it wasn't a typical weapon. It took a lot to get it. Replacing it wasn't an option. He'd have to go back for it or find some way to get it out of police custody if they confiscated it.

He rubbed his eyes, his synapses firing a million times a second. *Deep breath.* Just as he calmed himself before firing, he had to calm himself now. Some sixth sense told him the police would be here soon. He had to prepare. Since he knew he was being watched, he couldn't risk moving or changing anything. Instead, he hoped everything was secure. They could do their worst, but they wouldn't find anything.

He had several IDs. Passports. Cash. Credit cards. Disappearing was always part of the plan. Legends didn't get caught. He had an exit strategy, but he wasn't done. There was one last name on his list. That would make four, even if he'd been paid for three.

Only after the job was complete could he leave. Legends didn't have reputations for failing to carry out a contract. That wouldn't serve him or anyone. If anything, it'd make it look like he botched the job and ran away. Only cowards ran, and he had proven over and over that he was no coward. This wasn't the first time he'd done this, but this was the first time he'd committed to multiple hits. This was how he'd level up and become something they'd never forget.

He hid the documents and funds he would need on his person and dressed accordingly. They'd be here soon. He knew it. As his mother used to say, a little bird must have told them.

*       *       *

On the surface, Jim Parnell's apartment looked exactly as expected. It had the perfect amount of clutter and mess to indicate he lived here. The built-ins contained collectibles which he probably accumulated over time from working in the comic book store. He had a few different video game consoles and a modest collection of games. Surprisingly, he didn't have a single first-person shooter in the mix.

"Fridge is almost empty," Brad said. "Lots of opened condiments on the door. One or two expired things, but that's typical. His water pitcher is a quarter full. No milk. No eggs. No leftovers. The fruit drawer has a couple of apples and a grapefruit. Nothing that's likely to spoil too quickly."

"Parnell's supposed to be on vacation," I said.

"That's what his fridge indicates." Brad checked the rest of the kitchen and the nearby closets.

"The thermostat is turned off."

"That's consistent with travel plans." Brad moved into the dining room which consisted of a table. Half of it was taken up by a jigsaw puzzle. "I found dishes in the dishwasher, but they appear to be clean."

"Uh-huh." None of this was helping matters. I finished my search of the living room, but I didn't find anything damning. No loose floorboards. No hidden wall safes. No secret compartments in the built-ins.

Moving into the bedroom, I noted the half-made bed. Instead of making the bed, Parnell had pulled the top blanket up, leaving wrinkles and bumps in the bedding. Unsure what I may find, I slowly peeled down the covers to reveal nothing kinky or sexy, just creased sheets and crumpled blankets.

I checked beneath the mattress and behind the headboard. Nothing. Not even a dirty magazine, not that those were that common anymore, but given that Parnell had the comic book geek persona going for him, I thought he might have a few vintage *Playboys* stashed somewhere.

The rest of the search didn't turn up much of anything. No weapons or bullets. However, I did find an empty gun safe. The door had been left open, which was how I was able to access it so easily.

"Brad," I called, "what kind of weapon did the guy at the gun range say Parnell owns?"

"He didn't." Brad stepped into the bedroom, having concluded his search of the bathroom. "I'm sure I asked. He must not have known. We checked, but Parnell doesn't have an Mk22 or any sniper rifle registered in his name. From what I recall, he had a hunting rifle and a shotgun."

"No handguns?"

"Why? Did you find something?"

"No, but I was curious."

"Anything he uses to hunt the most dangerous game he wouldn't want linked back to him."

I gave my partner a random look. "Are you quoting Kipling?"

"Connell, and that wasn't a quote. It was the title."

"Are you sure that wasn't Kipling?"

"No, they were published together in an anthology. That's probably why you're confused."

I held up a copy of the book which I'd found on the top shelf of Parnell's closet. The only author listed on the cover was Kipling. "Apparently, you're not the only fan."

Brad took it from my hands and skimmed the dog-eared pages. "Based on the creases and stains, I'd say he must have reread that short story dozens of times."

"Clearly, it's his favorite." I took the book from Brad and held it with the spine up before flipping through the pages. However, nothing fell out. No secret note. No manifesto.

I backed away from the closet, hoping to gain some sort of perspective. Parnell couldn't be this careful. This was his home, at least part of the time. There had to be evidence hidden inside that would prove he and Wenchel were the same man and that they were responsible for the murders.

"Did you find anything in the bathroom?"

"Not really. The only thing I found was some heavy-duty cleaners and soaps." Brad went to the dresser and sifted through the items inside the drawers. "Have you looked in here yet?"

"No. That was my next stop."

He carefully removed every item from the first drawer before examining each article of clothing and checking the drawer itself. While he was doing that, I went into the bathroom to see what kinds of soaps Brad had mentioned. It was nothing too out of the ordinary, but it was the kind of stuff Emma kept in our apartment to wash off blood and bodily fluids after a day in the ER.

When I returned to the bedroom to share that with Brad, I stopped in the doorway. The dimensions felt off. The bathroom wall was straight. It didn't push outward until the very back to accommodate the bathtub/shower combo. Yet, the bedroom, which shared the same wall, cut inward from the doorway and made a straight line.

"Huh?"

Brad turned to look at me. "What's wrong?"

"This room's too small."

He looked around. "I'm not following."

I examined the wall more carefully, but it was a solid piece. No hidden seams. No secret panels. Returning to the bathroom, I looked again, but the dimensions didn't line up.

"Liv?" Brad peered at me from the hallway. "Talk to me."

Returning to the bedroom, I knocked against the wall as I moved toward the corner of the room. It didn't sound hollow, but it didn't exactly sound solid either. A shelf had been placed in the corner that ran from the floor to the ceiling. Beside it, to the left, was a mirror. I'd already looked behind the mirror, but there was nothing to find. However, the corner shelf wasn't the typical ladder or individual shelves stuck to the wall. Instead, this was a massive piece.

I felt along the side before exploring each of the shelves, finding a switch near the bottom. Originally, I thought it was for the lights, but that was in the middle. Pressing the switch, something popped. "Help me with this."

Brad joined me, pulling the side of the shelf away from the wall and revealing a small doorway. Flicking on his phone's flashlight, he shone the light into the opening. "The other day you were giving me shit for making you watch all those movies." He handed me his phone and stepped out of the way. "I'll take that apology now."

The opening couldn't be more than a three by six room. A few rifles, handguns, various scopes, suppressors, and ammunition lined the rack on the wall. Each piece meticulously placed. At the end of the opening was a chest of drawers that came up to my waist. Inside was a lot of cash, along with Jim Parnell's ID, passport, and corresponding credit cards.

I took a few photos. CSU would want to process everything. At least we found his stash, Parnell's stash. This didn't answer all our questions, but it was suspicious as hell. Did he have one of these slicks in every apartment he rented?

Brad called Voletek to update him on the situation before calling our find in and requesting a mobile crime unit to our location. It'd be best to make sure the evidence was properly catalogued. It'd also be nice to have a team search for other hidden gems that we might have missed.

"The gun's not here." Brad studied the array of weapons. "A few of these pieces would fit it, but the main hardware isn't here."

"How could it be? Parnell hasn't been back since we took him off the bus. He's had to stay in character. He's had to maintain his cover as Trevor Wenchel. Not to mention, we still don't know where the gun ended up."

"He wouldn't have left it behind. Wherever he tossed it, he must have a way to recover it. Maybe he put it in a dumpster and had someone pick it up for him." Brad eyed the stacks of cash. "How much do you think that is?"

"250K, maybe." We'd have to count it to make sure none of it walked away and we weren't blamed if it did.

The money was all in nonsequential bills. Most of the stacks were hundreds. There were a few stacks of twenties in the mix, which brought us down to $125,000. Once we were done, Brad went back into the bedroom and finished searching every inch of the dresser by the time CSU arrived.

We updated them on the finds, pointed out everything they needed to see, and signed the scene over to Officer Roberts who'd have to remain here until the cash was collected and transferred somewhere safe. I doubted it had been obtained through legal means, but we couldn't be too careful. Either Parnell would have a right to reclaim it, or it'd end up in evidence until the city figured out how to handle it and what to do with it.

"Did Jake find anything at Wenchel's place?" I asked as Brad and I made our way out of the building.

"Nothing damning. Nothing like this. I told him to look for hidden rooms and slicks."

I nodded, unsure how I felt about this. I should have been elated. Instead, this wasn't the break we needed. "If nothing else, we can bring Parnell up on gun charges."

"Unless those weapons link to other crimes or murders, it won't do much to slow him down."

"Maybe we can run down the weapons, figure out where they came from, and see if that'll lead to the sniper rifle we can't find. Once we find the seller, we can force him to talk. That could work, right?"

"Yeah." But Brad wasn't feeling any more optimistic than I was. "This is bullshit. We should be celebrating."

"That's hard to do without the smoking gun." I stared up at the apartment building. "You realize there's another key piece of evidence missing."

"What's that?"

"Parnell didn't have anything concerning his prior victims. No photos. No maps. No evil plan written down. We can't link him to the kills."

"He didn't have a computer, Liv."

"What?"

"No computer. No tablet. No device of any kind. My guess would be that's where he kept the incriminating evidence of his stalking and planning."

"Assuming he planned any of this."

"Oh, he planned it. Kills like that require recon." Brad froze. "Robard would be excellent at that."

"You think they're working together?" None of that made sense to me.

Brad jerked his chin toward a pickup/SUV crossover parked across the street. "How about we ask him?"

I rested my hand on my holstered weapon as we made our way toward his vehicle. "I thought he was locked down on base."

"I guess that changed after Overholdt was killed. After all, that proved Robard couldn't be responsible."

Brad went around to the driver's side while I kept an eye on things from the passenger's side, but the truck was empty. From what I could see, there were no weapons inside the vehicle. I checked the plate, but it was Robard's.

"Any idea where he could—" I stopped mid-sentence, pulled my weapon, and aimed. "Hands up."

The shadow which had snuck up behind my partner did as I asked. "I'm not armed," Robard said. "I wanted to check on a hunch."

"A hunch, huh?" I kept my gun pointed at him while Brad pushed him against the truck and patted him down.

Brad stepped back. "He's clean."

I gave the military sniper a warning look before holstering my weapon. "What kind of hunch?"

He jerked his chin toward the door. "Parnell's a braggart who's been able to go toe to toe with me and hold his own."

"Are you talking about at the gun range?" Brad asked.

Robard nodded. "It got me thinking, so once I was no longer confined to the barracks, I thought I'd do some investigating of my own."

"Why would you even care?" I asked.

Robard fought to keep the scowl off his face, but the harsh light from the streetlamp only made his expression appear that much more severe. "Some bastard killed two men who worked in the same building as Julia. I can't sit around and wait for him to decide to kill more people. What if he goes after her? What if she gets in the way of his next shot? I want this man stopped."

"You're sure it's Parnell?" Brad asked.

"No, but given the police cars, I'd say I must have gotten it right. Either that, or the two of you are way off base again." He snickered at the irony or the play on words. I wasn't sure which amused him.

"Where'd you get the Mk22?" I asked.

Robard looked increasingly uncomfortable. "Why does it matter?"

"We believe it's the same weapon the killer used. Yours is in custody. But we haven't found his."

Robard shrugged.

"Between us," Brad said. "You have my word you won't get in trouble for this."

My partner was lying, but Robard had tried to form a comradery with Brad from the beginning. Hopefully, this would work now.

"What about your word, Detective DeMarco?" he asked.

"It's Brad's case. I follow his lead."

Robard wasn't convinced.

"You want to protect Julia. This is how you do it," Brad said.

"I have connections to gun manufacturers. They provide prototypes and other essentials for us to use and test in the field. I've gotten friendly with a few guys. They can hook me up with whatever I want."

"Is that how Parnell got his own sniper rifle?" I asked. "After all, that ring you bought for Julia was nothing to sniff at, and I have trouble believing Uncle Sam pays that well."

Robard nodded. "I hooked up a few guys from the gun range. The weapons weren't supposed to be used as they were intended. They were only supposed to be used for target practice. Sport." He let out a shaky breath. "I fucked up. I've fucked up on a lot of things."

"Where were you when Yeger was killed?"

"It stays between us?"

"Yeah," Brad said. "It'll be our secret."

"I've been seeing a professional. Transitioning back to

civilian life is getting harder and harder after each mission. I wander sometimes. Have nightmares. Crowds and people stress me out. It's...not good."

"The military has—" Brad began, but Robard cut him off.

"This is my career. They hear things like that, and I'm done. That's why no one knows."

"What about Major O'Neal?"

"He knows I was with a woman. He doesn't know the reason for it. But he figured he should cover for me."

"And he didn't tell us because of Julia," Brad said.

Robard nodded.

"And you didn't want to tell us because you provided the weapon to the killer," I said.

"I didn't provide it. I provided a connection. There's a difference," Robard spat. "But I want to help now. You know I'm not guilty, so let me help you catch this guy. I know how he thinks, how snipers think. I can be a valuable asset."

"The police department has its own set of snipers."

"It's different. Parnell learned from watching guys like Balenti and me. He doesn't think logically. He thinks like a guy who watched the *Jackal* too many times and thinks he's playing some crazy game. He has the gun, and now he's running around like a lunatic shooting people."

"Any idea why?" I asked.

"I'm still trying to figure that out."

"All right." Brad pointed to our cruiser. "Let's go for a ride."

# THIRTY-THREE

We took Charles Robard to the scene of the last crime. He peered around the park. Given the recent shooting and the late hour, not many people were hanging around. Robard pointed to the bleachers near a soccer field. "I'd set up beneath there. It'd give a clear view of the courthouse steps, provide cover, and make an excellent perch." He indicated the metal seats. "Leave a balled-up jacket or towel right here and the barrel would be almost invisible."

I exchanged a look with Brad. Robard knew a lot for someone who wasn't involved. We'd have to dig deeper into his alleged alibi because, even now, he gave me the creeps. "What's your exit strategy?" I asked.

Robard turned away from the bleachers. "It depends."

"No one heard the shot," Brad said.

Robard smiled. "In that case, I'd pack up my things and walk out of here like nothing happened." Which was exactly what Parnell/Wenchel had done.

"Walk us through it." Brad stepped to the side, waiting for Robard to take the lead.

After careful consideration, Robard headed toward the subway station and bus stop. "I saw the video of the two of you. I know which way your suspect went during his escape."

"Would you have gone another way?" I asked.

"Probably not. There are more breakaway points, more congestion. This makes the most sense. He could change the play on the fly if something happened."

Brad gave me a look. It wasn't exactly regulation to divulge intimate details of the case with a potential suspect, but he wanted to know how or where Robard would have ditched the weapon. If the two men were working together, Robard may lead us right to it as a way to shake off any suspicion that remained. "We didn't recover the weapon. The shooter got rid of it before we arrested him."

Robard scanned both sides of the street. "You think it was in a briefcase."

"That's what Liv saw."

"Okay." Robard indicated several dumpsters. "You checked all of those, I assume."

"Yep."

"Inside and beside?"

"Uh-huh."

Robard studied the fire escapes, alcoves, and alleyways between the buildings before continuing his trek. "What about the bus stop?"

"We didn't find anything," Brad said.

Robard quirked his head at the plastic box before heading toward it. We followed behind. Robard examined beneath the bench seats before turning his attention to the large oversized schedule board beside it. One side contained the bus schedule and route while the other was covered with an advertisement for an exhibit at the museum.

After circling once, Robard knelt beside the board and popped out the side. "You didn't check everywhere." He moved away, hands raised, while Brad moved closer with the flashlight.

I kept my distance, keeping watch over everything in case Robard tried something. Regardless of his assistance, I didn't trust him. But given the black metal case Brad pulled from between the signage, maybe I should give the military sniper a second chance.

"Careful," I said, relieved my partner was wearing gloves.

Brad glanced at me before setting the case on the bench and examining the seam and hinges before opening the clasp and lifting the lid. Inside was the weapon, disassembled into pieces. Given the size of the case, I was surprised everything fit and even more surprised he'd been able to hide it between the two signs.

"How did you know it'd be there?" I asked Robard.

"A hunch."

"I'm gonna need more than that, buddy."

"Trade secret."

"That's not good enough."

"No, I'm serious. Balenti and I were talking one day about some things we'd seen over there. Parnell must have overheard."

"You told him he could hide his weapon behind a bus schedule?"

"No." The grin disappeared from Robard's face. "An IED. It took out everyone waiting for the bus, everyone on the bus, and another dozen civilians eating at a restaurant beside it." His cheek twitched. "I was supposed to take out the bomber. I never got a look at him. I expected a jihadist with a vest. Instead, it was a suitcase bomb that had been planted hours before we set up. Our intel was off."

"I'm sorry."

"Why?" His eyes held a challenge. "You didn't put it there."

Brad shook his head. It was best I let that one go. "So that's how you knew where Parnell would hide his gun?"

"I didn't know, but it's why I thought to look there." He sighed, rocking a little. I'd seen Brad exhibit similar behavior. Robard needed to get out of here. He needed space. To breathe. To think, or not to think. "Are we done? I have to get back."

"How about you return to the precinct with us?" Brad suggested, even though it wasn't much of a suggestion.

"I'd rather not. I need to get back. Bed check and all."

"We'll give you a ride."

Robard backed up, growing twitchier. "I'd rather walk."

"To your car? That's a long walk."

"I just...I...I'd like to walk."

"It's okay," I said. "Be careful out there. We'll be in touch. Make sure you don't give us the runaround."

Brad looked at me like I'd lost my mind. "You'll have to provide a statement about this. About how you helped us find it. The sooner, the better."

Robard sucked in a breath. "Yeah, um...is tomorrow okay?"

Brad nodded. "Are you sure you don't want a ride?"

"No."

I watched him head in the opposite direction. Before he even made it half a block, I sent a text to dispatch. Nearby patrol cars would keep him in their sights while he went for his walk. Someone would be waiting at his truck. Robard wasn't the shooter, but he knew Parnell. He could be his accomplice.

"Why'd you let him leave?" Brad asked. "He helped us locate the weapon. He could have known where it was because Parnell asked him to retrieve it."

"We didn't have enough to hold him. We'd take him back to the precinct, he'd make one call, and Winston would kick us both back to traffic."

Brad didn't believe me. "You're talking to me, Liv. I know you don't care about any of that. What's the real reason?"

"You know the reason."

Brad glanced in Robard's direction. He hadn't deviated off course. He kept walking, hands in his pockets, looking from side to side, taking in the sights, and sucking in lungfuls of air.

Two minutes later, a unit rolled to our location. Since CSU missed the gun the first time, we had to make sure we didn't miss anything else and that it hadn't been planted after the fact. Once everything was set in motion, we returned to the precinct.

Voletek was at his desk with a few evidence bags in front of him. He looked up as we approached. "I have good news and bad news. Which do you want first?"

"Bad," I said.

At the same time, Brad said, "Good."

Voletek snickered, looking from Brad to me. "Lady's choice." He rocked back in his chair. "Wenchel gave the officer watching him the slip. He said he had to use the bathroom, but since he wasn't allowed inside his apartment, he went across the street to a café. The officer followed him, but somehow that wasn't enough. I already issued a BOLO.

Lt. Winston ordered protection details for the attorneys involved in the court case."

"Why them?" I asked.

"The sniper took out the insurance agent and the judge. The next most likely target would be counsel."

"Wouldn't he only want to go after the opposition to the family's claim, assuming that's what these murders are about?" Brad asked.

"It depends. If our theory's correct and the claim denial is the reason for these revenge killings, Winston figures the killer could blame the lawyers on both sides, one for being incompetent, the other for ruining everything." Voletek picked up a sticky note. "Protection details are also keeping watch over the executives at Smith and Smith and anyone else who worked on Danes' policy, which was limited to Yeger and the man who signed off on the policy when it was first opened thirty years ago."

"Who is that?" I asked.

"Ron Johnson. He still works for the company, but he's only there part-time. He's well past retirement but likes working. I figured it couldn't hurt to keep an eye on him too, just in case."

"Don't you think Wenchel will try to flee the city now that we're on to him?" Brad asked.

"It depends."

"On what?"

"Whether he's finished the job."

"Did you find any proof he was hired to commit these crimes?" Brad asked.

"Mac said she's close." Voletek checked his e-mail, but he didn't have any waiting messages. "She thinks she may have found someone who heard someone was looking to hire a hitman."

"That sounds obtuse," I said.

"Is that the good news?" Brad asked.

Voletek shot a finger pistol at Brad. "No. The good news is you were right. Wenchel had a hiding place in his apartment too. It wasn't as grand as a secret room, but there were stacks of cash hidden in several hollowed-out books at the back of the shelf."

"Cash only? No IDs?" Brad asked.

"Just cash, but I found several empty books, so who knows what else may have been there or how much money he took with him. His apartment had a little trap door built into the closet which has to do with the pipes and utilities. Inside, I found a handgun and these." Voletek indicated the evidence bags. Besides the stacks of cash, which couldn't have been more than a couple grand, were boxes of ammo, everything from shotgun shells to 7.62 NATO rounds.

"No guns?"

"Nope, so why have bullets?" Voletek smirked. "Oh, and we dusted Wenchel's apartment and Parnell's apartment. Guess what."

"Same prints and DNA at both places," I said.

Voletek pointed at me. "DNA comparisons take a while, but I'm sure you're right. After all, the prints match."

"So we IDed our shooter," I said.

"I'd say so." Voletek glanced toward the lieutenant's empty office. "Only problem is we lost him."

# THIRTY-FOUR

He'd been right. The police arrived like clockwork. As he'd been told, they were a predictable lot. It wasn't that different from military operations. Everything moved on a timetable. Certain things took a certain amount of time.

What surprised him was how easy it was to walk away. He didn't expect the detective to let him go that easily. If anything, he figured he would have been forced into the back of the cruiser and brought in for more questioning. Maybe they hadn't found anything else. He'd watched from outside while they searched the place. He hadn't seen them come out with anything, but he hadn't stuck around that long either. He only stayed as long as necessary, and he knew once reinforcements arrived, his options would become even more limited. So he walked away.

The heft in his pockets reminded him he had options. He had a job to complete, but first, he needed to schedule a meet. They needed to talk.

Originally, he wanted to avoid face-to-face contact. He didn't want anyone to see them together. Frankly, he would have preferred if no one could identify him. However, that was never an option. They'd been in this together from the start. Things needed to be done, and he wanted to do them.

He always had an odd sense of the world. His shrink would say he had seen too much, but as long as he could remember, he always felt disconnected. An observer more than a participant. Distance shooting made him feel like he was part of it, not just watching it, but it allowed him the duality of remaining separate while being involved. Becoming a legend came later, when he realized he lacked purpose. He needed a goal, and this was a damn good one.

In years to come, he wondered if he'd be the subject of action movies or true crime shows. He wanted to be the whisper that sent shivers through grown men. He snorted. The cheesier the line, the happier it made him.

No, he wasn't running scared. He wasn't running at all. He'd discuss the added dangers with his partner, reassess the situation, revise the plan of attack, and devise a new exit strategy. By this time tomorrow, he'd have every name marked off the list and would be traveling elsewhere, basking in his success and lining up the next job.

\*     \*     \*

Since there wasn't much for us to do, Winston sent us home. It was late. I wasn't even supposed to be at work today, and Brad was halfway through a double. The only break he had was dinner with my family, which I didn't consider a break, particularly since he had spent most of that time talking to my dad about the case.

Before I got out of the car, I checked to make sure a unit was keeping tabs on Charles Robard. Fortunately, he hadn't given them the slip, and now, with Wenchel/Parnell in the wind, there was a slight chance the two could rendezvous if they were working together. It was best to keep tabs on the military sniper, just in case.

"Do you think we should have brought Robard in?" I asked.

"Maybe, but you were right. We wouldn't have been able to keep him there, and it would have done nothing but irritate Winston."

"You like irritating Winston."

"No, Liv, that's your hobby."

"I forgot. You like to keep your commanding officer happy. The reason I couldn't remember that is because you haven't acted like it since we transferred to homicide."

"You know the reasons why."

"I do. I also know Winston tried to make amends with you. I thought you let him."

"Yeah, until he—" Brad shook his head. "It doesn't matter. I just don't like it when he tries to use you to advance his career or throws you under the bus the second the wind shifts."

"It's a good thing he has Voletek there too. That gives him more options, so he can hedge his bet."

Brad turned to look at me and tucked a strand of hair behind my ear that had fallen loose from my ponytail. "How about you stay at my place tonight?"

"Why?"

"I'd like you to. C'mon, Liv. It's not that big of a deal. You slept over for weeks."

"Yeah, but we weren't sleeping together then. Is that what this is? Or is this something else?"

"What?"

"Regardless of whatever else we're doing, if you have a rough day, I'll be there. Sex. No sex. That's not the point."

He smiled at me. "I'd really like to not be alone tonight. Read into that whatever you like. I'm up for anything, but like you said, that's not the point."

"Okay."

I followed him up the stairs to his apartment, relieved when I didn't find a bunch of empty liquor bottles in the garbage or on the counter. Keeping up with whether Brad was drinking or staying sober on any given day required advanced mathematics well beyond my capabilities. He'd been drinking at my place, not to an extreme, but he didn't have anything stocked or opened in the fridge. Maybe I'd stop keeping it around too. I didn't want to be an enabler or encourage bad behavior.

"Do you want to talk about the case?" He took off his holster and put his gun in his nightstand drawer.

"Not unless you know where Parnell or Wenchel is going." I rolled my eyes. "What are we calling this guy?"

"Shithead."

"Besides that."

"Let's stick with Parnell. It's how we first IDed him."

"We need to find out whatever happened to the real

Trevor Wenchel, assuming there was a real Trevor Wenchel."

"Someone's working on that." Brad unbuttoned his dress shirt and tossed it on the chair. "As far as where Parnell would go, that's anyone's guess."

"He knows he's been caught. He should try to escape. He could have other IDs he could use."

"You heard Voletek. His photo's everywhere. Airports, train stations, bus stations, at the toll booths. They flashed his photo on the screen during the news. Cops are out in droves. We'll find him."

"Do you think he'll kill again?"

Brad tried to hide the concern, but I saw it.

"What? What did I miss?"

"You didn't miss anything." He waited for me to unclip my badge and put it beside my gun before he hooked his fingers into my belt loops and pulled me toward him. His expression softened. He looked like he wanted to kiss me. Instead, he bumped his nose against mine, kind of like Gunnie. "Hey," he said quietly, "do you think your mom is still holding the rest of the bridal party hostage?"

I snorted, which made Brad's eyes light up. He liked making me laugh. "Emma didn't send any S.O.S. texts, so I have to assume my dad made sure the captives were released unharmed."

"Vince had training."

"And lots of prior experience. He's been married to my mom for decades."

"That must be nice. Finding someone and knowing they'll always be there. For ever and ever."

"Til death do us part. That's the vow." I wasn't sure why we were talking about this. I hoped it only had to do with Emma. Sure, Brad may have slipped up the other day with the l-word, but I understood that. That wasn't a big deal. With anyone else, it would have been, but he was different. We were different. We'd said it a million times. Maybe we'd meant it more than we realized because it hadn't freaked me out to hear the words or to say them back.

"That's kind of morbid when you think about it."

"Don't say that to Emma. She's liable to have another

meltdown."

"Do you think she'll go through with the wedding?"

"I'd say there's an eighty-twenty split in favor of her tying the knot."

"That's better than the last time I asked. You had said fifty-fifty."

"Well, I thought she was going to kick Dino to the curb that day."

Brad gave me a gentle peck and backed away. Going to the bed, he pulled down the covers. "Do you want a t-shirt to sleep in?"

"Can I keep it?"

He gave me a strange look. "Why do women always steal my shirts?"

"I've never stolen one. I always left them when I've left, which means you owe me one."

"How?"

I shrugged. "I'd like to have something of yours."

"A trophy of your conquest?"

"I hadn't thought of it that way, but I guess that's true enough."

"Aren't you afraid someone will find it? Your mom? Emma?"

"Fine. I won't steal your shirt."

Brad searched the drawer and tossed a t-shirt to me, which he'd gotten in the academy. It was identical to the one I already had from my time there, except this one was larger. "You can keep that. That way, no one will ever think anything of it."

"You've done this before, haven't you?"

"What?"

"Sneak around."

Something flitted behind his eyes, but he didn't answer. "Are you ready for bed? Or do you feel like doing something else first?"

"We're really doing this?"

"Haven't you been paying attention? We've already had this conversation. That's been asked and answered several times."

"I meant fooling around. After what you said in the car, I

thought—"

He cut me off by kissing me. This was new and fun and forbidden, which made it a little dangerous. Thoughts of a conversation I'd had with Axel Kincaid came to mind, and I backed away.

"What?" Brad looked concerned. "Is this weird? We don't have to—"

"Do you think I'm an adrenaline junkie?"

Brad rubbed his eyes and laughed. "Of course."

"Really?"

"Liv, seriously, you specialized in long-term undercover assignments for the first two years we worked together. Why else would you volunteer for that shit if you didn't like the high?"

"Yeah, but it was necessary work."

"I'm not saying it wasn't, but you knew there were a lot more risks involved than in normal investigations or even working patrol. It's okay. You liked the danger, until you didn't. There's nothing wrong with that. You knew what your limit was and you did your best to stay safe."

"It made my mom and Em crazy."

"Me too."

"Which never made sense to me."

"I used to play the undercover game too. I knew exactly what you were up against. It was fucking terrifying having to watch from the sidelines." He sat down on the bed. "Why are we talking about this? Did something happen with the video footage?"

"No."

"Then what is it?"

"Axel told me the reason I was initially attracted to Sean was because of his profession. I was attracted to the danger, but when Sean turned out to be a safe bet, I got bored."

"First, don't ever listen to anything Axel has to say. He's been screwing with your head since the first time you stepped foot inside his club. Second, that's not why you were bored with Sean. He's a lying, manipulating, cheating son of a bitch. He didn't deserve you, and you picked up on that. That's all that was." Brad blinked. "Shit. Now you're thinking that's the only reason we—"

I grasped his face in my hands. "No. I'm not thinking that."

"Except you are." He pulled my hands away and held them. I could feel him tremble. "I thought we'd at least have one real date before you came to your senses."

"Brad, stop. That's not true." I stepped away from him. "You know I wanted this. We've skirted around it for so long. All those half-finished conversations. That entire time, I thought you weren't interested."

"Me?"

"You always had someone else to call. Someone waiting in the wings."

"We were never serious."

"Why not?"

"It was different each time. At first, I thought casual was what I wanted, but they always pulled away and moved on. I was a placeholder. What I wanted, they couldn't give because I wasn't giving it in return."

"What?"

He shook his head. "Too much therapy, but it makes sense to me. A part of me was closed off to them. Only you saw that side of me."

"But I'm not your type."

"Jesus, Liv, again with the blonde thing? I can't believe you don't get it. I didn't want to date a brunette because she wouldn't be you. I was looking for someone different, your complete opposite, because I wanted to prove it wasn't you that I wanted or needed. Not like that." He waved his hand at me. "Like this."

"But it was?"

"The whole damn time."

"Same," I said. "So why are we fighting?"

"I don't know."

I stared at him, seeing something only I could see. "Why am I here, Brad? If this was about picking up where we left off this morning, we would have been tearing off each other's clothes the second we made it through your front door. Tell me what's going through your head. Why didn't you want me to go home?"

"Parnell's on the loose, and when we had him inside that

interrogation room, he kept saying your name over and over. I don't know why. It's like he was committing it to memory or he already had and it rang a bell." He held up his hand. "Maybe I'm paranoid after everything that's happened recently, but I didn't want you to dismiss me so easily. I know every argument you would make, and I don't have a good rebuttal to any of them. Doing this," he gestured to the space between us, "means I have to trust you can handle yourself. I have your back. You have mine. But we have to watch ourselves first before we can watch out for each other. That's always been the rule."

"Oxygen masks on an airplane."

He nodded. "That's why the department has these stupid rules and regs. I understand. It's to keep us safe. I didn't want you to think this was me overstepping or forgetting the oxygen mask rule."

"You always keep me safe."

"And vice versa."

"I wouldn't have thought that."

He didn't look convinced. "Even if you didn't, you would have pointed out the obvious. Yes, your apartment isn't in your name since you sublet. It's not like he could track you down. Everyone's looking for him. We would have noticed. We're careful and more vigilant now than before. Hell, you clear your apartment every time you walk inside. But regardless, I'd feel better if you weren't there, which is why I wanted you here."

"You should have told me."

"You would have agreed eventually, but you would have argued. This was supposed to be easier."

"Instead, we argued about something else."

"It happens. I told you I wasn't any good at this."

"Neither am I, which is why we're going to figure this out together. We're partners. We work better together. I go where you go. That's the rule. Why would this be any different?"

# THIRTY-FIVE

I shot up in bed. The realization I should have had hours ago hit me like a ton of bricks. Why was I so stupid?

"What is it?" Brad looked around the dimly lit room. Dawn had broken, but the sun wasn't all the way up yet. "What's wrong? Did you hear something?"

"My dad."

"What?"

"Parnell kept saying my last name, but it's not just my name. My dad testified in that court case. Even though it was civil, they called him as a witness. Someone who could corroborate the findings for Ramon Danes' cause of death and the investigation."

"Shit." Brad tugged on a pair of pants. "I didn't even think about it. I should have."

"No. I should have." Scrambling for my phone, I dialed my dad's cell. If he didn't answer, I'd call the house. My mom would freak out, but this was too important to worry about that now. With any luck, I was wrong.

"Hey, honey," Dad's voice eased my jitters, "is everything okay?"

"I don't know." I glanced at Brad who was on his phone, requesting a protection detail to my parents' house. "We have reason to believe the sniper may target you."

My dad laughed. "Is this a joke?"

"No. I'm serious."

"Why would he come after me? That'd be insane."

"He took out the insurance agent and the judge. Last night, when Voletek was serving the search warrant, Parnell made a run for it." I glanced at Brad, who shook his head. "We have yet to locate him. Voletek assigned protection details to the attorneys and the head of Smith and Smith, assuming the sniper may target them, but Brad reminded me of something last night. Parnell had this odd fascination with my name, like he'd heard it before. DeMarco meant something to him."

"All right. Let me make some calls and find out what's what. In the meantime, stay on top of this. Don't come here. I'll be fine. Your mother will be fine. I'll make sure everyone is squared away, including Gunnie. Once that's set, I'll meet you at the precinct, so we can discuss these matters in person."

"Brad's requesting a protection detail," I said, watching him while he spoke on the phone.

"That's not necessary."

"But Dad—"

"Olive, no. They'll do little good anyway. From everything you've told me, this guy doesn't get up close and personal with his victims. If he knows what's good for him, he won't start now because I'll end him."

I snapped my fingers at Brad and shook my head. "Dad doesn't want the detail."

Brad gave me the same look I would have given my father if he could see me. "What do you want me to do?"

I held up a finger for him to wait. "Do you promise you and Mom will be okay?" I asked into the phone.

"Yes. Now let me go so I can take care of this. I'll see you soon."

I shook my head at Brad. "Tell them to forget it." I checked the time. "I'll meet you at the precinct. You better be there, Dad."

"I love you," he said before hanging up.

"Liv," Brad reached for my hand and gave it a squeeze, "he's got this. He'll be okay. For all we know, Parnell is long gone by now."

"Yeah, but if someone hired him or if he's working with someone else, that won't matter."

"Liv," Brad forced me to look into his eyes, "you're jumping to conclusions. Take a breath. You woke up in a panic. You need to think clearly."

"My subconscious figured out what I missed. If anything happens, I'll never forgive myself."

"It won't." He went to the dresser and pulled out some clothes. "We need to get going. You don't want your dad to get there before we do."

I hurried downstairs, took a quick shower, and dressed for the day. While Brad drove us to the precinct, I put my hair up in a twist and tried to think through every detail of the investigation. Jim Parnell was our shooter, but Charles Robard helped him procure the sniper rifle. We needed to bring Robard in again. He said he'd show in the morning, but I wasn't sure I believed him last night. Now, in the light of day, I wished I'd backed up Brad's play to force him to come back with us last night.

When we arrived, I headed to my desk, glad to see Voletek hard at work. On second glance, I realized he had on the same suit he wore the day before. He hadn't gone home. The coffee mug beside him was half-empty and cold. Several takeout containers were shoved to the side, and three paper cups from outside coffee shops filled his wastebin.

"What's going on?" I asked. "Did something happen?" If there had been another murder, I hadn't heard about it.

"Not really. We haven't located Parnell yet. The lab finished processing the bus stop, again, and they finished going over the weapon. They're pretty sure it's the same one used to kill Judge Overholdt and Ken Yeger. The results were inconclusive with our first vic. Too much damage. Too much nature."

"Trees aren't as hard as concrete buildings," I said.

"Don't ask me. I'm not the forensic expert." Voletek tapped his nameplate. "See? Detective."

"Are you okay?"

He rubbed a hand over his face. "I'm exhausted." He picked up a file and held it out.

I skimmed the results. The prints on the case containing the disassembled sniper rifle belonged to Jim Parnell. "I'm surprised he didn't wear gloves."

"He didn't expect us to find this. Cocky shit." Voletek indicated the conference room where Robard was waiting. "Around six a.m., he showed up to give his statement."

"I wasn't expecting that."

"I'm surprised he was allowed to leave the base or that he came here voluntarily." Voletek picked up his cup, drained the rest of the coffee from it, and pushed away from his desk. "The protection details haven't heard or seen anything. Maybe you were right. Maybe Parnell decided to get lost." He scowled, fighting to keep his temper in check. "I hate that he got away. I should have stuck him in the back of my car or cuffed him to the banister."

"An officer was watching him."

"It was my scene." Voletek took three steps toward the break room before stopping. "What are you doing here so early?"

"Waiting for my dad."

"Why?"

"We think the sniper may try to kill him," Brad said before I could.

Voletek leaned against the closest desk and crossed his arms over his chest. "What happened?"

I filled Voletek in on my suspicions and my reasoning for reaching that conclusion.

He nodded a few times. "Let me guess. Vince doesn't want to go into protective custody or have a patrol unit watching his every move."

"You hit the nail on the head," I said.

Voletek went to refill his cup and returned with another two. Brad grabbed one, and Voletek handed me the other. "I can call my pops and have him try to talk some sense into yours. They came up together. Vince may listen to him."

"I'm hoping I'm overreacting," I said. "Evidence is inconclusive. This is nothing more than a hunch."

"Except no one wants a sniper gunning for her family." Voletek squeezed my shoulder. "We'll figure this out. I promise."

I peered into the conference room, aware Robard was watching our exchange. "I'm going to talk to him. When my dad gets here, let me know. If there are any sightings or leads on Parnell—"

"I'll let you know." Voletek sunk back into his chair. "Here." He held out Robard's statement. "You might want to take this with you."

"Thanks."

Brad fell into step beside me. "Do you think the LT knows Jake worked all night?"

"I have no idea."

Lt. Winston's office was dark, his door closed. He hadn't shown up yet.

When we entered, Robard smiled at us. He appeared to have gotten about as much sleep as Voletek. I took a seat across from him and put the legal pad down on the table. "Did you leave anything out?" I asked.

"No," Robard said.

"Except the details regarding how Jim Parnell got his hands on a Mk22 MRAD with enough 7.62 NATO rounds to kill at least three people."

"Did you get yours from the same place?" Brad asked.

"Yes." Robard stared at the table. "I had no idea that's how he intended to use the gun."

"You're a sniper," I said. "How do most people you know use those kinds of guns?"

"I already explained that." Robard's fuse was shorter today than it had been. I chalked it up to lack of sleep.

"Right." I rocked back in my chair. "Do you know where Parnell is?"

"No."

"Do you know how to get in touch with him?"

"You mean like a phone number?"

"Yeah, like a phone number, e-mail address, dark web handle. Whatever."

"I have his e-mail address, I think." Robard looked from me to Brad. "Is it okay if I take out my phone?"

"Go ahead." Brad took a seat beside me.

Robard pulled it out and scrolled for a few seconds before putting the phone down on the table and sliding it toward us. "The only time we ever communicated was when I was hooking him up with my contacts."

"We're going to need those names," Brad said.

"I can't," Robard said.

"We could get a warrant," Brad said.

"Good luck. O'Neal would be back here, arguing it would put ops in jeopardy or risk exposing classified intel. The state department would agree. It'd be a mess."

"You think you're untouchable," I said.

"No, ma'am." His eyes held remorse.

"Did you teach Parnell how to shoot?"

"No." He stared at me. "I may have given him some pointers when he asked, but nothing more than that."

"What about your pal, Balenti?" Brad asked. "He claims to have taught you everything you know."

Robard chuckled. "I don't know. You should ask him."

I glanced at Brad. There was a good chance Voletek had already done that, but I wasn't sure.

"Okay, I'll give him a call." Brad stood. "Liv, can I leave you alone in here?"

"Sure."

My partner left, closing the door behind him.

"Is he afraid you're going to torture me?" Robard asked.

"He knows I'd never do anything like that. Not to a man like you. I'm sure you were trained to withstand all sorts of torture." I exhaled slowly. "Are you feeling better today? Last night, you were starting to come apart."

Robard gave a curt nod. "I just had to walk it off. Thanks for letting me have some space."

"Sure, no problem." I rocked back in my chair. "Why did you lie to me during our first encounter?"

"I didn't lie."

"You said you didn't know where you were. That you wander."

"That wasn't a lie."

"When we asked you again, you said you were with your therapist, that you couldn't afford for that to get out. That it'd end your career. Why change the story and give us details that could destroy you?"

He didn't say anything.

"Right, so I'm supposed to believe you now when you say you have no idea where Parnell is or what he planned to do. How about you tell me what he's planning next? You knew where he hid the gun so we wouldn't find it. But you gave it to us anyway. That tells me you're feeling guilty, responsible for the lives he took. So what's his play? Escape? Retreat? What?"

"I don't know."

"You knew where he'd hide the gun and where he was when he took the shot. In fact, you were in the same parking garage where he set up for his second kill that same morning and you were in the wildlife reserve the same day he was out for target practice and murdered Ryan Dugrey who, as far as I can tell, did nothing but take a hike to his favorite spot only to get his brains splattered into the dirt."

"Bad luck. Bad timing. I don't know what to tell you."

"The truth would be nice."

He laughed. "Is this where I try out my Jack Nicholson impression?"

"You don't think I can handle it?" I returned his smile. "That tells me one thing. You're covering something up. What the hell is it?"

"Nothing."

"Bullshit." I slammed my palm on the table, which made him flinch. He was jumpy. On edge. He hadn't been faking the panic attack last night. "Why were you there? Are you mentoring him?"

"You're out of your fucking mind."

I had hit a nerve. Finally. "How does it read to you? You can't expect me to believe Parnell was stalking you and decided he'd drop bodies wherever you happened to be. That'd be ludicrous."

"Would it?" Right there, in his eyes, Robard believed that.

"I hate to break it to you, but you're not that special. I doubt Jim Parnell was stalking you. I have an even harder time believing someone with your level of training wouldn't notice a tail. The reason you rose to the top of our suspect list was two-fold. First, you were there, at the crime scenes. Second, your girlfriend connects you to the victims."

"Tangentially. I never met either of them, I don't think. And I most certainly don't have any ties to Judge Overholdt."

"What about Ramon Danes?"

"Who?"

I searched his eyes, but I didn't see any of the telltale signs that he recognized the name. "Ramon Danes."

"No. Who is he?"

I didn't answer. Instead, I studied him. "You know what's going on here."

"Lady, the only thing going on here is I'm trying to help and you're trying to accuse me of a crime you know I couldn't have committed. Sure, my truck was parked in that garage, but I wasn't there. I may have been at the wildlife reserve, but I didn't see Parnell or his victim. And yes, maybe those two men worked at Smith and Smith with Julia, but they mean nothing to me. I had no reason to kill them, and you know I couldn't have done it."

"You didn't pull the trigger, but you gave Parnell the means to do it."

"I didn't give him anything," he spat, rising from his chair. "I provided a connection. Whatever happened after that wasn't my business."

"You got a commission, though? A finder's fee, right?"

"I wasn't involved in the transaction. I had nothing to do with those murders. What I was doing at the park and at that garage is my business. I already explained those things to you."

"Except you lied."

He paced back and forth, but he remained on the other side of the table. Without turning, I knew Brad and Jake were watching us from the bullpen. If Robard tried anything, they'd burst through the door in a second, but I wasn't worried. "I want to help. I'm doing what I can to help. Neither of us wants to see anyone else get hurt. I'm telling you the truth when I say I had nothing to do with these murders. I didn't know Parnell was planning anything like this. If I had known, I would have reported him. I wouldn't have helped him get a weapon like that. I'll do whatever I can to help you find him and stop him, but I want to make one thing clear. I don't know why he's doing this or what he'll do next."

# THIRTY-SIX

By the time my dad arrived, I'd finished speaking to Charles Robard. Technically, he was free to go. He had come here of his own volition, and regardless of my suspicions, we couldn't hold him, let alone arrest him. But he hung around anyway.

"What's wrong, honey?" Dad asked, glancing toward the conference room.

"I don't like him watching us."

"But he's not the shooter."

"Liv thinks they're working together." Brad put a cup of coffee down in front of my father. "For what it's worth, I think she's right."

Dad narrowed his eyes. "Okay, so what is he getting out of this arrangement? According to everything you've said, this is about a kid who ODed. Neither Robard nor Parnell have any known ties to Danes, so why seek revenge for the lack of an insurance payout?"

"My guess is someone put them up to it," I said. "Robard's motivated by money, and Parnell's motivated by something else. Glory, maybe? I'm not sure."

Dad spun to face Voletek. "What do you think?"

"Is this a pop quiz? I'm exceptionally bad at those."

My dad snickered. "I can see you have Manny's smartass attitude."

Voletek shrugged. "I had to get something from him besides the fear of a receding hairline and a constant craving for burnt coffee and stale donuts."

"Police work's in the blood." My dad waited for an answer to his question.

Voletek glanced at the conference room. "Robard's untouchable. He knows it. By hanging around, he could be messing with us. That's what Parnell did from the moment we brought him in. He pretended to be someone else. He played his little game, and when things got too hot, he used a phone-a-friend to get him the hell out of here. But when I showed up to search his place, he knew I was coming. He expected to see me. He had his escape plan mapped out. Every word, every syllable. At first, I thought the officer screwed up—"

"He did," my father said.

"Yeah, but he got played. Parnell wasn't under arrest. We didn't have enough for that. We just had enough to conduct a search. I didn't want him there, so he waited outside. It's like he knew my play, and he didn't argue or fight me on it, like every other person whose house I searched. It was weird."

"Like he'd been coached," Brad said.

My dad thought about it. "He had a ride or disguise waiting. That's how he slipped the officer. How many people knew what you were planning to do?"

"The judge who signed off, the LT, and us."

"The techs downstairs knew," I said. "Simmons ran the comparisons. She knew what we hoped they'd prove."

"Ellie wouldn't have tipped the shooter," Brad said. "I don't think anyone here would have done that."

"That leaves the courthouse," I said. "Have you looked into Judge Overholdt's enemies?"

"There's too many to count," Voletek said.

"He's a judge. That's a given." My dad looked around the bullpen. "Does intelligence know anything about what's been going on?"

"I haven't looped them in."

"I did," Brad said. "I thought Cap could help. Mac's been asking them a ton of questions about dark web contacts and contract killers."

My father pointed to the double doors. "I'll go pay my old

partner a visit and see if he has any idea what's what. Don't worry, Liv. I'm not leaving. I'll stay inside the building and away from the windows." He jerked his chin toward the conference room. "Is anyone monitoring his phone activity while he's here? If Robard is working with Parnell, they must have a way of communicating."

"There's been nothing. Mac's keeping an eye out." I hadn't shared that with anyone, but Brad wasn't surprised and Voletek pretended not to have heard what I said.

"All right. I'll be upstairs if you need me."

I slumped into my chair. "Something's going on."

Voletek tapped his pen against the notes he'd made while speaking to my dad. "Here's everything your father could remember about Danes. I took the liberty of reviewing the file and every incident report and mention I could find. I even went through the records room to make sure we weren't missing something that wasn't digitized. Ramon Danes was a nobody addict who got mixed up in stuff he should have avoided. He gained intel from his cellmate concerning cartel connections and how drugs were being smuggled into the prison. That's how he got released early, I think. It fits our timeline, but I can't prove it. It's not like anyone wrote this in an official report."

"That was the case Det. Tony Vale was working?" I asked.

"He was part of a narco task force which was focused on cutting off the cartel's local connections. They even assisted the DEA, but it never resulted in the giant bust they expected."

"Because Danes died?" I asked.

Voletek rocked in his chair. "I can't say for certain."

"Vale wouldn't tell us anything," Brad said. "He should have. You'd think if his CI was murdered and his case fell apart, he'd mention that. But he didn't. All he wanted to do was tell us how great retirement is."

"If we live that long," I reminded him.

"Did he actually say that to you?" Voletek asked.

"More or less."

"Could Vale be on the take?"

Brad snorted. "His office looks like the kind of thing you'd find in a Vegas hotel, but that's due to his fancy new private sector title."

"It's not that new," I said, but Voletek's question made me wonder. "Vale was demeaning and antagonistic. Very old-school. Very much a mess with your head for shits and giggles kind of guy. Cartel leadership wouldn't tolerate that. I doubt they would have paid him to look the other way. Even if they had, they would have offed him when he became too annoying."

"Let me look into his closure rates." Brad slid in front of his computer and searched for Vale. "Not bad. Nothing spectacular." He scanned a few things. "He worked narco for years. He made a few big busts, but he never arrested any major hitters. At least, not that I can find. He may have assisted, but he wasn't primary."

"Whatever he was working on with Danes should have been big," Voletek said.

"Instead, he retired soon after." I went around the desk and read over Brad's shoulder. "Did he have plans to do so?"

Brad skimmed the pages, but we couldn't access Vale's personnel file. "I don't know. From what he said, it sounded like he'd originally been reluctant to leave the force until he found out how great life is on the other side."

"Do you think that's an act?" Jake asked.

"I dunno. Maybe," Brad said.

"I'm gonna check on some things upstairs. I don't want my dad to have too much fun with Captain Grayson. Let me know when the LT gets in." I headed for the door.

"I'm not your secretary, Liv," Brad called.

"Are you sure?"

He crinkled his nose and stuck his tongue out at me playfully. Maybe too playfully. But Voletek didn't find anything suspicious, so I hoped no one else would either. I was too in my head about a lot of things right now. Worrying about spilling relationship beans was a waste of time and space in my brain, at least for now.

When I stepped through the double doors into the intelligence unit, Detective Sullivan chuckled. "I had a feeling I'd be seeing you." He jerked his chin toward Captain Grayson's office. "Where's your better half?"

"He and Voletek are running down leads." I peered at his

partner's empty desk. "Speaking of, where's Loyola?"

"He's sleeping in this morning."

"Lucky man."

"I'll give him shit for it later." Sullivan scratched the back of his head. "Do you really think a sniper is gunning for your pops?"

"I hope not."

Sullivan nodded a few times to himself. "How did your mom take the news?"

"She doesn't know."

"That ought to be interesting."

"Have I mentioned I'm so glad I have a place of my own?"

Sullivan laughed. "How come I haven't gotten an invite yet?"

"You did. You just couldn't make it."

"Yeah, yeah, likely story." He rubbed a hand over his mouth. "You came up here for a reason. What do you need?"

"A look at a retired detective's personnel file."

"The Cap can get that for you."

"That was my hope."

"Anything I can do in the meantime?"

I gave him a rundown of everything in the works. "Something is up with Robard and that gun range. I haven't figured out how to touch him though."

"I'll get you something."

"How?"

"Don't look a gift horse in the mouth."

"Okay. Please and thank you."

"Yeah, no problem." He jerked his chin toward Grayson's office. "Get going. You're not getting paid to hang around and gab to me."

Not needing to be told twice, I knocked on Grayson's door before pushing it open. He and my father looked up, not surprised to see me. "How's it going in here?"

"It'd be better if we had Parnell in custody." Grayson steepled his fingers. "What's your take on this, Liv?"

"I don't know."

"That makes it hard to determine why someone would want to pop Vince."

My father rolled his eyes. "If the shooter's smart, he's

already skipped town."

"They're never that smart." Grayson studied me. "What do you want?"

"A look at Tony Vale's file."

Grayson tilted his head to the side. "I'm gonna need a good reason." So I told him everything I knew. Grayson rubbed a hand over his mouth. "Any idea why Vale wouldn't talk to you?"

"He acted like Fennel and I were the two stupidest cops on the planet." I glanced into the bullpen. "Obviously, he never met Sullivan and Loyola."

Captain Grayson chuckled. "All right. Let me see what I can pull up. Take a seat."

I dropped into the chair beside my dad and waited for Grayson to access the files. After entering his credentials, he opened the file and read. "Vale didn't take an early retirement. He'd already put in his twenty. It looks like when his case fell apart, he called it quits. I've seen that happen time and time again. It's not that odd."

"Do you know if he wanted to retire? Some guys count the days."

"There are no notes or mention prior to his official notice. That doesn't mean anything. Lots of times that's between him and his CO. I can ask around."

I turned to look at my father. "Do you remember anything about that?"

"I wasn't in charge of narcotics, honey."

"Yeah, but—"

My dad shrugged. "I don't know. I signed a lot of forms, approved a lot of leave, a lot of retirements, and a lot of transfers. I can't remember everything that happened. I told you everything I could about that case, but I don't recall getting Vale's walking papers at the same time. All I know is when the civil case came around, I got subpoenaed. Maybe I knew Vale had left by then, or I thought they summoned me since I had captain bars which are far more impressive and carry more sway with a judge and jury than a detective's shield."

More thoughts and theories flooded my brain. "I should get back to helping. Are you planning on sticking around?"

"I'll be here all day," Dad said.

"Where's Mom?"

"She went to her sister's."

"Did you tell her?"

"I told her you needed my help and we didn't want to risk work following us home. That's all she needs to know right now."

"Okay." We'd be in the doghouse for this, but better safe than sorry.

On my way back to homicide, I stopped to see Mac. Robard hadn't made or received any calls or texts since we ran into him outside Parnell's apartment last night. She checked where he'd gone, but after leaving us, he walked back to his truck, drove to his house, and stayed in his neighborhood until showing up at the precinct first thing this morning.

"I'm surprised he was allowed off base," I mused.

"He's proven he couldn't be the shooter, not after the last murder, so they must have let him go." Mac looked up at me. "I found some disturbing things. I'm not sure they're related, but I'd say there's a good chance they might be."

"Tell me."

"After chatting with some lovely folks on the dark web and getting absolutely nowhere, I decided to mix things up a bit. One thing led to another and I ended up down a rabbit hole concerning that gun range. It links Robard and our sniper together. Unfortunately, it doesn't connect to victims one, two, or three. Dugrey wasn't big into distance shooting. He never paid for access to that range." Before I could ask how she knew that, she told me she checked the range's receipts and charges on Dugrey's credit card statements. "Sixty percent of the people who go there are casual customers. They buy ammo and take some practice shots. A few take gun safety classes. It's the usual, what you'd expect. However, the more hardcore crowd, your Robards, Balentis, and Parnells, spent a lot more time and money there. They had memberships and passes. They bought a lot of ammo in a lot of different calibers, and they made that place their hangout. The people I spoke to online said if that's where I wanted to pick up exotic weapons or specialty pieces, like the suppressor, that's where I should look. So I did." She clicked a box and opened a video. "That's security footage from the gun range."

"Did we get a warrant for this?" I asked.

"We did, but the gun range didn't turn over everything." She pointed to the screen. "They omitted this part."

I couldn't think about the legality of that right now, nor did I want to ask any more questions for fear I'd dig myself into a deeper hole. "What does it show?"

"Arms dealers." She let the video play, pointing at the screen at various points. "The range is closed. This happens after hours. Based on what I've watched so far, it happens on a regular basis."

"Is Robard running it?"

"No."

"What do you mean no? He admitted to having connections to dealers, but he won't go on record. The only reason he told us was because he believes we can't touch him."

"It's not him," she repeated.

"But that's what he said."

"Listen to what *she* said. After all, that's how the punchline works." She pointed to the video. "Robard's not the ringleader. In fact, he's never even been at the range when these deals happened."

"He gave them the supplier."

"Okay, maybe. But it doesn't look like he has anything to do with it." She looked up at me. "What do you want me to do with this?"

"Have you IDed the arms dealers?" I watched two men I didn't recognize exchange cases, one presumably contained guns, the other cash.

"All I can say for certain is the guy who operates the gun range is definitely involved, but I don't recognize anyone else."

"Let me call the ATF and FBI and see if they know anything about any of this. In the meantime, keep digging. Robard has friends with contractors and overseas dealers. He said he hooked Parnell up. Let's see if we can nail that down for no other reason than being able to keep Robard here a while longer. If Parnell bought the murder weapon or any of its parts at that gun range, the footage must be here."

"I'm on it." I was almost out the door when she added, "We finished pulling the footage of Parnell leaving for his trip. He took the van to the airport, where he got into a cab."

"Don't tell me he and Wenchel aren't the same person."

"No. Well, I don't know, but I doubt either has a twin. That'd be too freaky. The problem is we lose track of the cab for about fifteen blocks. When we pick it up again, using DOT footage, Parnell isn't in the back. He got out somewhere."

"And turned into Wenchel."

"Probably."

# THIRTY-SEVEN

Since Brad had been dealing with the Feds, I passed along Mac's intel and let him make the call. I didn't want this to turn into one of those too many cooks situations. Plus, I liked to avoid dealing with the suits when possible.

While he handled that, I went back into the conference room to speak to Charles Robard. "We know your friends were dealing guns out of that range. Did they plant you there to make the connections for them?"

"No."

"Really? You've lied too many times for me to believe anything you say."

"So why are you talking to me?" He had me there.

"I don't know what else to do."

He studied me carefully. "I'm not involved in that. If I were, I wouldn't have gone looking for Parnell. I wouldn't have helped you find the gun."

"You could be doing that to throw us off your scent?"

"I'm not."

"Let's say I believe you," which I might have, "why were you looking for Parnell?"

"I already told you."

"Tell me again."

"I didn't know he was planning to kill anyone. If I had known, I would have stopped him."

"Is that what you were going to do if he'd been at home? Were you planning to kill him?"

"No, of course not."

"So what were you going to do?"

Robard pressed his lips together and stared at his hands.

"You have some issues you're working on, but you made it clear that your military service is important to you. You don't want to lose that. If this comes to light...correction, when this comes to light...you stand to lose everything. When we apprehend Parnell, you have no idea what he might say. Even if you have nothing to do with this killing spree, you put the gun in his hand. He could try to cut a deal and turn on you, especially if this operation is as big as it seems."

"I want to stop this as much as you do," Robard said. "But I am not at liberty to discuss these matters."

"That's rich. For the record, when I said I eat this stuff up, I was lying. I don't eat this stuff up. I think it's a bunch of bullshit." I got up to leave. "We will find Parnell. If you help us locate him, we'll go easier on you."

"I don't know where he is."

"Do you know any of his other aliases?"

"How many does he have?"

"At least two, but I'm sure there's more. A lot more."

Robard reached for the legal pad and pen, wrote something down, and slid the paper toward me. "You didn't get that from me. Do you understand?"

It was a phone number and nothing else. "What is this?"

"A way to contact the people who sold Parnell the sniper rifle. Make sure they don't know you're a cop or you're dead."

"That's convenient." I tore off the sheet of paper. "Why give me this? How can you trust me not to give you up?"

He stared into my eyes. "I know you won't, Detective DeMarco."

I wasn't sure how he knew that, but he believed it. I nodded once and returned to the bullpen. Making contact with arms dealers wasn't on the top of my to-do list, but if they had details that would help us apprehend Parnell, I'd be remiss not to reach out.

Before doing anything, I looked up the number. It wasn't registered, which meant it was most likely a burner. Why was I not surprised?

"Liv," Brad put down the phone, "that gun range has been under investigation for a while."

"I thought you spoke to the FBI."

"Not by them."

"ATF?"

"CID."

I glanced back toward the conference room. "Are they investigating Charles Robard?"

"They wouldn't say."

"Did you tell them they should be?"

"I may have mentioned it."

"Okay, good." I jerked my chin at his notes. "What can they tell us about this?"

"They're tracing the sales back to the source, which they believe to be private military contractors who were supposed to clean up after allied troops pulled out but instead decided to make a quick buck reselling the abandoned weapons. Usually, things like that get sold or absorbed by the local factions, so at least they're keeping the guns away from them. Unfortunately, they're doing so by loading them up and selling them on our streets, where they stand to make a hell of a lot more."

"Does CID know anything about the buyers?"

"They figured it was mostly gangs and thugs. They weren't too concerned with who was buying, which tells me the sales weren't being made to other gunrunners."

"They're selling the weapons off individually. That can't be a very big operation."

"No," Brad shook his head, "they're selling them off to gun clubs and ranges in bulk, and those are getting sold and distributed locally."

"Like a warehouse and hundreds of big box stores?"

Brad pointed a finger at me. "Bingo."

"Does ATF know?"

"Some alphabet soup agency does. CID is working with federal law enforcement to figure out the distribution network and how far-reaching it is. Right now, they suspect this is happening in at least a dozen states. Unfortunately, it also means the details they have won't help us gain more intel on Parnell. However, this should be enough for us to flip the gun range owner. Jake went to pick him up. Hopefully, he'll be able to tell us everything about Parnell, the deal they made, and where we can find the killer."

I stared down at the phone number Robard gave me. It didn't fit with what Brad had told me. "Robard said he put Parnell in direct contact with these guys." I handed him the sheet of paper before picking up the receiver and dialing Mac's extension. "Did you find any footage of Parnell buying a weapon?"

"None," she said.

"How much is left to go through?"

"I did this as quickly as possible, checking only for Parnell. Speed may have compromised the results, so Epstein is going through everything again. But I don't think I missed him. I just can't say for certain. Human error and all."

"All right. Thanks." I put the phone down. "Parnell didn't get the gun from the range. He got it directly from the source."

"This is the source?" Brad flicked the sheet of paper.

"According to Robard."

"Why would he give this to you? You don't trust him. You made that clear. Is he hoping to trap you?"

"There's only one way to find out." I reached for the phone, but Lt. Winston stopped me.

"DeMarco, my office. You too, Fennel."

Getting up, I followed the LT into his office and stood in front of his desk. Brad pulled the door shut and joined us. Winston pointed emphatically toward the conference room but didn't say a word. Instead, he shook his head and dropped into his chair.

"He said he'd show up in the morning to give his statement," Brad said. "That's why he's here. We didn't arrest him. We didn't do anything."

"I'm surprised you didn't." Winston stared at me. "I hear that's DeMarco's doing. Didn't I tell you this wasn't your case?"

"I'm assisting Detective Voletek," I said.

Winston sighed. "Your father's in the building. It's my

understanding you believe he may be the sniper's next target. Do you have anything to substantiate that?"

"Not exactly, but that's what circumstances indicate."

"Sir," Brad interrupted, "we don't want anyone else to get killed while we get to the bottom of this. In fact, we should have a detail watching Tony Vale, but he refused and sent them home."

"That threat assessment is based entirely on Judge Overholdt's murder?"

"In connection with Yeger's," Brad said.

"That's a stretch. How does that figure into any of this?"

Brad updated the lieutenant on everything we'd learned about the gun range while I silently watched. It was best not to remind Winston I was still in the room.

When Brad finished, Winston nodded a few times. "Voletek's bringing in the gun range owner. That should help. In the meantime," Winston turned to look at me, "you can reach out to that mysterious phone number. Make sure you use a spoofed number. The only reason I'm letting you follow up on this is because you have extensive training undercover. It'd be a waste not to put some of that to use. But do not blow this up like you did the original arrest. Do I make myself clear?"

"Yes, sir," I said.

After being dismissed, I made sure everything was in order before dialing the number. It went to an automated voicemail, so I hung up. I wasn't sure what I'd been expecting. I should have figured it'd be something like this, but I had hoped for more.

"Jake's back," Brad said. "Fingers crossed this guy knows where Parnell is and is willing to give him up."

# THIRTY-EIGHT

He pulled open the door to another of his cover apartments. Unlike the previous two, this was a motel room he rented a few weeks ago. He knew this job had the potential of getting messy. This was his backup plan. The man who hired him had said he may need one, but he hadn't expected things to go south this quickly. If it hadn't been for those two detectives, he would have gotten away with it.

*DeMarco*, the name meant trouble. He knew it the moment she introduced herself. There was a reason that name was on his list. At first, he thought it was kismet. Now, he was convinced it was a curse.

After locking the door, he went to the trunk at the foot of the bed, unlocked it, and removed a Remington bolt action. He hadn't planned on losing the Mk22. The police had it now. The man inside told him they found where he hid it. It was evidence now, so he'd have to go back to the basics.

He'd learned on the bolt action. That was the weapon he'd seen the greats at the range use for target practice. The ritual of sliding in the round and pulling it back with that metallic ratchet excited him. It wasn't ideal for taking calm, measured shots, but he could keep it together. This wasn't his first kill. He'd already popped his cherry. He could last longer now. Force himself to relax, to be steady and still.

Once the final target was eliminated, his business would be concluded and he'd disappear into the shadows. *Shadow. Ghost. Whisper.* He tossed a few pseudonyms around while he emptied out the trunk, taking all the cash and travel papers he had. Two identities were burned. He'd have to use the third to get out of town. The others held up better. He'd bought them off homeless men who had wanted to disappear. They were probably dead now from drinking or drugs. But he had allowed them to live on by using their names and making them upstanding citizens. The third name had been a doctored ID, something he'd bought off a guy in the back of a shop. He'd need something better, but he'd get that once he was elsewhere. Then he could start over again.

His partner, the man footing the bill and helping him along the way, said he'd monitor things at the precinct, so he could stay one step ahead. The heat was on, just like the song. He needed to know how close the police were. It was bad enough they had burned his covers and posted his photo everywhere. Before doing anything, he'd have to change his appearance and wipe down the place.

He checked the passport photo again. *Black hair dye it is.*

*       *       *

Ted Barnes, the owner of the gun range with a side hustle in arms dealing, had already spoken to Detectives Fennel and Voletek several times. So had everyone else at the gun range. Barnes had provided a few helpful details, but now that we knew he was involved in illegal activities he'd want to conceal, we had to question everything he said. Still, we were pretty sure Parnell was our shooter. All we needed to do was find him and figure out why he was on this killing spree.

Barnes wouldn't talk until he was threatened with his own charges. Failing to comply with the search warrant opened him up to all sorts of things, but the real kicker was what we'd found on the footage he concealed. Luckily, Voletek had gone to bat on that one, and Winston couldn't hold any of what Mac had done to get the footage against me.

"Tampering with evidence and obstructing justice are crimes," Voletek said as I watched from the other side of the two-way glass. "Add to that multiple counts of arms dealing, and you're looking at lots of hard labor ahead of you. Decades of hard labor. I'd like to help you out. I really would, but you have to help me out first. I need you to tell me everything you know about Jim Parnell, starting with where he is right now."

"How should I know?" Barnes asked. "We aren't friends. He comes to the range to shoot. That's it."

A knock sounded at the door, and I turned to see an officer escorting Robard toward me. "DeMarco, he wanted to speak to you."

I gave Robard an uncertain look. "Sure. Thanks."

I stepped toward the doorway, aware Robard was enthralled by what was happening inside the interrogation room. "What do you want?" I asked, pushing him into the hallway so he couldn't see what was happening inside.

"Barnes can't help you. He never liked Parnell. The guy freaked him out. Parnell didn't fit the type, so Barnes was always suspicious of him."

"What type?" I asked.

Robard gave a half shrug before gesturing to himself. "Me. Balenti. Guys you'd expect to see in a motorcycle club or setting traps in the woods." He stared at me. "Did you call the number I gave you?"

"It went to voicemail."

"Did you leave a message?"

"No."

Robard nodded, but he stared at the room behind me. I doubted he could see the interrogation from here, but I wasn't sure.

"What do you want?" I asked.

"Has he given up any names?" He jerked his chin at the room.

"Why? Are you afraid he'll mention you?"

"What I wanted to tell you was I remembered Parnell had a second phone. The last time I saw him at the range, which was the day before the first murder, he was putting some things in the locker before heading out to take practice shots, and his phone rang, except I could see his phone on the shelf."

"He has multiple identities. We know he has multiple phones."

"This one was pink, like the kind parents get for their kids to keep track of them. Y'know, with no other function other than communicating with approved numbers and emergency services." Robard cocked his head to the side. "Let me guess. You don't believe me. That's fine. It doesn't make a bit of difference to me."

"Why are you helping?"

"You know why."

"Do you know who called Parnell or why?"

"I have no idea. All I know is he left in a hurry after that."

"That would be on the footage," I said. "Did he get into his car?"

"I assume so, but I can't say for certain." He nodded toward the interrogation room. "Would you mind if I watch some of that?"

"Yes, I would." I pointed to the end of the hallway. "This is a restricted area. I'll take you back to the conference room."

"I could leave."

"Feel free."

Robard gave me a curious look. "Nah, I'd rather hang around for a while, if it's all the same to you."

"Careful, Julia might get jealous."

He chuckled. "She knows me better than that."

"If that's true, why wouldn't she marry you?"

Robard's eyes went hard. "She won't say yes until I promise to remain stateside. That'll never happen."

"It might, if we arrest you. You can't go anywhere once you're stuck in a jail cell, but I don't think she'd be particularly pleased about that either."

He smiled again, amused as if I'd made a joke.

After escorting him back to the conference room, I paid Mac another visit. There was no way of knowing if Robard's intel was legit, but I was desperate. However, desperate always proved detrimental to solving cases. It led to mistakes, but I couldn't help myself, not with a clock ticking and my father in the crosshairs.

"Got it." Mac pointed emphatically at the screen. "There

he is, leaving the gun range."

"Just like Robard said. I need to know where he goes afterward. He had a call, possibly on a burner we don't know about."

"Some sort of secret two-way communication?" she asked.

"That's how Robard made it sound." More than anything, I wanted to search him to see if he had a phone that would correspond with Parnell's. I didn't doubt the possibility since I wasn't convinced they weren't working together. However, given everything that had happened in the last twelve hours, it appeared Robard had decided to turn on his partner. I wasn't sure why, but if I took him at face value, it was because people were getting killed. He hadn't been that upset when Yeger got his brains splattered against the wall or when Dugrey met his end in the woods, but those men worked with Julia. "Dammit."

Mac gave me a worried look. "Did I do something wrong?"

"It's not you. I keep spinning myself in a circle. I want it to be Robard. I want him to be involved. It makes sense. But it doesn't, and it makes me crazy. All I know is he's a liar."

"That doesn't make him a killer." She blinked. "Okay, it does, but that's because he's a professional killer. Sniper. Whatever. You know what I mean."

"That's what Parnell wants to be." I pointed at her. "Thanks for that."

"Um...you're welcome."

"Now all I need to know is where Parnell went after he left the gun range."

She dialed up the city feeds and traced his movements. From the range, he drove to the comic book store, went inside for a while, left, presumably for lunch, and boarded a bus. I wrote down the bus number.

Mac pulled up more feeds. Scanning the times and moving the footage ahead, stop by stop, until Parnell got off the bus. Once he was no longer on public transportation, he was harder to track. As he moved down the street toward the high-rise office buildings in the business district, all I could do was watch his back disappear off screen. She searched other cameras, but we couldn't pick him up again.

"I'm sorry, Liv."

"Don't be. I have an idea of where he may have been going."

# THIRTY-NINE

That had taken longer than he expected. Unlike his preferred weapon of choice, this couldn't be broken down as easily. An oversized case couldn't camouflage this weapon as a musical instrument. Instead, he had to go with a golf bag. Unfortunately, lugging around a set of clubs was harder than he imagined. He didn't have the same frame or musculature as Robard or Balenti. If anything, he looked like a guy who worked in a comic book store, which made him the least likely suspect. At least, it should have.

As he set up in a vacant office across the street from the precinct, he wondered how he messed up. He never left prints or DNA. Even if he had, he wasn't in the system, so they'd be meaningless. Stealing the van shouldn't have been problematic. He took precautions so it couldn't be tracked or traced, but maybe he took too many.

He'd have to revise for the future. Was there such a thing as overplanning?

After adjusting the magnification and zooming in on the back door, which led into the rear parking lot at the precinct, he checked the area. Additional ammunition was within reach. His side arm was hooked to his thigh. No one should interrupt him, but if they did, he'd handle them. He hadn't come this far to get caught.

His partner, accomplice, benefactor, at this point he wasn't sure what to call the man, had made it clear that full payment required crossing out every name on that list. Plus, how would he ever achieve legendary status if he only completed two-thirds of the job? With percentages like that, he shouldn't have bothered at all. When he went into this, he promised the man all or nothing. He'd come too far to turn back, not that he ever had any intention of turning back.

This was the last shot he needed. Killing a cop where they lived would make him a legend. He'd be the most sought-after contract killer. The man without fear. The man without limits. No hard lines. No nothing. Finally, he'd be able to reinvent himself into a person no one could bully or kick around.

He adjusted the sights and checked the wind gauge. A test fire was in order, but he didn't have a suppressor. He had to hope the calibrations he'd made to the weapon last time had held and that external factors wouldn't interfere. Unlike the shot that killed the judge, this wasn't about distance. This was about making a statement.

When the door to the parking lot opened, he peered into the scope. The female detective had emerged. He took a few calming breaths, hoping this would be the perfect opportunity. He'd tried earlier this morning, but it was too late. His target had already gone to the precinct. Setting up elsewhere and waiting may have been smarter, but now was the time to be bold.

A second figure emerged behind her, and he smiled. Showtime.

$$*\qquad*\qquad*$$

"Are you sure about this?" Brad asked.

I turned. "No."

"Okay, so what's the plan?"

"I have no idea."

"Winston won't like this." Brad stood in the doorway, watching me. "I get it. I do. But we don't exactly have evidence."

"Vale was a detective. He should want to assist the investigation." I held up the USB Mac had given me with copies of the footage she pulled. "Parnell was headed in that direction. All Vale needs to do is give us copies of the security footage from outside the office building. If it shows Parnell entering, then we ask to see more."

"He won't show us if it'll incriminate him. That's what you're thinking, isn't it? You think Vale's involved."

"He might be. We won't know until we find out. He shut us down so quickly the first time."

The door behind us opened. Brad moved to stand beside the door, his back to the wall while we spoke. However, the person emerging wasn't a cop. It was my father.

"Liv, I'm glad I caught you. Are you headed to see Vale?"

I glared at Brad. "You told on me?"

"No." Brad glanced at my dad. "No offense, sir."

"None taken." My dad cocked an eyebrow at Brad. When they first met, my partner had been starstruck, but that had worn off after several dozen family dinners and other events. "If that's where you're going, let me handle this."

My dad must have lost his mind. "I hate to break it to you, but you're not a cop anymore, Dad. You retired, remember?"

"So did Vale. We have things in common. You want both of us in protective custody. We can bond over that."

"You want to make the approach," Brad said. "You want to see if he'll open up to you."

My dad smiled. "It can't hurt to try."

"It could be dangerous," I protested.

"You and Brad will be nearby if things take a turn, but I can handle myself. I haven't been out of the game that long." He stepped into the parking lot. "I already signed the forms. Grayson approved. It's about damn time my daughter and I get to team up on the job." He turned to face Brad. "No offense."

Brad didn't answer. Something had distracted him. I turned to see what had caught his attention, and that's when he shouted, "Down," and barreled into us.

A crack of thunder sounded, but it wasn't from the heavens. It was from a high-powered rifle. I hit the ground hard, my side catching on the mirror of the closest parked car and knocking it off. My dad landed beside me. He pulled his piece and got to his knees, keeping his head down while he crawled toward a better cover position.

"Brad?" He didn't land on top of us. Instead, the force had knocked him closer to the precinct door.

He gasped a few times, shock and pain on his face. I didn't see blood, but for him to have gotten thrown, he must have been hit. Was he wearing a vest? We'd talked about it after the incident at the courthouse. But I wasn't sure if he put one on underneath his clothes. We'd gotten dressed so quickly this morning and left soon after.

"Shit." My father grabbed Brad's collar and dragged him closer to the car.

The sound had caught the attention of our colleagues inside. Two came out the side door.

"Sniper. Get down." I pointed in the direction the shot had been fired.

Brad tried to cough, but no sound came out. "Fourth floor. Go," he barely managed to whisper.

"Br—"

"Go," my partner insisted.

"We got him, DeMarco," the officer said. "We'll make sure he's okay."

Even from here, I could see movement on the fourth floor. "Notify ESU. Tell dispatch I want everything shut down. He's not giving us the slip this time."

After casting one final look at the windows, I raced down the street. The building wasn't that far away. The fourth floor meant he'd have to come down. I wasn't sure how many entrances or exits there were. The building used to be offices, but most of them had shut down in recent years, leaving the space available for rent. The city had been in negotiation to buy some of the empty spaces to expand the precinct by creating dedicated areas for the civilian workforce, but that hadn't happened yet.

I was halfway up the steps when I heard footsteps below me. Glancing down, I spotted my father taking the stairs two at a time. He had his piece down by his thigh while he ran up flight after flight.

When he met me on the fourth floor landing, he tapped my shoulder. "Let's go."

I pulled open the door, and he went inside, gun aimed. I entered low, aiming from left to right. The reception area was clear. The elevators were to our left, but the lack of illuminated lights above and below told me the sniper hadn't used that as a means of escape. We hadn't passed him on the stairs. Either he hadn't left yet, or he took the other staircase down.

My dad continued moving forward, checking each of the offices as we passed. The large windows and glass doors made it easier to see inside each room. Dad stopped in front of the sixth room on the left.

Aiming, I came up beside him, but the room was empty. However, the open window told me everything we needed to know. This had been where the sniper set up. A bullet remained on the desk, standing upright, the sun glinting off the shiny metal.

"He's sending a message," Dad whispered.

"He's close," I said. "He hasn't left." Continuing down the hall, I checked each room, hearing my dad's soft footfalls behind me. The end of the hallway opened up, breaking into a larger reception area on one side and a kitchen on the other. I gestured to the door that led to a second staircase directly in front of us. "There."

I was halfway across the expanse when the elevator to my right dinged, the doors opening. Spinning, I aimed, but the car was empty. Instead, I heard the faint rustling, like the plastic wrapper from a snack cake crinkling, coming from behind me.

My father was already at the staircase door. He shouldered it open, peering down the steps while leaning against it. He turned back to me and shook his head. Silently, I pointed toward the sound. It had stopped almost as soon as it started, as if someone had stepped on the clear cellophane without realizing it was there.

Dad nodded. "I'll check the stairs. You check the elevator."

It was a ploy, albeit one I didn't like. Dad moved into the stairwell, the door closing with a bang. Reaching into the elevator, I blindly hit a number and stepped away as the doors closed. Then I ducked behind the reception desk and waited.

Five seconds later, the sniper edged to the office door,

made sure the elevator was headed down, and hurried to the stairs. As soon as he reached for the handle, I moved out of cover and into position behind him.

He stepped through the door, rifle on his back, side arm in his hand. I wasn't sure where my father was set up, but I knew he was waiting. However, I knew he didn't have a vest. Flashes of Brad on the ground tried to distract me, but I couldn't think about that now.

Grabbing the stairwell door before it closed, I stepped inside, unsure what I'd find. The sniper wore a navy blue baseball cap, probably with a sports team logo on the front, and a heather gray hoodie beneath a black denim jacket. His hair was black. The clothing gave him the appearance of having bulk. Was that Jim Parnell?

"Police," I announced. "Drop your weapon. Hands in the air."

He slowed, stopping on the landing below me. He held his hands in the air, like a referee awarding a field goal. He kept his finger on the trigger. He had balls. Any second, he'd turn and fire. That was the only reason for the hand placement. It wasn't like he was an amateur. Quite the opposite, actually.

"Put it down. Nice and slow," I warned.

He chuckled, turning toward me. Once he made a ninety degree revolution, my father came up the stairs from below him, gun aimed.

"She said put it down. Twice. Don't make her ask again." My dad kept his distance, but he kept his gun aimed.

Taking that as my cue, I made my way down the stairs. The sniper faced me. He'd changed his hair, but it wasn't enough to confuse me again. There was no way this guy was a triplet.

"Jim Parnell or whatever you want to call yourself, you're under arrest. Put the gun down unless you want me to put you down."

Parnell winked at me. "I'm not here for you, Detective DeMarco."

Before I could do anything, he spun toward my father. A gunshot boomed, echoing in the stairwell, and Parnell hit the ground, blood blossoming from his chest. My father didn't fire the shot. Instead, he aimed above me.

Spinning, I joined him, surprised to find Charles Robard on the landing above. His hands were in the air, his handgun on the ground. He knelt down, interlacing his fingers behind his head. Robard didn't even wait for me to ask.

"Cuff him," I said to my father, handing him the silver bracelets while I moved closer to check Parnell. There was no pulse. Blood dribbled out of the center hole in his head. "Fuck." Turning, I stared at Robard. "What did you do? How did you get here? Where did you get the gun?"

Robard exhaled slowly. "He needed to be stopped."

"Why? Were you afraid he'd turn on you?"

"He would have killed you." Robard looked at my father. "Are you okay?"

My dad nodded. "Yeah, thanks." He hauled Robard to his feet. "How did you get here?"

"The precinct's going crazy. When Fennel said the sniper was across the street, I knew where he'd be."

"Did you give him that tip?" I asked.

Before Robard could respond, ESU stormed the stairwell.

"We're code four." I indicated Parnell. "He shot Fennel. He," I pointed to Robard, "is another story."

# FORTY

"Are you sure you're okay?" I asked.

"I got the wind knocked out of me. That was it. I'm fine, Liv. Promise."

I gave Brad a look. He should go to the hospital to get x-rays. Winston was a stickler about such things, but since everything was crazy at the moment, the lieutenant hadn't had time to berate my partner or force medics to check him out.

"Voletek," I called, "you're coming with us."

"Absolutely." Jake glanced around the busy bullpen.

My father and Captain Grayson were in the conference room. Robard had been moved into one of the interrogation rooms where officers were keeping an eye on him. EMTs, the coroner's assistant, and CSU were in the nearby office building dealing with the scene. Detective Lisco was overseeing so Voletek could go with us to pay Tony Vale a visit.

We didn't have time to wait. Not when news of Parnell's death would spread. If Vale was involved or unlucky enough to be another of Parnell's targets, he could be dead or in the wind. Either way, we had to find out sooner instead of later.

The drive didn't take long. No lights. No sirens. We didn't want Vale to know we were coming, but given his years on the force, I suspected all he'd have to do is make a call, ask some questions, and he could find out whatever he wanted.

Twenty plus years of loyal service afforded him a lot of friends and racked up a lot of favors.

Jake requested two patrol cars meet us at Vale's office. We didn't know what to expect, but he wanted to make sure no one else tried to give us the slip. When we parked, he got out of the car.

I hadn't come down from the adrenaline high yet, so I was firing on all cylinders. Hypervigilant. Given that Brad remained mobile, I had to assume the extent of his injuries hadn't sunk in yet either. We hadn't had time to talk. I'd heard another officer say Brad saw the light glint off the scope's lens, but I didn't know for sure. All I knew was my father would be dead if it hadn't been for him.

"I'll take lead," Jake said. "No reason you should get in trouble after the day you've had."

Unlike the last time we were here, we didn't wait for the receptionist to tell us Vale could see us. Instead, Jake marched down the hallway, flashing his badge and ignoring the panicked, frantic protests from the receptionist who chased after us before reversing course and rushing to her desk to call and warn Vale, unless she was calling for building security, which would make things even more interesting. I'd nearly shot someone today and was still a little itchy and raw. Who knows what could happen if security showed up to escort us out?

Jake barged into the office. The workers in the large room looked up, watching as Vale came to meet us at the office door. "Tony Vale?" Jake held out his shield. "I'm Detective Voletek."

"Manny's kid?" Vale asked.

"Yeah. I need to talk to you. I apologize for barging in, but it's urgent. Time is of the essence." Jake gestured to the room from which Vale had emerged. "May we speak in there?"

Vale stepped back. "What's going on?" He glanced from Jake to me to Brad.

"Do you know Jim Parnell, a.k.a. Trevor Wenchel?"

Vale raised a confused eyebrow. "Should I?"

"He knows you. Well, he says he does. It's a mess really. I wanted to give you the heads-up concerning what may be coming down the pike. Y'see, Parnell's in custody. We're still sorting out his name and identity and all that. Maybe you know him by another name?" Jake held out a photo ID.

I could see it on Vale's face, the way his pupils dilated slightly. He knew Parnell. But that wasn't enough to prove it.

"He doesn't look familiar," Vale said.

"He came here the other day. We have security footage that shows him leaving a gun range, detouring to work, and then coming here."

"I don't know anything about that." Vale sat in his chair. "I'm sorry, but I can assure you that man has never been inside this building."

"Then you won't have any problem showing us the security cam footage."

"Not unless you have a warrant."

"Okay. Would your boss feel the same way? You're head of security, right? I'm guessing he wouldn't like you not cooperating with us. I bet he'd like it even less if his chief security officer was involved in a string of murders." Jake turned toward the door. "His office is down that hallway, right?" He pointed. "Maybe I should have a chat with him."

"Do whatever you like, but unless you have a court order, this is harassment. Don't they teach anything at the academy?" Vale turned back to me. "The PD is nothing but nepo babies."

"Fine. Have it your way." Jake turned to leave, winking at me before stepping out of the office. *Your turn*, he mouthed.

Once the door closed, I made sure Jake was gone before turning back to Vale.

"What are you two still doing here? Run along. Or do I need to draw you a map?" Vale asked.

"Seriously, Tony, you need to cut the crap. We know what's going on. Parnell's been arrested, and he's freaking the fuck out. He killed three people. One of them was a judge. We caught him trying to kill a cop." I glared daggers at him. "Not just any cop. A retired police captain."

"Oh? Anyone I know?"

"Don't play me. You know damn well Parnell was gunning for my father. You put him up to it."

Vale laughed. "That's the most ridiculous load of bull I've ever heard."

"Parnell told me. He told us." I indicated Brad. "He wants to cut a deal. He figured we'd be the most likely to give it to him since that last hit, the one he failed, landed a little too close to home for me."

"Liv nearly killed him," Brad said. "She wanted to march down here and put two in you, but I talked her out of it."

Vale snorted. "Is this how they taught you to do good cop/bad cop? Because I'm not buying it."

"I don't care what you believe. The simple fact is Parnell's gonna give you up. He's going to get a reduced sentence, maybe even some cushy witness relocation thing by handing you over."

"No one would believe that. I was a cop."

"You were," Brad said. "But narcotics never quite hit the nail on the head while you were there. Things got bumbled. The efforts on your last big case never paid off. The cartel continued to do their thing and that was it. They'll start looking into all that. Every questionable act. And I'm sure they'll find something."

"You're fishing. I wasn't dirty. Everyone knows that. Now get out of my office." Vale pointed emphatically at the door.

"I'm not here for revenge. I want to give you a chance to tell your side of things. Admit the part you played and help us nail Parnell, or you'll go down for all of it." I dropped into the chair in front of his desk. "The only way you can save yourself is to tell us the truth."

"I can smell the desperation on you." He pointed at the door again. "Get out."

"Just one last thing." I took out my phone and dialed the number Mac had texted me. It had been the only number Parnell had called from the pink burner phone. When I heard buzzing coming from Vale's top drawer, I pointed toward his desk. "You might want to answer that."

Vale opened the drawer, but instead of pulling out the phone, he pulled a gun.

Brad didn't waste time drawing down on him. I remained in the chair, knowing if I went for my gun, Vale would fire, which would cause Brad to fire, and someone needed to

"That was a bad move, Tony," I said. "You're going to have a hard time explaining that one. First, we find you with the burner phone that links you to Parnell, and then you pull a gun on us." I shook my head. "You're outgunned and outmatched."

He didn't look convinced until Jake returned with a few members of building security who had been watching the scene unfold from another office.

"Put it down," Jake said.

Once Vale lowered the weapon, Jake spun him around, slammed his chest against the desk, and cuffed him. "Anthony Vale, you're under arrest. I'm sure you remember how the rest goes, so say it with me."

\*     \*     \*

I was almost finished with the paperwork when Major O'Neal arrived. Robard hadn't said much since the incident. He'd kept his mouth shut and asked for a lawyer. Even now, with Vale in custody and the evidence we collected from Parnell, I had nothing that linked Robard to any of this. He knew a lot, which told me he was involved, but I wasn't sure how. He saved my father's life and possibly mine, but he also silenced someone who could have testified against him. I wasn't sure what to think.

"DeMarco, Fennel, get your asses in here," Lt. Winston bellowed.

Brad got out of the chair slower than usual, wincing when he moved. By now, his side was red and purple from where the bullet had punched against his vest. If he hadn't been moving and it hadn't glanced off him and into the brick wall behind him, I doubted the Kevlar would have been enough to save him.

"I'm okay," he whispered, his hand lingering on my low back for a moment before he gestured that I go ahead of him into Winston's office.

"Liar," I retorted.

O'Neal looked up as the two of us stepped inside. "My apologies for our last encounter. This was a criminal investigation. We hoped to handle this ourselves, without involving civilians."

"Robard was leading the CID investigation into the arms sales," Winston said. "He thought Parnell was looking to deal on the side. That's why he hooked him up with his contacts."

"You were going to put arms dealers in contact with gunrunners?" I asked.

O'Neal shook his head. "That number was a front. A decoy we set up. Since Parnell was acting separately, we gave him weapons we could trace, hoping he'd lead us to whoever he planned to sell to, but it turned out he wasn't looking to deal."

"That's how Robard knew where Parnell was and where he was set up," I said.

"It's why he was in all the locations where the sniper was." Brad exhaled, forgetting he shouldn't do that. He put a hand against his side and stared at the ceiling for a moment. "Why weren't we informed? Why didn't anyone notify us a sniper was on the loose?"

"By the time we realized it, it was too late." O'Neal looked at Winston. "Is Robard free to go?"

Winston waved his hand in a dismissive gesture. "Yeah, fine. The next time something like this happens, I better be read in, or I'll arrest every person involved in your operation for obstructing a police investigation, and I can guarantee the charges will hold up. Do I make myself clear?"

"Yes, Lieutenant." O'Neal stood up straight, practically clicking his heels together before pulling an about-face and heading out of the office.

Winston watched him go before turning to Brad. "Was that what it was like when you served?"

"Not quite."

Winston nodded. "You did good today. Captain DeMarco wouldn't be alive if it hadn't been for you. Good job, Fennel."

Brad appeared uncomfortable with the compliment. I knew I was, but I was grateful he'd done something. "Yes, sir."

Winston narrowed his eyes at the way Brad held himself. "Did you get checked out yet, son?"

"No, sir."

"All right. Turn in your reports and get yourself to the ER. Let's make sure nothing's broken and there's no internal bleeding. I don't need one of my best homicide detectives down for the count."

"Yep."

Winston turned to me. "I heard you took out the side mirror on one of the cruisers."

"Do you want me to pay for it?"

Winston laughed, as if I'd made a joke. Maybe I had, but if so, it wasn't intentional. Our CO was too mercurial for me to figure out if he was on our side or against us, which usually made life more difficult than necessary. Truthfully, I missed working for Cap, even if it led to a lot more whispers and nasty rumors. Maybe I'd figure Winston out one of these days. Or maybe he'd finally get a promotion or whatever it was he wanted, and I wouldn't have to deal with him anymore.

"You did good, DeMarco. When you're finished with everything here, go with your partner to the ER. If you could knock a mirror off a car, I'd hate to see what it did to you in return."

"Yes, sir."

"Liv," he called before I could follow Brad out of the room, "I'm glad Vince is okay. Taking initiative is important. It's key to being a good detective. You and Fennel have demonstrated that time and time again, but the reason I ride you so hard, force you to go home, force you to stop, is because without getting rest you can't think clearly and your reflexes are slowed. Unless you're firing on all cylinders, someone's bound to get hurt or worse. I don't want to see that happen. Do you understand?"

"You took me off the case," I said, "even though I was right. That wasn't fair."

"It didn't matter because you found the killer anyway."

I wasn't sure if I should walk out or sit down. Instead, I remained where I was. "Why did Vale do it? Why did he want those people dead?"

Winston sighed. "The desire for revenge is something that doesn't go away. Vale may have played it off, but I spoke to the guys in his unit. He had been tight with Ramon Danes. Danes was his everything. His friend. His CI. I don't know. Maybe there was more to it than all that. Vale hung his career on Danes coming through. When he was killed, everything fell apart. But Vale was smart. He walked away. That was the right move, where he screwed up was by not letting it go and not getting out that frustration."

"But the civil case was decided years ago. Why act now?"

"Vale recently got a promotion. More money. More time on his hands. And since he was working security for a tech firm, he spent a lot of time on the dark web. He stumbled across some contract killers, hooked up with Parnell, and the two proved that bad idea plus bad idea doesn't equal good idea."

"The perfect storm."

"Isn't it always?" Winston rocked in his seat. "Murder never makes sense. All I know is Vale wanted someone to pay. According to his coworkers, the guys had been teasing him and giving him a hard time about working with no good junkies before moving up the corporate ladder. That may have triggered him, reminded him of what the judge had said about Danes, what everyone had said, or maybe there's something else going on. All I know is Vale won't talk. Laura Mackenzie found evidence on his work computer that links him to the dark web, where we believe he hired Parnell. The security footage from the office shows them together. We know money was exchanged. The DA will build a strong case. We got him."

"Not soon enough."

Winston pressed his lips together. "This is the homicide unit, DeMarco. It's never soon enough."

# FORTY-ONE

"My dad knows about us," I said.

Brad put his hands on my thighs and sighed. "Are you sure?"

"Before he left the precinct, he asked how long this has been going on. I told him it's new and not to tell Mom or anyone. I don't think he will, but he wants us to be careful. Dating your partner gets tricky."

"How would he know? He was paired off with Cap for years."

I laughed. "He's seen things. But he's not worried about you. No talk about breaking your kneecaps or disposing of your body, so that's good. Although, it probably helped that you saved his life today."

"That's not why I did it."

"I know." I put my hands on the pillow beside his head and leaned down to kiss him. "Have I mentioned how grateful I am?"

"You don't have to. I love Vince and your whole family. I'd do anything for them. For you."

He pointed to the bruise on my side. "Y'know, some couples get matching tattoos. We don't need to be like those people. Our bruises don't need to match."

"Our scars basically do."

"Have I mentioned how much I hate that?"

"Only a million times."

"Well, I do."

My phone rang, but before I could grab it, Brad picked it up. He read the display, quirked an eyebrow at me, and hit answer. "Liv's busy." He listened for a moment. "No. She's going to be busy for the foreseeable future. I don't suggest you call back." He chuckled, though it sounded more menacing than pleasant. "Damn right." He put the phone down.

"Who was that?"

"Axel."

"Kincaid?"

"How many Axels do you have saved in your phone?"

I stared at my partner for a long time. Brad didn't say the words, but he'd made it clear. My dad wasn't the only one who knew. Axel knew. Brad wanted him to know. They'd been in competition for my affection since my undercover days. I wasn't sure if Brad had claimed victory or thrown down the gauntlet. Only time would tell.

"We're doing this now?" I asked.

Brad laughed that velvety sound I loved. "We've been doing this. It's about time we do it right." He sat up. "Let's go out. It's first date time."

"Now?"

"Yeah, Liv. Right now."

# ABOUT THE AUTHOR

G.K. Parks is the author of the Alexis Parker series. The first novel, *Likely Suspects,* tells the story of Alexis' first foray into the private sector.

G.K. Parks received a Bachelor of Arts in Political Science and History. After spending some time in law school, G.K. changed paths and earned a Master of Arts in Criminology/Criminal Justice. Now all that education is being put to use creating a fictional world based upon years of study and research.

You can find additional information on G.K. Parks and the Alexis Parker series by visiting our website at
www.alexisparkerseries.com

www.ingramcontent.com/pod-product-compliance
Lightning Source LLC
Chambersburg PA
CBHW020735250626
47155CB00003B/774